Advance Praise for
RUBY FALLS

"Imaginative, unique, spine-tingling, and just the right amount of eerie, *Ruby Falls* is what a reader wants a psychological thriller to be."

—SANDRA BROWN, *New York Times* bestselling author

"*Ruby Falls* will sweep you headfirst into the life of Eleanor Russell, an actress setting up house in the glamorous Hollywood Hills with her handsome new husband, Orlando. Secrets abound in this bang of a book, a haunting tale sure to give readers chills. A stunner with some serious Gothic vibes."

—KIMBERLY BELLE, internationally bestselling author of *Dear Wife* and *Stranger in the Lake*

"A tribute to Daphne du Maurier's *Rebecca*, this unnerving story about a Hollywood starlet haunted by her past will captivate you right up until the shocking ending. A must-read for anyone who loves an expertly plotted thriller with multidimensional characters."

—EMILY LIEBERT, *USA Today* bestselling author of *Perfectly Famous*

"In 1968, young Ruby Russell loses her father while touring an underground cave. She recalls the moment his hand left hers, and nearly twenty years later, his disappearance remains a mystery. Ruby has reinvented herself as Eleanor Russell, married the man of her dreams, and is acting in a feature film. But as her new life begins to go awry, the mystery surrounding her past and present collide in a well-crafted and head spinning twist that I did not see coming. *Ruby Falls* is a skillfully plotted page turner!"

—WENDY WALKER, national bestselling author of *Don't Look for Me*

"What a lovely ride! With fun twists and whip-smart language, clever Deborah Goodrich Royce leads readers down a familiar path—until she doesn't. Lyrical and filled with page-turning suspense, I gulped every word and enjoyed every bite. I promise *Ruby Falls* will become your next favorite book!"

—MAUREEN JOYCE CONNOLLY, author of *Little Lovely Things*

"*Ruby Falls* is a fantastic combination of a sweeping Hollywood story folded into a twisty thriller. Fans of *Rebecca* will be enthralled with how the classic story is woven into the masterful plot of *Ruby Falls*."

—VANESSA LILLIE, Amazon bestselling author of *Little Voices* and *For the Best*

"Brimming with Hollywood nostalgia, this mesmerizing and thrilling page-turner is impossible to put down. Deborah Goodrich Royce's second novel, *Ruby Falls*, has all the elements of an addictive read: fascinating characters, quick pace, and an intriguing story full of suspense. Masterfully plotted, the story of Eleanor Russell, a young impressionable actress, plagued by a childhood trauma, unfolds against the backdrop of a film production remake of *Rebecca*, in which she stars. A haunting, unforgettable thriller."

—DANIELA PETROVA, author of *Her Daughter's Mother*

"Mix a dark childhood trauma, a fragile young actress, and a hasty, ill-advised marriage. Add old Hollywood glamor, dashes of enchantment, and lashings of noir suspense. Now shake—and prepare to be shaken. Much more than a mystery, *Ruby Falls* is about stories—the ones we tell ourselves, the ones we tell others, and the dark gaps in between."

—ELKA RAY, author of the Toby Wong Vancouver Island mystery series

"*Ruby Falls* is a psychological tour-de-force that grabs you on page one and doesn't let you go until the end. A compelling, engrossing, and truly suspenseful thriller that takes place in the mind of one woman struggling to overcome her demons."

—KRIS FRIESWICK, author of *The Ghost Manuscript*

RUBY FALLS

Also by Deborah Goodrich Royce

Finding Mrs. Ford: A Novel

RUBY FALLS

A Novel

DEBORAH GOODRICH ROYCE

Post Hill
PRESS

A POST HILL PRESS BOOK

Ruby Falls:
A Novel
© 2021 by Deborah Goodrich Royce
All Rights Reserved

ISBN: 978-1-64293-709-1
ISBN (eBook): 978-1-64293-710-7

Cover image by Melanie Willhide
Cover typography by Cassandra Tai-Marcellini
Cover concept by Becky Ford
Interior design and composition by Greg Johnson, Textbook Perfect

"Ruby Baby"
Words and Music by Jerry Leiber and Mike Stoller
Copyright © 1955 Sony/ATV Music Publishing LLC
Copyright Renewed
All Rights Administered by Sony/ATV Music Publishing LLC, 424 Church Street, Suite 1200, Nashville, TN 37219
International Copyright Secured – All Rights Reserved
Reprinted by Permission of Hal Leonard LLC

"Sweet Dreams (Are Made Of This)"
Words and Music by Annie Lennox and David Stewart
Copyright © 1983 by Universal Music Publishing MGB Ltd.
All Rights in the U.S. and Canada Administered by Universal Music – MGB Songs
International Copyright Secured – All Rights Reserved
Reprinted by Permission of Hal Leonard LLC

Post Hill Press
New York • Nashville
posthillpress.com

Published in the United States of America

To Ana, Lisa, Howard, and Grant—
all gone too soon.
It was an honor to walk with
you for a way when
we were young in Hollywood.

"I stand amid the roar

Of a surf-tormented shore,

And I hold within my hand

Grains of the golden sand—

How few! yet how they creep

Through my fingers to the deep,

While I weep—while I weep!

O God! Can I not grasp

Them with a tighter clasp?

O God! can I not save

One from the pitiless wave?

Is all that we see or seem

But a dream within a dream?"

—A Dream within a Dream,
Edgar Allan Poe, 1809–1849

"It is the nature of grief to keep its object perpetually in its eye, to present it in its most pleasurable views, to repeat all the circumstances that attend it, even to the last minuteness; to go back to every particular enjoyment, to dwell upon each, and to find a thousand new perfections in all, that were not sufficiently understood before; in grief, the pleasure is still uppermost..."

—*A Philosophical Enquiry into the Origin of Our Ideas of the Sublime and Beautiful,*
Edmund Burke, 1729–1797

PROLOGUE

THEN

1968, Lookout Mountain

I was standing with my father in the pitch-black dark—the blackest dark I'd ever seen in the few short years of my young life—and the blackest dark that I've seen since, which is a considerably longer span.

The surrounding air was dank with flecks from falling water.

A disembodied voice rose up from the mist, then swooped back down to submerge in it. First amplified then muffled, the sounds changed places, each taking its turn at prominence. The drone of the voice, the roar of the falls, and the clammy damp came at me from all directions—from the sides, from above and below—to seal me in a viscous coating and stick me to my spot. The waterfall could have been anywhere. Next to me? Yards away?

I dared not move a muscle.

The woman's words transfixed me with a tale of scuba divers. Fearless swimmers who, over the years, had plumbed the depths of a fathomless pool. In wet suits and tanks, in masks and flippers, down they had plunged into icy water, in an effort to find its bottom.

No search had been successful.

The roiling cascade dropped into a lake that continued, it seemed, to the center of the earth. To China. To horrible depths my imagination was fully engaged in conjuring.

Cold drops of perspiration ran down my face, my arms, and the back of my neck. I was concentrating hard—trying to locate the source of her voice, trying to pinpoint the crash of the falls, trying not to move and tumble in, and trying most heartily not to be afraid—when my father let go of my hand.

That was it, really—that was all he did. He loosened his hand from my grip. And he disappeared, never to be seen again, while the tour guide never stopped talking.

July the 12th, 1968. The last day I saw my father.

James Emerson Russell was Sonny to most—from the son in Emerson, I imagine. Or maybe from his position in his family of origin. I don't really know. He was just Daddy to me, what a little girl calls her father.

He was handsome, that Sonny. It is not just my memory. It is what people still say when they don't stop themselves from talking about him. And, they say it just like that. "He was handsome, that Sonny, I'll grant him that." As though his visage were something they grudgingly bestowed on him. Then they change the subject on seeing me.

He was long and lanky—six feet even—impossibly tall to me then. A slight stoop to his walk, crinkly blue eyes, and a halfway receding hairline.

His taste in attire ran to western and that was how he was dressed that last day. Jeans and a checkered shirt. Madras, my mother had called it. Snaps down the front and a turned-up collar. Cuffed sleeves rolled up to reveal strong forearms, all covered in downy blond fuzz. He wore cowboy boots and he carried a hat. In a nod to convention, he would not have worn it indoors. Men did not do that then. Then again, men did not tend to walk out on their children in the middle of tourist attractions, either, but that hadn't served to stop him. I guess my daddy picked his proprieties from a smorgasbord of options.

He wore a watch and his wedding ring, too, and a belt with a silver buckle. He had surprisingly soft hands for a man. I had held his hand for the longest time, twirling his ring, until the darkness commandeered my attention when the lights were abruptly switched off. Then I just stood still, clutching that hand and willing him to protect me. Those large, soft hands that belonged to a man who would use them to wrest himself free of his daughter.

But how, you might ask, could a full-grown man vanish from the middle of a clump of tourists visiting Ruby Falls in Lookout Mountain, Tennessee, on a sweltering summer day? More precisely, how could a man disappear from a cave *under* Lookout Mountain—when that very act would require accessing the elevator (through the lightless cave), traversing the entrance lobby, crossing the parking lot, starting his car, and driving away—leaving his own flesh and blood child standing frozen under the earth beneath him?

In the end, nobody remembered seeing him do any of those things. And his car, a 1962 Cadillac de Ville, in a vibrant shade of turquoise, remained where he—we—had left it in the parking lot.

It is an unsolved mystery. And it turns out that people who experience an unsolved mystery in their lives become inordinately keen on unsolved mysteries as a topic in general. I am one of those people. My father disappeared from Ruby Falls in the summer of 1968, when I was six and a half years old. He left me alone and mute, unable to move, even once they put the lights back on and herded the crowd past the stalactites and stalagmites and the God-forsaken falls toward the elevators, en route to the streaming sun above.

The tour guides had to pick me up, when it became evident that I was not ambulatory. They groused the whole way up to the surface that I was stiff as a corpse, which, as they made clear to each other and to me, added to the overall creepiness of my father's de-materialization. Had they been superstitious people (and who, really, isn't?) they might have thought some sort of black magic was being performed by us.

Lest I forget to mention—my name is Ruby. Not believable, you say? Well, it is true. My name is Ruby (not Falls, if my name were Ruby Falls, that *would* be unbelievable). My name is Ruby—Eleanor Ruby Russell—but called Ruby from birth, in the way that Southerners do, being extremely fond of middle names.

Thus, I became famous for a while at the age of six and the press had a field day with my name.

Little Ruby Left in Ruby Falls!
Did Ruby's Father Fall in Ruby Falls?
Ruby Took the Fall in Ruby Falls!

You can imagine, I am sure, the extent to which the headline writers amused themselves. I might have been entertained, too, except for obvious reasons. Namely, my age at the time of the incident. But, trailing a close second to that was the fact that my mother shielded me from the newspaper clippings that she studiously pasted into a scrapbook. I was a teenager when I discovered that macabre memento.

Strangely—though what about this case wasn't strange?—my father had chosen my name. My mother hated it—Northerner that she was, she considered it a countrified name—but my father had won the day. That did not look good for him, in the end. Or what everyone has questioned, from that day to this, as being the end or not. Kind of suspect to insist on calling your daughter Ruby, then abandon her and vanish into thin air in the middle of Ruby Falls—bad form no matter how you slice it. It could be taken as intent.

But intent to do *what*?

My mother had not been with us on our outing that day and the staff had had a hard time figuring out what to do with the rigid child on their hands. Understandably, they had no idea that my father had been the one to leave me alone in the cave. They figured I hadn't come to Ruby Falls on my own—considering that I was only six years old—but no one had taken much notice of me, or whoever might have been along with me, for the first half of my descent into the cavern. When questioned, some thought they had seen me with a man. But there was no longer a man to be seen with me.

There were no security cameras to review, no credit card records to comb. There really was no way of verifying when and with whom I had entered the cave. Or who might have exited without me.

And I wasn't saying much.

The police were called. They drove out to the mouth of the cave to have a look at the little girl who was found on her own at the bottom of it. It came to be closing time and no one knew what to do with me, so the policemen stuffed me into the back of a squad car and took me back to the station.

It was around ten o'clock that night, I later learned, after numerous hands of pinochle, when my mother understood that my father and I were not just dawdling over dinner and telephoned the precinct. Margaret Russell—her husband's social superior in every way: birth, breeding, and means—identified herself, as if the Tennessee cop might know her. Officer Brady gave his name in reply.

And then they got down to business. Officer Brady matched up the child my mother described with the small, silent, staring creature he saw on the bench before him. Pink and green flowered shorts?—check. White eyelet short-sleeved blouse?—check. White socks, red Keds, blond page-boy haircut, and big brown eyes?—check, check, and check.

Aunt Hazel, at whose house we had been staying on our annual Southern trek to see my father's people, drove my mother to the station to fetch me. The women floated in on drafts of Jungle Gardenia and bourbon (in fairness to them, it was after eleven p.m. by that point). All scarves and heels and shirtwaists, their pumps clattered their arrival just seconds after their scent had pre-announced them.

My mother confronted the officer. Just what did he mean by this? In the face of Peggy's perfection—her beauty, her cat-eye glasses, her touch of eyeliner and frosted lips—he shouldered the responsibility. He was sorry, he said, for her troubles. He could not say what had happened to my father. He looked to me to save him.

And I was not talking.

Reminded of her duties by Officer Brady's glance in my direction, my mother swished over to peer at me. I must not have looked good for, big as I was, she reached down to pick me up. For the first time in hours, my body began to uncoil. Her smell, her warmth, her vitality—her utter familiarity in a world that had become a funhouse—seeped into my cold, hard bones and, on the spot, sedated me.

I fell fast asleep in her arms.

Sometime later, my mother laid me on the back seat of Aunt Hazel's Comet station wagon. The women took me back to my aunt's and put me in my pjs. They ladled some broth down my throat, offered me Jell-O, which was thought to be curative, and put me to bed, where I remained for the better part of the summer.

My condition, and my father's absence, grounded my mother and me in Chattanooga.

She, answering questions and chain-smoking.

I, face to the wall.

1

NOW

1987, Roman Holiday

"Ellie?"

"Ellie?"

"Mrs. Eleanor Russell Montague, darling wife of mine, are you breathing?"

I am standing in the catacombs in Rome, scarcely a few feet into the entryway and I find myself immobilized. I cannot step forward and I cannot step back and our tour group is moving away from us. Sweat pops out on my upper lip and trickles down my spine. And as to the particular subject of my breathing, my husband is correct. I don't seem to be able to do it.

"I…I…" I don't want to go into details—not now, not here—with him. This happens to be our honeymoon and it isn't the time to spoil things. "I think I'm feeling queasy. Maybe it's something I ate?"

This newly minted husband of mine stands before me, looking straight at what I'm sure must be my blanched and clammy face. My beautiful new husband, Orlando. He is English, of course. Consider the elegance of the name.

When I attempt to open my mouth again, my tongue sticks to the roof of it and makes a very unattractive smacking sound before I am able to form any words.

"I think I'm getting sick," I fudge and look around for a guide. "*Posso uscire? Non posso scendere. Uscita, per favore? Aiuta!*" The Italians are so lovely when you try to speak their language. They let you butcher it and come to your aid most graciously. I call out with a bit more volume. I try not to appear wild-eyed as I rapidly scan the room. Who the hell knows if I'm saying it right, but I really *must* get out of here!

A kind woman in uniform approaches me.

"*Si, si, signorina.*" That much I understand and quickly correct her.

"*Signora,*" I say, offering my left hand as proof. My wedding ring is so exquisitely lovely—so delicate, so tasteful, so clearly an heirloom from my husband's family—that I proffer it to warm the heart of the guide and get her to help me out of this place as fast as she possibly can.

She appears to be nonplussed.

Nevertheless, she says, "*Seguemi, Signora,*" and I am grateful. At least she makes me feel that I am totally normal to panic this way underground. I guess she's seen it all. She walks briskly through a cordoned-off area to lead me away from the land of the dead and back to the realm of the living. I feel like Persephone, ending winter and initiating spring.

"Are you coming?" I look back and smile sheepishly at my husband—rumpled in his tan linen suit and Borsalino fedora—and laugh a little at what I hope he'll chalk up to my utterly charming kookiness.

"Of course, darling." Orlando is perfect. "I've already seen the catacombs."

Orlando *is* perfect. He accompanies me into the sunlight. He takes me to a little café and orders wine for the two of us.

"*Due bicchieri da vino rosso, per favore.*" Orlando's accent is better than mine.

"*Certo, signore,*" the waiter says.

Orlando touches my forehead. "Do you think you're coming down with something?"

8

I know. This would be my opportunity. The perfect moment to tell my new husband about my circus sideshow of a childhood. We've just been in a cave. He's seen me freak out. Now would be the time to tie it all together in a nice neat bow. One cave with the other. Cave of now with cave of yore. It is exactly the time to trot out that old tale. We could laugh about it, even. Darling, he might say, let me take care of you. Step into the void that your dear old dad has left. Dear old deadbeat dad, he might add. No, he wouldn't do that. He is too kind to say that. It would be indelicate and might further injure what he must just be beginning to suspect is his already-injured wife.

The waiter plunks down a carafe of red and a little dish of olives.

"*Grazie,*" I say as I readjust the olive bowl.

"*Prego.*" He walks away.

I turn back to Orlando. "I was feeling a little off this morning. Maybe it's just a cold."

I know! I've blown it—have already let the moment pass. I should tell him, but I can't. I will. I mean, of course I will. It isn't like it's a secret or anything. It's just too much to go into right now. The old story. The old name, Ruby. The scene of the crime, Ruby Falls. I will tell him all of it. It's just too ridiculous to explain right now. I will tell him when the time is right. We have a lifetime together, after all, to dig up these old skeletons.

"I'm feeling better already," I say and take as big a swig of wine as decorum permits at three o'clock in the afternoon.

"I'm so happy, my love," he says and takes a more delicate sip.

We linger there for hours, allowing the light to lapse. To intensify first in an ochre glow that centers between two buildings and catches us in the face. The sun and the wine both flush us, enhancing our honeymoon heat. We drink, we chatter, our hands find each other on the table, our knees find each other below.

When the light is gone and the wine is still flowing, we order carbonara. The Roman food of the gods. Eggs and cheese and bacon and pepper. Pasta cooked *al dente*. It nourishes us and comforts us and maybe it arouses us. Carbonara: soother of babies, calmer of tempers, aphrodisiac to lovers?

"This is sublime, this pasta." I have really never tasted anything quite like it and I struggle to find the words. "And it's also subliminal. It rises from subliminal to sublime, like something imaginary becoming tangible. Right there, on your tongue. It's beyond that. It's seminal. I'm eating a seminal meal. I'll never forget it. The meal of my life."

Orlando snorts affectionately. "Are you drunk? You're sounding a bit daft."

I push my chair back suddenly. "Let's go make love right now," I whisper.

"Are you sure? Your seminal sublimity is still sitting on your plate."

"Orlando, please," I continue, throwing whatever caution remains to me fully into the wind.

He cocks his head for a moment. Then he laughs and calls for the check. "Your wish is coming through to me, loud and clear. Nothing subliminal about it."

A breeze has sprung up from the south, warm and a little humid. My gauzy skirt billows and collapses, like a bellows, as we stroll through the dusky streets of Rome. Orlando holds my arm to steer me in the right direction.

I stumble once, when we enter our hotel lobby, and Orlando grabs on harder.

"*Buona sera*," the doorman says, pretending not to notice.

"*Buona sera*," I reply, working not to slur my words.

In our room, Orlando insists I lie down and places a cool cloth on my head.

"You're so young, my darling," he says. "Sit up a bit and take these. For whatever might be ailing you."

Even in my current state, I recognize the double allusion to my earlier claustrophobia and my present tipsiness.

"I'm almost twenty-six years old," I say, gulping down the aspirins. "If I live to be a hundred, I'm a quarter through. Anything short of that, I'm much farther along."

"Don't wish your life away."

I reach up to pull him down beside me. But Orlando moves away to sit beside the bed.

"Sleep is what you need. I'll just be here." He clicks on a light and picks up a book.

"Come to bed, Orlando. Please."

"Not now. Sleep."

I sigh and close my eyes. In time, I think, as the wine overpowers my concentration, I will tell my husband my story. I just don't want to ruin this. Everything happens in its own sweet time.

I look up to catch his eye. His smile could not be more tender.

How did I get so lucky?

2

FLIGHTS OF ANGELS

We have been in Los Angeles—pronounced Los Angeleeze by my Anglo-import husband—for about eighteen hours, and the real estate agent is meeting us at our hotel at nine. This city is where we intend to live. To make our life together. Neither of us has ever lived here before. I've never even been here before. But, together, this is the place we have chosen. It is a fresh, clean start for both of us.

For us—a *we*—not a *he* and a *she*.

Our breakfast has been served—with a vase of sweet waxy gardenias—on the patio of room sixty-four of the Chateau Marmont Hotel. The bellman who brought us up said it was Howard Hughes's former apartment. But, for these few days, it is ours. It is a bit of a splurge, but it's worth it. An extension to our honeymoon, which only so recently ended.

This same bellman said that in the old days, Mr. Hughes sat on this very patio, holding binoculars to his eyes. Peering over the railing, he studied the bathing-suited starlets assembled for him near the swimming pool below. I walk to the edge to gaze down at the pool, its chairs, umbrellas, and tables. Except for a small dark man in a sun hat who is sweeping, it is empty at this early hour. I squint my eyes and imagine those women, trussed up and on display. They had to have known that

Hughes was above them, a hawk staring down at some rabbits. After all, it's the reason they came.

I lean out over the parapet. Vertigo is not my trouble. I lean out farther, feeling the edge of the short porch wall pressing hard into my thighs. It is claustrophobia that is my weakness. A little farther still, testing my sense of balance by lifting my hands in the air.

"Look at this," says my husband right behind me, startling my hands back to the railing. He gestures toward the vista. "Isn't it breathtaking?"

He walks back to the table and I join him as he pours another cup of coffee for each of us.

"It really is beautiful," I say. And it is.

We look out over the entire valley of Los Angeles which, at this very moment, is streaky with pink and white clouds. Turning my head, I see there is an equally impressive panorama of the Hollywood Hills, stretching eastward toward the morning sun.

"Oh look!" I gasp. "I think I see snow-capped mountains over there. In the far distance."

"That would be the San Bernardino Mountains and Lake Arrowhead. We'll take a drive there one day."

"How do you know that?"

"I like to study maps. Train schedules. Airplane schedules. Things like that. I like to know where I am and how things work. You've married a bit of a nerd," he says.

"Good thing I did, because I can't find my way anywhere."

"My love, it would be my honor to guide you through life. Or, at least, to the bedroom." He winks at me as he opens the morning papers.

We are each wrapped up in a hotel robe with our feet tucked into slippers. I am surprised at the early morning chill. Surrounded by cascading bougainvillea, I had expected the heat of the southeast that starts off early and steams upward into the day. Of course, I know Los Angeles is basically a desert and deserts cool off at night, but it is nevertheless a disconnect in my brain. I see tropical plants and expect tropical heat. Hard wiring.

"Feeling a bit peckish, love?" Orlando breaks my reverie. He is looking at me across the top of the newspaper. If any other person had asked me this question while I was stuffing a second croissant into my mouth, I might think he was calling me fat.

"I'm not sure what you mean by that." I try laughing a little as I say this, to whitewash my defensiveness.

"I don't mean anything. Just asking if you're especially hungry this morning." He goes back to his reading.

Self-consciously, I set down the croissant and brush the crumbs from my lips. I don't know of a woman alive who is able to tolerate comment on any aspect of what, when, and how much she eats. It really is the third rail of feminine subjects.

"Actually, I'm full," I say to the air.

The telephone rings, the distinctive *bring bring* of a vintage table model, the heavy kind with the cloth covered cord that connects to the wall. It must be a vestige of the Hughes era.

Orlando snaps the paper shut and stands up to answer it.

"Oh! Please let me get it," I say. "It might be my mother calling me back."

Obligingly, he steps aside as I dash to the bedside table.

"Hello?" I say, a little breathless, as I turn to smile at my husband, who has followed me into the room. "Oh, hi, Mom. I was hoping it was you. Thanks for calling me back."

Orlando returns my smile.

"Yes, I know I've been hard to reach lately. I'm sorry. But I have some news for you. Are you sitting down?"

Feeling a jangle of nerves, I hold out my hand to Orlando. He walks three steps to reach me and—instead of taking my outstretched hand—places his hands on my shoulders. He keeps them there, pressing firmly, and kisses me once on the forehead. Through him I find my courage.

Looking straight into his eyes—the most astonishing shade of green—I deliver the news to my mother. "I'm married, Mom!" I say, making sure to add an exclamatory note. "My husband's name is Orlando Montague."

I twirl the cord around my index finger and pause to straighten my ring.

"It's an English name. Orlando is British. Well, actually, he's Anglo-Chinese."

My mother asks if I can repeat that.

"I said he's half English and half Chinese. His father met his mother in India during the war. He was stationed there with the British Army and she was fleeing the Japanese in China. She got on the Burma Road and eventually landed in Calcutta. Isn't that amazing?"

I need to slow down because I am definitely talking too fast.

Orlando looks at me and I gain strength from him, though my mother's barely controlled hysteria is rising on the other end of the line.

"Three weeks. We've been married for three weeks, Mom."

Orlando presses a little bit harder and it makes me feel rooted in him. I hope he can't hear my mother through the receiver. Though it is not her style to raise her voice. She makes her displeasure known with intensity, not volume.

"I know, Mom. Yes. Yes. He's an antiques dealer just like Daddy! Well, kind of…what? Um, no. No. Different style of furniture."

I push the receiver closer to my ear, in an effort to contain her alarm. She is revving up her engines.

"We knew each other six weeks. It was a whirlwind romance! The best kind, right? Anyway, I know you'll just love each other."

Actually, I fear they will hate each other.

"Look, Mom, I just wanted you to know, okay? I'm really happy. I've never been so happy before in my life."

Why did I say that? I shouldn't have used that phrase. That is the thing they always say on soap operas before the axe falls—before the cancer diagnosis or hidden twins or un-dead-ex-wives come down from the attic.

"I can't talk any longer, Mom. We're in LA and we're going out shopping for a house now. Our very own house!"

As if on cue, the doorbell rings. Orlando keeps his hands firmly on me, and I am connected to the phone, so—pinioned like that—neither one of us moves.

"I have to go now, Mom. The realtor is here. I love you!"

I hang up and give Orlando a peck. And then I try to turn, to bolt for the bathroom and my clothes. To regain my composure after that phone call has ruffled it. But Orlando squeezes me for a moment more.

"What did your mother say?" he asks.

"She says she can't wait to meet you." I smile brightly.

"See, darling. I told you it would be all right." His smile is even brighter.

3

THALIA AND MELPOMENE

I might as well tell you before I continue that I happen to be an actress. I have spent the past two years starring in a daytime soap opera in New York City. I was named "Ingénue of the Year" by *Soap Opera Digest* in a readers' poll.

I *am* an actress. It is my profession. But, more than that, it is my essence. My core. My San Andreas fault; if you were to dig down deeply enough—or scratch the surface enough—that is what you would get. An actress.

I was not born knowing this about myself. It was an acquired awareness. Up until the incident—my mother's genteelism for my father's desertion—I suppose I thought I was exactly who I seemed to be. In truth, I am certain I never gave the subject much thought. Other than the normal childhood fantasies—that I was a princess switched in the hospital at birth or a foundling left on a doorstep—I was just a little girl named Ruby.

My first glimpse of this character trait came about six months after my day in the cave. It took that long for me to speak again and, once I did, I was not the same girl I had been. As I grew older and more self-aware, I became intensely conscious of playing a part in life. It came naturally to me, as though I had lived my first seven years as a false self, and this new self—this person-who-wasn't-who-she-pretended-to-be—was who I really was.

First off, I jettisoned the name. At seven, I found the nerve to ban anyone from ever calling me Ruby again. In fact, it was the first thing I said.

We had returned to Michigan in September of the year my father disappeared. The Tennessee police had exhausted their questions and effectively discontinued the search for him, though they claimed they were still looking. I learned years later that they had even used divers to explore the underground lake for remnants of my father, due mainly to the vestigial presence of his car in the parking lot. Could he have fallen in? Committed suicide? But—as I could have told them already—no diver has ever been able to find the bottom of that pool of water.

The Tennessee doctors had washed their hands of me. Unworriedly, they advised my mother to let nature take its course. They said that I would talk again when I was good and ready. Psychology was never mentioned.

Silently, I began second grade. My mother had organized everything for me at school. She met privately with the principal and the teachers. I am not quite sure what she told them but, knowing her, I suspect that they were scared of her. Peggy Russell could be imperious. Because of her— or really because my story had been splashed all over the news—I was given a wide berth. I did my assignments and turned in my worksheets and drawings. But I was never called upon to write on the blackboard or answer a question in class.

It was January of 1969, not long after I had celebrated my seventh birthday in December. That had been a grim affair with only me, my mother and grandmother—cake and ice cream for me, Salems and coffee for them—followed by an equally desultory Christmas.

On that January morning, I set off as usual for school.

Swathed against the Michigan winter in the standard uniform of undershirt, tights, dress, sweater, zip-up leggings, coat, hat, scarf, mittens, and boots, it was difficult to walk.

Five houses down, as I squeaked through the snow, the Kowalski kids fell out their front door—all seven of them. Though we Russells may have been a small family—smaller still after my father's exit—the Kowalskis were considered large by anyone's standards.

The Kowalskis exuded a group identity, which may be common for children of large families. They were like the Soviet bloc nations—hard to distinguish one from the other and all controlled from a central command. In their case, it was Dickie, who was the oldest at twelve. They were all pretty bad, but Dickie was the worst of the bunch.

My mother had a thing or two to say about Mrs. Kowalski and the litter of children she had produced in eight short years. My father had always reminded her that Mr. Kowalski had had a fair bit to do with it. He also joked about the milkman.

That year, when I was in second grade, all seven Kowalskis were finally enrolled in school. And all of them exited their house at the exact same minute that morning. These were the Kowalski children, at that moment in time: Dickie—age 12, Barb—age 11, Mikie—age 10, Renee—age 8, Chuckie—age 7, Philip—age 6, and Missie—bringing up the rear at age 5.

Being an only child made me highly unusual in my neighborhood. It also made me defenseless.

Dickie made eye contact first and immediately began to close in on me as he launched into the lyrics of the Dion song, "Ruby Baby." His little alto voice rang out in the cold air, making a cartoon bubble of condensation that quickly disappeared. "Ruby, Ruby, Ruby will you be mine?"

Dickie Kowalski did this every time he saw me. Every time. Even at age seven, I recognized his lack of imagination.

And just like always, his siblings backed him up with the chorus—the syllables of which were supposed to be "hey-hey"—but the Kowalskis pronounced them "hep-hep."

To escape them, I sped up my shuffle. I was doing a pretty good job of putting some distance between us—sliding on the hard pack of snow—but I was starting to get winded from breathing so hard and fast into the scarf wrapped around my mouth and nose.

"Now, I love a girl, I said-a Ruby is her name," Dickie sang on. He didn't have a bad voice.

"Hep-hep. Hep-hep," the others trilled behind him.

I worked harder to glide my feet back and forth.

"I said, the girl don't want me but I love her just the same."

"Hep-hep."

They were definitely getting closer.

"Oh, oh, Ruby, Ruby, I'm-a want ya. Like a ghost I'm-a gonna haunt ya."

At that, I broke out into the closest thing I could manage that resembled a full run. All I could hear was Dickie now. I didn't dare turn around to see which of the other Kowalskis were keeping pace with him. I lowered my head like a torpedo and worked my padded legs as hard as I could.

Just as I dared to hope I had ditched him, I felt Dickie's hand on my shoulder, which caused me to stumble and face-plant in the snow.

Seizing the opportunity, Dickie decided that the best course of action would be to tickle me and immediately jumped on my back.

I despise tickling.

Dickie endeavored to dig his fat, mittened fingers into my tufted torso.

"Ruby, Ruby, Ruby will you be mine?" he gasped along with his efforts.

"Hep-hep." His siblings caught up and encircled us.

By now, Dickie had given up singing and was maniacally working to make me laugh, pushing his fingers deeper into my coat and miraculously connecting with my rib cage. Twist and turn as I tried, I couldn't release myself from under Dickie Kowalski.

His brothers and sisters had become like a witches' coven—intoning the syllables: Hep. Hep. Hep. Hep. Over and over again. Not even bothering to sing them. Just chanting them in a monotone.

Thrashing face down in the snow, Dickie Kowalski sitting on my back, I was beginning to despair. Would he ever tire of this? Or would we die this way, Dickie and I, frozen in the snow like a misshapen beast?

Would his dimwitted siblings have the sense to pull him off me or would they freeze to death, too, drooling all around us?

But lo, like an answered prayer, my hand hit on a rock. Not a very large rock, but useful, just the same. I could just grasp it in my left hand and, if I managed it correctly, I could swing that arm over my right shoulder to connect somewhere on Dickie Kowalski's person.

Hep. Hep. Hep. Their mantra fortified my resolve.

Closing my eyes and clutching the rock, I raised my head back as far as I could, and, cobra-like, lifted myself up onto my right elbow. Supporting the full weight of Dickie Kowalski this way, I reared back and around to slam him in the head with the rock.

"Aaaaaarrrrrrgggg!" I screamed, as I did it.

"Aaaaaaarrrrrggggg!" he screamed, as he received it.

Dickie jumped off me, holding his mitten to the side of his now bloody head.

"What's the matter with you, Ruby Russell? Huh? Are you crazy?" he yelled at me. "We were just playing!"

The mouths of all six of his brothers and sisters hung open, like guppies, as they stared at me.

"Dickie Kowalski," I said, my voice surprisingly strong after its hiatus. "Don't you ever touch me again. Ever. I mean that, Dickie. And don't you ever call me Ruby, either. My name is Eleanor."

Enter Eleanor Russell, stage left.

4

SWEET DREAMS

Orlando shifts gears seamlessly, gliding us up and down the hills of this city of angels. If I close my eyes, I can pretend we are flying.

This is our maiden drive in our new Volkswagen Rabbit convertible, not counting the trip home from the dealership. Our car is red with a black canvas top—not my first choice—but it was the only one they had on the lot.

It really is a fantastic-looking car. Square and boxy—nothing like the aerodynamic designs coming out of Detroit these days, where you can no longer tell one make from another. It is certainly the most distinctive-looking car that still fits our budget.

Mindy, the leggy looker of a real estate agent, is in the front passenger seat, and I am folded into the back behind her. The top is down, the cassette player is blaring, and the sun radiates upon us. It is a perfect California day. Seventy-two degrees and sunny. Not cold, not hot. No sensation of weather at all. Annie Lennox and the Eurythmics are smoothly, sweetly singing about dreams. And this is pretty much my dream come true. My husband and I—driving down the highway—the wind in our hair.

Well. Except that he is in the front seat with Mindy, and I am in the back seat alone.

I have tied a scarf around my head, old Hollywood style, to keep my long red hair from whipping straight up in the air like a twister (after leaving the soap opera, I needed a change from my natural blond). With my sunglasses and lipstick, I look like a movie star. Which, I guess I sort of am. A soap star, anyway.

"Just hang a left here, to go up into Beachwood Canyon," Mindy says to Orlando.

"Is this the part of the Hollywood Hills we talked about?" I shout to the back of her head.

"Very much so." With the agility of a gymnast, Mindy swivels in her seat to address me. "This and Los Feliz are the areas that'll have the old Hollywood feel you want. Maybe Silver Lake, too, but that's pretty far east. Currently, there are some charming little bungalows just to the west of the canyon that are within your price range. Closer to the Cahuenga Pass."

Mindy faces forward to direct the price range comment back to Orlando. Very traditional of her to assume he is the source of our money. It doesn't bother me.

"I like to drive up first through Beachwood Canyon so you can see the pretty little village area at the top. It'll give you a nice feel for the neighborhood. Then, we'll come back down the canyon and head into the area with the houses I'm going to show you," says Mindy. It is a Hollywood-worthy gesture, I reflect, to stage manage our entrance this way.

"Brilliant," Orlando says to her, as he shifts gears and sings along with Annie Lennox. "Sweet dreams are made of this."

Who am I to disagree?

At the top of Beachwood Canyon, I see that Mindy is right. It is just about as charming as anyone could imagine. We enter the little commercial area—almost a town square—through stone columns. Lampposts—ribbed cement cylinders topped with frosted glass acorn-shaped globes, just like in the old film noirs—meander in all directions as they follow the sloping curves of the streets.

There is a cute little market, shops, and a restaurant. And the houses surpass my imagination. You can tell that the early builders in these hills, once they fled the constraints of their communities back East, really cut loose and constructed whatever fantasy houses had appealed to them. You want to live in a Spanish castle? Fine! You want to live in a California craftsman? Great! You want to play Snow White in a little thatched cottage? Knock yourself out! Minus the seven dwarves, it is all here, surrounding us.

Circling back down to look at the neighborhood Mindy has in mind for us, I notice the Hollywoodland Realty Company. Mindy's company. That's why we picked her.

"Hollywood," I say to myself, softly. "Our new home."

"Turn right here, on Scenic Avenue. There's a pretty little street up ahead. Primrose Avenue. Don't you love the name?"

Orlando makes the requisite turns and there we are, on a mixed-use residential street. There are some dreary mid-century apartment blocks tucked in among tiny Spanish-style colonials, squat bungalows, and right in the middle, a perfect—*the* perfect—rose-covered cottage.

"That's it!" I scream from the back seat.

Mindy seems surprised. "How did you know?"

"How did *you* know, Mindy?" I am nearly standing up to get a better look. "That's the house I've seen in my dreams! Stop, Orlando! Please stop! That's our house!"

Indulgently, Orlando pulls to the curb. "Are you sure? That one might not even be for sale."

We both look at Mindy, like puppies awaiting a treat.

"Well, it is for sale. It's one of the ones I was going to show you today. I was going to start over on Ivar and work my way back here. As I told you this morning, we have six houses to see." Mindy is a little petulant now that I have spoiled her game plan.

"Do you really like it?" Orlando turns around to face me.

"It's our house," I say, as though this were self-evident.

"How much?" Orlando directs the question back to Mindy, taking charge of the financial arrangements. How traditional of him. Again, I don't mind.

"This one is at the higher end of your range. I was saving it for last."

"I don't want to look at the others!" I say like a child. "Orlando, may I speak with you?"

"Of course, darling."

"Out of the car, I mean." I smile at Mindy to soften my request.

"Ah. Yes, of course." Orlando smiles at Mindy too, as a kind of apology for me, his willful wife. Mindy doesn't know that the money is mine. Why would she? Orlando looks and sounds like nobility. I look and sound like I'm twelve.

Orlando exits easily, flipping his seat forward so that I might do the same. I need to grab onto the back of it and give myself a little heave to get out.

I latch on to Orlando's hand and pull him over to the quaint picket fence—I am not making it up—the white picket fence that encloses the perfect postage-stamp-size front yard.

"This is it, Orlando. I'm certain. This is where we're meant to live."

"Darling, I appreciate that it's charming." He reaches out to touch a vibrantly colored rose—a blend of pink, red, and orange—that hangs off a picket. "But it would be prudent to go and look at all of the other options."

"Orlando," I laugh, "we got married after knowing each other for six weeks! We're not prudent! Why start now?"

Orlando pauses. He touches the strange rose again—then another, then a third—from the profusion of these roses cascading over the fence. He looks at the façade of the house, the two wicker chairs on the front porch cushioned in cabbage rose chintz, the purple clematis climbing a trellis, the pastel hollyhocks standing tall.

He looks at me.

And then, just when I am afraid that I might not have understood him as well as I thought I did, he reaches out, picks me up and twirls me around. He kisses me on the lips and says, "Welcome home, my love."

We haven't even looked inside.

5

AS THE WORLD TURNS

"Welcome to Los Angeles, Kitten." My agent, Howard Silver, kisses both of my cheeks. He has always called me Kitten. I think he calls all his clients Kitten. But, that's okay. I always feel special with Howard. He has that charismatic way of focusing his entire attention on the person he is with at the moment. He holds me by the shoulders and examines my face before he ushers me through the reception area and into his private office. There, he offers me a seat on a slick black leather chair and, forgoing his desk, takes the black leather sofa opposite.

His handsome assistant, Kyle, without being asked, brings us each a Waterford stem glass of water, floating with wedges of both lemon and lime. It is the perfect Howard touch. The kind of quick and abundant gesture, without even asking, that makes you feel fussed over but with no cost in calories.

"Gosh, Howard, I didn't know how nice your offices were!"

"Why do you think I left New York, Kitten? This beats my old cubicle on Madison Avenue, wouldn't you say?" Howard gestures toward the wall of glass that appears to tilt vertiginously down over Sunset Boulevard and the sparkling sea of LA beyond. The city shimmers, probably from air pollution particles, and very much resembles a rolling ocean.

"You deserve it," I say to him and mean it.

Howard Silver is the closest thing to a father figure that exists in my life. I have known him since I first arrived in New York after college in 1983. I wanted to be an actress—I'd studied theater and film!—and he was a junior agent, a few years out of law school, by way of the mailroom at William Morris. I worked as a hostess at Fiorello's, across from Lincoln Center, and Howard came in almost nightly. He was always dating one or another of the young ballet dancers and there, in that artistic quarter of the city, the slightly older man and his younger male companions did not stand out.

We just clicked, Howard and I. The sex part was not an issue, so that cleared an entire junk heap out of the way, for openers. But beyond that, Howard Silver is a truly kind person. I saw it the first day I met him when I was struggling with delivering an order and he came to my rescue. And, from that day to this, he has rescued me more than once.

"How are you doing, Kitten?" Howard asks me.

"I'm doing very well, Howard."

"You're feeling better about the—uh—misunderstanding? Because you look good. You look great, even. Better than ever. And you're one good-looking girl for a girl," he teases.

"Thank you, Howard," I say. "You've always been my biggest fan."

"I have plans for you, Kitten. Now that that mess is all over and you're out here. The sunshine and fresh air will do you good. Already have done you good. I have so many people who are dying to meet you. Despite what happened, you're a hot commodity."

"That's great. I can't wait. But I have something to tell you. I wanted to tell you personally."

"Should I sit down? I am sitting down. Should I recline?"

"Stop! I'm about to tell you a happy thing!"

"Oy. I'm bracing myself."

"Howard! Seriously!"

"Okay, shoot."

I take a deep breath and open my hands wide. Broadway style. "I'm married!" I say.

Howard looks blank.

"I just said I'm married. I've gotten married. To a husband."

Howard slowly nods his head. "I know what married means. Are you pregnant? Is that why you did this?"

"No! I'm not pregnant. Why on earth would you say that?"

"Why?" Howard's voice stuns me with its sharpness. "Well, because I was in New York with you not even six months ago in April. You were collapsed on the floor of your apartment because that diva had you written out of *The Finger of Fate*. You couldn't understand how you could be fired despite the popularity of your character. You were weeping because you thought you'd never work again. You were afraid she'd ruined your reputation."

I can't believe he is dredging this up!

"And, as far as I know," he goes on, "and I'm pretty sure I know what I know, you weren't even *dating* someone then, much less about to be married. So, it occurs to me that you might have gotten into your cups one night and then discovered yourself in the family way. And that you decided to go forward with the whole thing because you're lonely or you need a new hobby. Or something. And that might be why I'm sitting here listening to you tell me that you're married!"

Howard comes up for air and turns to the window to study the view. After a moment, he adds, "That's why I said that."

"Well. I don't even know what to say to all that. I thought you'd be happy for me. Anyway, I'm not pregnant."

"That's good," he says, facing me again. "We both have too much invested in you to have you toss it all away. And, mark my word, a baby right now would kill your career. So. Now that we have that out of the way. Tell me. Who is it?"

"His name is Orlando Montague."

Howard's laugh starts slowly, a little gurgle arising from his belly. It bubbles up, spurts, stops. He breathes. Wipes his eyes. Regains his composure.

"Kitten! That sounds like a gay porn star!"

"I assure you he's no porn star. He's an aristocrat!"

28

At that, the dam breaks. Howard's smile grows wider. And then a whoop bursts out of him, like a dog bark.

"Howard, really. I don't know why you're laughing!"

"Sorry. Surely you see the absurdity of this?"

"There is nothing absurd about my *life!*"

"Oh, Kitten, if that's true, you're the only person on the planet who can say that."

"I get it. But don't you see how wonderful that makes what just happened to me? I met Orlando, we fell madly in love, and we were married in a little church in a Tuscan village. At sunset, for crying out loud! Absurd maybe, but pretty damned good!"

Howard sighs. "Of course, it's good. When do I get to meet your Mr. Montague? And precisely what type of aristocrat might he be?"

"English, of course. The very best kind."

"Ahhhh." Howard takes a long, theatrical sigh. "Well. Only the best for my girl."

6

A RAVEN AND
A WRITING DESK

I hear the screaming. Mournful and rhythmic. Someone lets out a wail, takes a rasping breath, and the process is repeated. It comes to me from far away, at the other end of a tunnel. It sluices through a channel—around a corner and up some stairs, through a string of shuttered doors, gelatinous like plasma—to find me where I cower. It emanates from the basement. Or it could even be outdoors.

Wherever its source, it freezes my very core.

I feel the screamer's anguish. It enters me completely as a permeating blackness. Not darkness as in lack of light, but darkness as devoid of good. Like paper dipped in ink, my body cannot resist it. What soaks into me is desolation. I am wholly inconsolable. Bereft of—well, I know not what. Who is it that is screaming? Where am I? When is this?

And then I see my husband, next to me in bed. He is looking straight into my eyes, but his face is not right. The muscles are twisted up, contorted in a grimace. Orlando's eyes are bulging with emotion. Fear? That's it. He is afraid, too. He has heard it, too. There *is* someone screaming.

"Ellie." Orlando's voice is ragged, and he speaks in a heightened whisper. "Eleanor, are you all right? What is it?"

"Orlando. Listen! We have to help that woman!" I am also stage-whispering. I am not sure why. Unless we think that *we* are in danger. Well, why wouldn't we be, with a screaming person so nearby? Something horrible must be happening.

"Ellie, what are you talking about?"

I can't make sense of his question. And, why is he holding me away from him? He has clasped onto my shoulders with locked straight arms, his elbows rigid and unyielding.

Orlando blinks his eyes. He does it a few more times. Then, his face composes itself and begins to reassemble. Finally, he speaks, "May I turn on the light?"

"Orlando, we need to find that woman!"

"Ellie, sit up. Come on, darling. Upsy-daisy." My mother used to say that. "Here, take a sip of water."

He reaches to the bedside table and holds a glass to my mouth. He succeeds in pouring half down my chin, my neck, my chest. My nightgown is now soaked.

"Orlando, we need to help that person! I know you heard it. I saw your face!"

"Ellie, that was you."

"What?"

"The screaming came from you."

"It did not!"

"Darling, it did. I was right next to you. You woke me with it. Your eyes were wide open and staring at me and, I'm embarrassed to admit it, you frightened me!" He laughs a little and rubs his hands through his long black hair, washing the demons out, it looks like. "Not like I was worried *for* you. I was actually scared *of* you. You looked strange and ominous.

"But, look at you now!" He perks up. "Lovely and sweet as normal. Wet, but sweet."

"I…I don't know, Orlando. I heard someone screaming. I *heard* it. It was so sad and just, I don't know. Just empty."

He sighs. "It's almost morning. Nearly five. Let's have some tea. There's nothing in life that can't be made better by a nice hot cuppa. I'm going to put on every light in this room and then I'll go to the kitchen to make our tea. And I'll bring it back to you, all right? Maybe you should change that nightgown."

The matter settled in his mind, he gets up from the bed. He wears his pajama bottoms only. His long, dark back gleams in the glow of the lamps as he leans over to turn them on, one by one. The room is stacked with boxes from our still-unfinished move. The walls are painted the palest pink. Mindy, the realtor, assumed we would have the color changed— Orlando being a man and this being the master bedroom. Orlando just laughed and said the pink flattered me so we would keep it. It flatters him, too.

My husband's tender care, the rosy walls, and the light of the lamps start to settle me. Still shaking, I walk to the window. The sun will rise soon and blast the cobwebs out of my brain. This is our house, after all, the one I chose. The one I had dreamt of. Flowers outside. Flowers inside—chintz curtains from Laura Ashley. I put them up yesterday. Cascading bowers of pink and green, tumbling over themselves from ceiling to floor. I hope it reminds Orlando of home. Of how I imagine his home in England to be.

I intend this to be our English cottage in Los Angeles.

I must have been dreaming just now, but I have no recollection of it. Just the screams. And the black despair. Nothing else. I scared myself. I scared my husband. God, I probably scared the neighbors. I need to shake this off. And Orlando is right, I need to change my nightgown.

"Still wearing that nighty?" Orlando is back with the tea tray. "Come on, love. Let your husband undress you."

Which I do. And he does. And the tea grows cold.

* * *

"I have a surprise for you," Orlando says when he comes back with a second round of tea. This time he has added toast and marmalade.

"I hate surprises."

"No you don't."

"How do you know?"

"I just know. I give very good surprises and you would be a foolish girl to refuse them."

"Okay, I surrender. But let the record note that it's against my will. Go ahead, surprise me."

"I'll just pop off to the garage then."

"Is it a puppy?"

"Don't even go there! It's definitely not a puppy. A puppy is the last thing we need right now."

"I don't know. I kind of wish we had a puppy. Or a kitten! I'll take a kitten."

"This is not an à la carte menu of surprises, my dear. There's a surprise I have for you and that's the surprise you'll get."

"Fine. I'm ready to receive."

"Aren't you magnanimous." He kisses me and darts out of the room. He is gone so long I doze off.

I wake to a rumbling. The room jiggles in a sharp, short shudder, as though we—the contents of the room and I—are in a box that a giant has picked up and shaken. The teacups rattle on the tray and the tiny pitcher of milk tips over. Reaching to stop the spill, it hits me that this must be an earthquake. What is it I'm supposed to do? Get under the bed? Go outside? Stand in the doorway? That's it, I am sure. I am meant to stand inside the doorjamb.

Then, just as suddenly as it started, it is over. Other than car alarms ringing outside, it is as though nothing at all has happened. I look around the room. Everything is as it was, except there is now a box sitting on the bed, right next to the tea tray. Orlando must have left it there while I was sleeping.

"Orlando?" I call out.

I reach out to touch it. It is about the size of a shoebox and wrapped in yellow paper with a white satin ribbon tied in a bow.

"Orlando?" I call a little louder.

I pick up the box and shake it, like the unseen giant just shook me. I picture a tiny person inside the box, shaking a smaller box still; a tinier person in that one, shaking an even smaller box; and so on *ad infinitum*.

Its contents make a noise as they shift from side to side. Not a sound of glass or metal. More of a soft, papery sound.

"Orlando!" Now, I actually yell. "Orlando? Come back! I want to open my present!"

Still no response.

"Okay, I give up! You're right. I do like surprises. I'm sorry I pretended I didn't!"

I get up from the bed and slip into my bathrobe.

"I'm coming to find you!" I pick up the box and set off to discover my husband's whereabouts.

The sun is shining in through the back windows of the house. Its angle is low and slanting and dust motes float in the motionless air of the rooms. I walk down the hall, through the still un-curtained living room, around more unpacked boxes and into the empty kitchen. The kettle is there on the burner, extinguished but still hot. He isn't in the house.

Then I remember he mentioned the garage.

I walk out the kitchen door and through our little garden. Varying-size clay pots are scattered everywhere, filled with flowers and greenery—gardenias, orange trees, hibiscus and bougainvillea. The air is chilly. The dew on the flowers will be all the water nature will provide them for the day. It hasn't rained for months and doesn't look like it will do so any day soon.

Quietly, I pad in my bare feet on the cold terra-cotta patio. I round the corner of the garage, recently Sheetrocked and fitted out with glass double doors to serve as an office, and there I see my husband. He is turned away from me, bent over the large secretary that just arrived from my mother—the old Georgian writing desk that has been in our family for generations. Angry as she was at our marriage, she still sent a lovely wedding present.

I walk into the room. It really will make a nice office, opening wide the way it does onto the patio, with a partial view of the hills looking just the right angle to the left. That is how all views are in the Hollywood Hills—I am coming to understand—sliced up and served in fragments. You never really see the whole of anything.

"Boo!" I say when I am nearly upon him, surprised he hasn't heard me approaching.

Orlando lets out a gasp and whirls around to face me.

"Eleanor." It is all he says but his voice is cold.

"Hi!" I force a cheery tone, to combat the chagrin I am feeling at his implied rebuke. "Did you feel that?"

"Feel what?"

"I think it was an earthquake."

"I wasn't really paying attention. You startled me."

"I'm sorry I surprised you, but I've been looking everywhere for you. I found my present, but I didn't want to open it without you." I look over his shoulder at my desk. "What are you doing?"

"I was just admiring the wood on this fine piece of furniture. Burled maple."

"I suppose. We've had that for ages."

"How long would you say? Did your parents acquire it?"

"Oh, no. We've always had it. It belonged to my mother's family in Connecticut for years, before her grandfather moved to Michigan. I'll ask her to tell me the whole story again. She's told me before, but I never really listened."

"You should pay more attention, Ellie. Or your life will pass you by and you won't have even noticed."

"Well, that's a grim thought! Anyway, you didn't notice the earthquake."

"I'm sorry, darling. Your screaming started me off on the wrong foot today. Let's go back into the house and begin this day all over again. It's still a little chilly out here."

"All right." I allow him to take me by the arm and lead me toward our cottage. "Can I open my present now?"

"Of course."

Orlando makes another pot of tea and we sit at the kitchen table. I tear into the wrapping and open the box inside. There, in creamy stock, sits a stack of letter paper. Embossed at the top in deep forest green is the name, *Eleanor Montague*, which touches me profoundly. I have a career established as Eleanor Russell, but I am moved that he's printed this paper with my married name. I take it as a sign of his love. Of his commitment. Of his permanence in my life.

I dig down under the pile to reveal the bundle of envelopes, clasped in their paper band. Creamy like the paper, with pale green tissue lining. Flipping them over, I see our address, done English-style, no house number, just the name of the house, the street and the city: *Rose Cottage, Primrose Avenue, Los Angeles*. In a nod to modern convention, he has included the zip code.

"Orlando, this is beautiful. I can't wait to write a letter!"

"You can keep them in your wonderful desk. In one of its nooks or cubbies. It seems to have many compartments."

"The perfect stationery in the perfect secretary."

"And all for the perfect wife."

7

L.A. BABY

Rounding a bend in the mountain pass, that special LA cocktail of sun-filtered-through-smog hits me in the face with brilliantly diffused midday light. I am not actually staring into the orb of the sun, but the light grows so much brighter that I can locate its shape behind the scrim of air pollution. I lower my visor and pull to the right to make my way onto the Warner Brothers lot.

This is when I pinch myself. After a lifetime of watching movies—every Saturday of my childhood and even more in college—I still can't believe I am in the land of making them. The soap opera set did not have this effect on me.

My audition today is for one of the new Brat Pack–style films that are cropping up by the dozen. John Hughes is the man of the hour and any actress who looks remotely passable as a teenager is auditioning daily for some sort of ensemble picture featuring a varied collection of precocious youths. Wholesome and new—freshly hatched out of an egg—is how Howard is positioning me now that I've left the soap opera.

I'm still getting used to the cultural divide between soaps and features. On a soap, the makeup is ladled on with a spatula and hairstyles are stiff and set. The wardrobe is purchased at Bergdorf or Saks and is upscale urban dressy—everything from ladies-who-lunch to ball gowns. On days when we were draped in furs, we had our very own Pinkerton guard who followed us around the set; when we were dressed for bed it was always in a negligée and peignoir. Though I was in my early twenties on *The Finger of Fate*, once I was tricked out that way, I could have passed for older. Thirty even. Now, for these youth-centric films, I only need to brush my hair, add a little lip gloss and mascara and I'm good to go. I also need to navigate the diction and vocal pitch—definitely younger and breathier, but not quite Valley Girl.

"Eleanor Russell," I report to the guard, who checks my name off the list of visiting starlets and directs me to the appropriate bungalow on the far side of the lot. Back I drive, keeping the faux New York City streets to my right as instructed. The incongruity of those streets—empty and pristine, with the hills of Griffith Park rising up behind them—causes me to pause.

You can make anything look real in Hollywood.

"Welcome to Los Angeles, Eleanor. I'm Jake Tapsall." The casting director is a thirty-something guy in jeans, and he sits with the director and producer, who are theme and variation of the same. "This is Max Height, our director, and Michael Gold, our producer. Please have a seat."

I take the lone chair opposite them, seated three abreast in front of a rectangular folding table, and shift to cross my legs. I've worn a jean skirt and *Flashdance* kind of loose-necked top, pairing them all with slouchy socks and sneakers to convey that I could still be in high school. I've added hoop earrings to suggest that I could be the sexy cool girl in high school.

"I must confess," Jake continues, "I was a huge fan of yours on *The Finger of Fate*. You and Nikki really had some intense competition going in your storyline. And you were so good at playing crazy! Did you guys ever watch?" He directs that question to the other men.

"No," says one, and the other just shakes his head.

"I was surprised when you left the show so suddenly." Jake seems fixated on this topic. "What did they do with your character?"

"I went to prison." I shift again and recross my legs the other way, trying to smile in an offhand way.

"Right." He laughs. "Prison!"

Michael and Max stare at me as though I actually went to prison myself.

"What is Nikki like?" Jake presses on. "I'm a huge fan."

"She's lovely," I say, my canned response to any queries about the character played by Sylvia Long, the biggest soap star in the United States—the woman whose sister I portrayed on *The Finger of Fate* and the woman who probably had me fired.

"So!" I change subjects, determined to steer this conversation in a new direction. "I really like the character of Missy in your script. She's a bit of an enigma. High school senior, yes, but a girl on the verge of womanhood." I sound like an idiot.

"Yeah," Max, the director, speaks. "Missy's cool."

"Yeah," I dumbly repeat. "She's cool."

"Want to give her a try?" asks Michael, the producer.

"Let's see what you do with her before I give you any direction," Max adds.

"All right. Am I reading with you, Jake?"

"Yep," he answers. "I'll play Buck."

"Great," I say and stand up to turn away from them for a moment, to gather my thoughts. One deep breath and I turn back around, fully (I hope) embodying Missy, the slightly slutty teenager with the sensitive heart of gold.

"Buck," I begin. "We need to talk."

* * *

An hour later, I wearily pull onto Primrose Avenue and thank heaven for small favors when I find a parking spot directly in front of our house. I have no idea how that reading went but I suspect it wasn't a triumph. Max, it turned out, had a very clear vision of Missy and I'm not sure I'm it. He asked me more than once if I could make my voice sound like Demi Moore's, raspy and low. They'll probably just end up hiring her.

Orlando is working at home today, just like every other day since we arrived in LA six weeks ago. He is currently searching for a space on Robertson or La Brea to set up his antique shop.

Oddly, that is also what my father did. My dad may have favored jeans and a cowboy hat, but he was actually an expert on early American antiques. In fact, he met my mother when they both worked at Parke-Bernet Galleries in New York. She as an intern. She says he did not dress in western garb on the job, instead cutting a dapper figure in suits. But I can't really remember him looking that way.

That similarity—though Orlando deals in Asian antiques—is probably one of the reasons I was attracted to my husband. That is surely what my shrink would say if I were still speaking to her.

"Hello!" I call as I push open the front door. I love how its mullioned glass panels open onto the front garden, letting in the maximum amount of light. "Orlando?"

I drop my bag and keys onto the little table to the right of the door and head off toward the kitchen and tea. If I spent a weekend at someone else's house, I would be fine if there were no liquor or food. But no coffee or tea? I'd have to go on a search mission.

"Orlando?" I call again. He must be out in the office. We have just had a phone and fax line installed out there. I put the kettle on and walk out the open back door to find him.

All at once, a tiny streak of black crosses my path and I stop short to stare at a small kitten, who freezes to look back at me. In a flash of instinct, I just manage to reach out and pick it up. It meow-squeaks up at me and digs its needle claws into my hand.

"Hey," I coo. "It's all right." I hold it closer to my chest and stroke its head. I haven't had a cat since my old Siamese, Charlie, died two years ago. A few more high-pitched mewls are followed by the beginnings of a full-fledged purr. I stand there in our garden, holding this little life, listening to its oversized motor, and I fall headlong in love.

"You're back!" Orlando walks out of the office. "What's that you have there?"

"Isabel," I say.

"Isabel? Whose cat is that?"

"My cat. Our cat." I correct myself. "Her name is Isabel."

"Did you go to a pet shop?"

"No. She was here. Just now. She let me pick her up. She's purring!"

"Eleanor." Just like my mother, when he uses my full name, I know he is serious. Although my mother would string together all three names: Eleanor Ruby Russell.

"Orlando." I use his name right back at him. "I've wanted a dog or cat so badly and I think we have to see the perfection in this. Isabel just appeared, an answer to my wish. Kind of like you did when I met you on the airplane."

"Darling, I don't think it's quite the same thing."

"It's exactly the same thing!"

"Do you even know how to care for a cat?" I can see him softening.

"Of course I do! I've had four different cats in my life and two dogs. I definitely know how to care for animals."

"How do you know she's a she?"

"Well, I haven't really checked. But I decided long ago that my next cat would be black and I would call her Isabel. Come on, Orlando, you have to admit it's meant to be."

Just then the tea kettle starts to whistle.

"How about this?" I say to him. "You run to the store for litter, a box, and some cat food, and I'll have tea ready when you get back. It's almost four." Four p.m., I have learned, is hallowed ground for an Englishman. All life stops for tea, precisely at four. If you were an invading army, you would be wise to hit England at four. You'd sail right into the country, completely unobstructed.

"Ah!" He relents. "Anything for you."

8

ETERNAL SUNSHINE

It's another sunny day in LA. When we arrived here—that first day of unmarred sunshine—I felt compelled to go outdoors, to make hay while the sun shone, as my grandmother would have said. The following day was cloudless, as well, and outside I went again. Then the next day, and the next, and the next. After a point, I realized that this was just it. It was always sunny and 72 degrees in the city of Los Angeles. If I intended to do my laundry, pay my bills, or vacuum the living room rug, I had better stop waiting for a rainy day and just get on with it.

"B Bel!" I call as I prepare my kitty's food. Isabel, wouldn't you know it, has turned out to be male. So his name just morphed into B Bel for Isabel-the-Boy. He skitters happily into the kitchen, snaking around my legs and purring loudly. I can barely put down the bowl without falling over from his entanglement with my person.

"Good morning." Orlando enters the kitchen fully dressed. "I'm off to look at that space."

"Oh, wonderful. I hope it works. La Brea would be terrific since it's so close to our house."

"Yes. I think so too. We just need to negotiate price." He pours a cup of coffee. "Would you like one, my love?"

"No thanks. I'm over-coffee'd already. So, about the rent? What do you think we can afford? I mean I haven't booked a film yet and my soap savings are dwindling. And my next trust payment isn't due until the first of the year."

"Don't worry your pretty head about that. I've got it covered."

"Okay, because I just wasn't sure. With the special funds we've drawn for the house and car, my quarterly distributions are going to get much smaller. My trustee has explained all that to me and he's warned me to be a little more careful and…"

"Eleanor." Orlando cuts me off sharply and then laughs a little as he continues, "I said I have it covered. You might try listening."

I study his face, trying to connect the look in his eyes with his laughter.

"I'm sorry, darling," he says. "You were just prattling on and not really paying attention. I told you I have it covered. You don't need to worry."

I suppose he means to telegraph to me that the conversation is over. That it's all right to discuss my money in all of its nuances but his money is in some mysterious pool that we aren't going to talk about. I don't know what resources Orlando may have, but we have paid for everything in our marriage, thus far, with distributions from my trust fund. And my trust fund is not that large.

My mother's family were minor Midwestern industrialists—a degree of success and comfort, generation-skipping trusts established for the grandkids and all—but that was nearly a hundred years ago and they certainly were not the Fords or Carnegies. My great-grandfather had invented a part that was indispensable in the early years of automobile manufacture but eventually had become obsolete. On top of that, he had five children, and those children all had children and, before you know it—shirtsleeves to shirtsleeves in three generations.

"Fine," I say. The word all women use to signify that they are deeply ticked off.

"Ellie. Don't be a baby."

"I'm not the baby, here, Orlando! You're the one who just flew off the handle and became exceedingly rude! I don't like the way you spoke to me. Really. I don't."

"I said I was sorry. You're not very good at listening this morning, my poppet."

"Orlando, don't patronize me. And that was not an apology. When someone says he's sorry but if you hadn't done what *you'd* done he wouldn't have had to do what *he* did that he is now sorry for, it means he's not at all sorry for what *he* did but is, instead, sorry for what *you* did to make him do it!"

"Darling." Orlando moves over to me and places both hands on my shoulders. "You seem tired today."

"I am not tired! I just got up. I'm angry that you spoke to me so disparagingly. That you continue to talk to me like I'm a five-year-old. And a bad one, at that!"

"I didn't realize you were such a grudge-holder, Ellie."

"I'm *not* a grudge-holder! We're in the middle of discussing something that just happened three minutes ago. That doesn't qualify as holding a grudge."

"Look, I need to go. I can't just stand here going around in circles with you." And, with that, he sets down his mug and turns on his heel toward the living room.

"Orlando!" I follow after him. "Please! Don't leave in the middle of an argument! I can't stand that!"

"We're not arguing, Eleanor. *You* are ranting." His tone is cold and distant.

"That's not true! You started this!"

"Well you're certainly not letting it finish gracefully," he concludes as he walks out the front door, neglecting to close it behind him.

"Orlando!" I shout to his retreating form.

Before I can even analyze what just happened, B Bel slips out the front door and the open gate, and heads in the direction of the street. "Bel!" I cry as I run after him, still in my pajamas and robe.

Bel darts into the road with me hot on his heels. Orlando has pulled off to the left toward downtown Hollywood, and I imagine he doesn't see either of us in the rear-view mirror as we streak from left to right. On the opposite side, Bel easily makes his way between the pickets of our neighbor's white wooden fence. I've seen this property, of course—our cottage faces it—but I've never met its occupants. In fact, I haven't actually seen the house, obscured as it is by the profusion of plants crowding the front yard.

I hesitate for a moment—I am now officially about to trespass—then I lift the latch of the gate. The fence is badly in need of a paint job and the gate practically falls off its hinges at my touch. I wonder if I should prop it open or close it behind me. I opt to shut and refasten it, which takes a little effort.

I pause to take stock.

The house is set far to the back of the premises, with an expansive and entirely overgrown yard in front. The enclosure is an utter bramble. Tangles of old growth roses—the exact same color as those at our cottage—wind around other trailing and spiraling vegetation, the identity of which I could not name. Great masses of all of it clump up the sides of trees, which rise dizzyingly around me. I recognize honeysuckle and think I see jasmine, as well. Those three plants—rose, jasmine, and honeysuckle, along with the ones I don't recognize—combine to create a perfume that is overwhelmingly sweet and cloying. I am starting to feel hot and nauseated.

"Bel?" I call out in a heightened whisper as I visually scan the setting. The house is directly in front of me, at the end of a long, straight path. Its doors and windows are shut tight. It appears to be a cottage, similar to ours, but it has not been maintained as well as ours has. Its yellow paint is peeling, and a faded trellis has loosened off one side and flaps with a little ticking sound against the stucco wall. As I set off toward it, I notice that the walkway beneath my feet—what little I can see of it with plants encroaching from both sides—is red brick in a beautiful herringbone pattern. The property must have been lovely at one time. But the shabbiness of the house and the overgrown garden make me think that it might be abandoned. *Suddenly Last Summer* was my mother's shorthand code for a garden that had grown wild to the point of choking off its surroundings. This garden certainly meets that standard.

It is then that I notice the cats.

There is an orange tabby sunning itself where a pinpointed ray of light penetrates the canopy to brighten a little patch of path directly in front of me. It is lying on one side and opens a bored yellow eye to check me out as I pass. Farther on, a black cat—a larger version of Bel with the same white chest patch and green eyes—sits sentry to further passage. "Hi there," I say to him. Surely he must be Bel's father. Whoever he is, I need to circle around him when he doesn't budge an inch.

Cats are everywhere, I now see. Lying about, sitting on a few rusted iron benches that pop up out of the undergrowth, scampering through the tall grasses to chase each other around. As I make my way through this wonderland, calling Bel's name from time to time, I reflect on my fight with my husband.

It was our first fight and it has left me feeling remorseful. I am utterly consumed with guilt and fear. Why do men do that? Turn everything around and make you feel that you are completely to blame? Why specifically did *Orlando* do that? It is a trap that, once set, I cannot avoid falling into. I feel horrible now, like I've done something irreparably wrong and there won't be a way to fix it. On top of it, why did he just walk out? I am never able to walk away from any discord. Once I'm in an argument with someone I love, I just can't concentrate on anything else until it's resolved.

This property goes on forever. I am approaching the house and still don't see my cat. Should I just go home and trust that Bel will return to me? It is dawning on me that this must be where he came from originally. And who feeds these animals? This is the strangest place—right in the middle of the Hollywood Hills and yet a world apart. Vacillating, I make a decision to circle around the house and look for him in the back. "Bel?" I call out once more.

Even larger trees flank the left side of the house and I am fully submerged into deep shade when I follow the path in that direction. "Bel?" I try again. Just then, his little black form—at least I think it is him in the shadows—flits across my feet and disappears in front of me. "Bel! Stop it. Come here!" No cat I've ever met responds well to being chastised, but I'm feeling strange and anxious and I want to get out of this place. "Bel? Come on! Bel!"

"Ruby."

Just like that. I hear the voice behind me and my blood stops moving. No one—I mean no one—ever calls me Ruby anymore. I haven't used that name in nearly twenty years.

"Ruby." The voice says again. I am not imagining it. There is someone following me—a woman—and she is calling me Ruby.

Slowly, I turn around to face her.

An old woman stands before me. A small, skinny old lady in a faded floral housecoat. Her hair is a mass of short silver curls, her eyes are a piercing blue, and she is looking directly at me.

"I'm sorry," I blurt in a run-on sentence, "to be on your property but my cat ran over here and I was scared he'd get hit by a car and I just followed him here to bring him home."

"Ruby." She says it again.

"I...I...do I know you?"

"Ruby."

"Look..."

"It's the name of your cat."

"Oh!" I nearly collapse with relief. "My cat! Well, um, no. I called him Isabel. But then I found out he's a boy and now I call him Bel."

"I called him Ruby when he was born."

"You did?" I am stupefied.

"I did. And then he disappeared. Did you take him?"

"No! I would never take someone's cat! I mean, he came to my house and I thought he was feral and I just adopted him. I didn't know he was your cat. I'm so sorry."

"Did you post a sign to say you'd found a missing cat?"

"Uh, no. I didn't. I just figured he was wild."

"Did he act like a feral cat to you?" She is pretty tenacious for a little old lady.

"No. No, he didn't. He let me pick him up. I'm sorry." Suddenly I am overcome with light-headedness and feel like I'm going to pass out. I reach out for the closest tree.

"Here," she says as she holds out her hand to me. "You don't look so good. Come into my house and sit down a minute."

This is all so strange—this garden, this old woman, these cats—that I am struck with visions of witches in the fairy tales of the Brothers Grimm. I don't think I should go into her house. I really don't. But I can't see a way out of it. And I do think I'm going to keel over.

"Come, dear," she says, and—in an instant—she transforms from a witch into a fairy godmother right before my eyes. An old and wrinkly fairy godmother, but her menace has disappeared and warmth exudes from her.

Inside, she offers me lemonade. "The sugar will do you good," she says.

I drink it and gasp at the sweetness.

"Extra sweet is the way I like it!" She winks.

"This qualifies as sweet," I say. But it is somehow refreshing as well.

"Ruby."

My agitation returns. "Why do you keep saying that?"

"That name seems to cause some unease for you, my dear. Did you ever know a Ruby?"

"Uh, sort of."

"I see," she says, and I think she does, but she quickly changes the subject. "My name is Dottie. Dottie Robinson. I was born in this house back in 1907. It was one of the first houses around here. There were orange groves to the south, but this land up here didn't have much. My father settled us here for the view. And the air. But the view is gone now. We're surrounded by apartment buildings."

I don't mention the thatch of her garden, which wouldn't allow her to see anything even if she were surrounded by nothing at all.

"So, Ruby…"

"That's *not* my name." I say that a little too emphatically.

"Of course not, dear. You haven't told me your name. The cat's name is Ruby. Remember?" She talks to me like I'm demented. I wish people would stop talking to me that way. "Would you like to keep him?"

"Oh yes! I'd like to keep him very much. I really love him." And I surprise myself by starting to cry.

"Here, dear." She whips out a tissue that was tucked up into the sleeve of her housecoat. I can't very well refuse it but I'm not sure that it's entirely clean. In fact, this house must be crawling with fleas. There are cats everywhere inside, too.

"Don't worry. We don't have fleas." She reads my mind!

"No, of course not. I didn't think you did."

"Now, really dear, if we're going to be friends, you might as well be honest."

"I…"

"Let's start with your name. It's not Ruby, that much we know. But there are thousands—millions—of other names that you could have. Names like Peggy or Sonny or Eleanor."

I stand up so quickly that my chair falls over. "I have to go." I almost can't get out the words. She *is* a witch.

"I'm not a witch, dear," she says in a matter-of-fact tone. "I'm just your friendly neighborhood clairvoyant. That's how we said it in the old days. Such a nice word." Dottie pauses and appears to consider the prettiness of that word. "Any-who-how!" She gets herself back on track with that silly expression my grandmother used to use. "Psychics—that's your modern term—are not witches. Though people have often confused us."

"I have to go," I repeat and stumble toward the door.

"Don't forget your cat," she says as she hands me little Bel. Where did she get him? I never even saw him enter the house.

"Oh, thank you! Thank you so much. I promise I'll take very good care of him." I step outside and turn away from her.

"I know you will, my dear. And, one more thing." I pause to listen to her. "You're not crazy. Don't let anyone make you feel you're crazy."

"I won't." I say and start to turn away.

"Oh, and Ruby?"

I freeze. My voice comes out as a whisper. "What?"

"Don't you think that's a better name than the one you're using?"

I cannot think of a thing to say. I pivot and run down the garden path clutching sweet Bel to my chest, putting as much distance as I can between myself and this neighborhood patch of enchantment.

Away from these rumblings of Ruby and back to my life as Eleanor.

9

VERTIGO

Orlando has been gone all day. He left for his meeting at nine a.m. and I haven't seen him since. This is the first day I've been alone in our cottage and it comes on the heels of our unsettling argument.

I napped for a bit this morning and woke with a start—in that sweaty damp of a childhood fever—wondering if I had dreamt that strange encounter with the woman across the street. Dottie. Between the fight with my husband and my meeting with the neighbor, I am feeling a bit unstrung.

As the day has stretched on, I have tried to occupy my time, both constructively and not.

I have paced and sat and tried to read. I have ambled out to the office and trudged back in to go through each of the rooms in the house. That endeavor doesn't take long since there are only five of them.

I have climbed the stone steps that steeply rise through a eucalyptus grove behind the office and stooped to pull a few weeds in the overgrown terraced gardens. The scent of these trees—normally so refreshing—overwhelms me now.

Each time I return to the house, I stop to check the answering machine. Orlando might have called while I was outdoors. He has not.

Finally, in a bid for composure, I go to the market to get what I need to prepare dinner. A nice candlelit meal will be just the ticket to make up for our cross words this morning. Since we only have the one car, I travel by bicycle with a basket in front—no easy task through the Hollywood Hills. Between the uphill passages and the already-narrow lanes further pinched by parked cars, I am spent from physical exertion and mental vigilance. My fatigue at least helps to mitigate my anxiety.

Once home, I put the kettle on for a cup of tea and turn the radio dial to classical. The gentle notes of Brahms rise up from the little box on the counter to soothe me.

Roast chicken is what I have decided to make. Stuffed with lemons and garlic, rubbed in olive oil, salt, and rosemary; served with mashed potatoes, wilted broccoli rabe, my grandmother's gravy (always use the potato water), and a bottle of Chianti—memories of our time in Italy— should set just the right note of comfort and rapprochement. How can he stay mad at me if I've roasted a chicken for him?

Bird in the oven, potatoes peeled, table set with candles, I am running a bath to further take the edge off my jangled nerves when the phone rings. I slip once on the bathmat, barrel down the short hall to our bedroom, and grab that extension before the answering machine picks up.

"Hello," I say with a happy up-note, to show Orlando I am no longer angry.

"Kitten." It is Howard. "Throw on something gauzy and romantic and get over to the Paramount lot within the hour. They've fired the lead on this new untitled gothic film and they're going to meet three actresses tonight. Only three, Kitten, and you're one of those three. If you get it, you would start rehearsal tomorrow."

"I can't!"

"You can't what?"

"I'm cooking dinner and I just…I don't know." The thought of a starring role suddenly terrifies me. "I mean, I haven't even seen the script. Plus, I don't have a car."

"What do you mean you don't have a car? You just bought one!"

"Orlando has it. He's been gone all day and I don't know where he is and I just can't, Howard. I promise I'll be more amenable tomorrow, but tonight I can't."

"Listen, Kitten, this is a big role—the lead—in an important studio picture. And they are only seeing *three* girls. Do you understand what that means? It means they take you seriously. That your recognition on that soap amounts to something. If you refuse to show up for this, you won't win friends or influence any people in this town. Look, they had Meg Ryan and it didn't work out. I don't know why, she's too contemporary or something. You, my love, are not a modern-looking girl. You were born to play this part. Now, get your ass over there!"

"Howard, I said I don't have a car. Even if I *wanted* to go, I couldn't."

"I live five minutes from you. Get dressed and I'll be right over. Seriously, Kitten, you need to do this. Your career needs this. You need this. Your agent needs this!"

"Oh god, Howard, I had a fight with Orlando and I'm cooking dinner and I just need to fix things with him."

"I'll have you back in less than two hours. In plenty of time for your make-up dinner with Mr. Wonderful."

"You don't know him."

"But I know *you*. And I know you need to get some work right now and get back on the horse that threw you."

He's right, of course. I need to get back to work. And I can do it. I can. Plus, Orlando and I had that fight about money. If I get a movie, our financial worries will ease up. "Okay," I relent. "Give me fifteen minutes."

I turn off the spigot, drain the tub, and dash out to the kitchen to lower the oven temperature to 300 degrees. I had just put the chicken in. Surely it can cook for two hours at 300. I trot back to the bedroom, nearly falling over Bel, who is now fully into the game of racing me from room to room, and throw on my gauziest dress. I shake out my hair—this new red is definitely dreamy and romantic—and touch up my face minimally. There. I look like the girl in Dracula. How's that for gothic?

True to his word, Howard arrives in exactly a quarter of an hour.

* * *

At eleven p.m., I am picking at the dry, overcooked chicken and draining my glass of wine. My date for the evening—B Bel—sits opposite me on top of Orlando's plate. He waits very patiently for me to hand him little bits of chicken, the fatty parts I don't care to eat.

Orlando has still not returned.

The cat and I both jump at the ring of the phone. Once again, I dash to pick it up while Bel makes his way toward the chicken.

"Hello?" My tone is more tentative this time.

"Kitten?" Damn it, it's Howard again. "Are you sitting down?"

"No, Howard, I'm standing up."

"Well, sit down. I have big news for you. *You* are the new Lavinia Lange!"

"Bel, put that down!" The cat jumps off the table dragging a drumstick. "Just a second, Howard." I run over to Bel and wrestle the chicken out of his jaws.

"Hi, Howard. I'm back."

"Are you all right? I just told you that you have officially been offered the lead role in the new Frank Walders film at Paramount!"

"That's great, Howard. I'm happy. Really. So, what's the offer?"

"A hundred and fifty thousand, which is pretty damned good since this is your first feature. You start tomorrow with a week of rehearsals, then you go right into nine weeks of filming. They're shooting the whole thing in a soundstage and around town, so you don't have to travel. Five-day work week, unlike location shoots, which are six. No per diem since there's no travel. So, how's that, Kitten? You've got the job, you've got the money, you've got your career back on track and you don't even need to leave hubby dearest."

"Who are you talking to?" Orlando's voice is close behind me and causes me to jump from the proximity and unexpectedness of it. He is practically touching me and I didn't even hear him come in.

"Darling!" I spin to face him. His eyes are dead, flat cold. "It's Howard! I've just booked a movie! I start tomorrow! I made dinner, too!" I cap my string of superlatives with a sweeping arm gesture toward the table, the chicken detritus, and the sputtering candles that are now down to about an inch of their length.

"We need to talk," he says.

Four words that strike terror in the heart: We-need-to-talk.

"Uh, Howard, I need to go."

"Eleanor!" Howard *never* calls me that. "I will personally drive to your house at 7:30 tomorrow morning. Get your ass out the door and get that ass in my car and I will drive you to the set. Is that clear?"

My head is spinning out of control. What is the matter with everyone?

"Yes. It's clear." I click down the receiver, turn to my husband and force my face to smile. "Are you hungry?"

Orlando smiles back at me in his normal, loving manner. "Yes, I am!" he enthuses. "Dinner looks fantastic." He sits at his chair at the table and, with a little theatrical flourish, shakes out his napkin to place on his lap. Am I imagining things? Wasn't he just icy with me and speaking in a threatening tone? "Sorry I was gone so long. Great news, though. The space is terrific. We've worked out all the details and I can immediately schedule my containers to arrive from London to get the place stocked up."

"Oh, Orlando, that's wonderful! I'm so happy for you—for us! And, I have news too! Like I said, I just booked a film!" I pour a glass of Chianti for him as he carves up the chicken. I decide not to ask him where exactly he's been for the past fourteen hours. Better to just concentrate on the now.

"Looks like you got started without me," he says as he examines the table.

"I'm sorry," I say, on my guard again. "It's just so late. I didn't know where you were. Anyway, I just picked at it."

"I like sharing our meals together, Ellie. I would not begin dinner without you."

"I love eating together, too. But the chicken was ready hours ago and I never heard from you. Where were you?" My gut instantly tells me that this is the wrong question to put to Orlando tonight.

"Eleanor." He looks me straight in the eye. "If this marriage is to work, we need to trust each other."

"What are you talking about? We're newlyweds! And you're questioning whether or not the marriage will work?"

"You're being dramatic. I'm not questioning our marriage, Ellie. I'm simply stating that, as a married couple, we need to trust one another."

"That's not exactly what you said, Orlando. If someone says, *if* this marriage is going to work, it implies that he thinks it might not!" Even I hear myself being petulant and argumentative.

"Eleanor." I wish he would stop saying my name. "Don't be so literal. You're acting like a child."

There is no way off this merry-go-round unless I forcibly stop the spinning. "You're right. I'm sorry." I rise and cross over to kneel next to his chair and rest my head in his lap. "I love you, Orlando. I'm so happy for you about the new space."

"Thank you, my love. Would you pass the potatoes?"

I guess that's all the reprieve I'm going to get, so I get up and go back to my place.

Orlando never asks any questions about my movie and I decide not to mention Dottie. He finishes the chicken and the bottle of Chianti. To my infinite relief, we make love on the living room rug, in front of a crackling fire. Orlando falls asleep and I lie there, stroking Bel and convincing myself that this day that had begun so badly is ending well after all.

Orlando has his antique store.

I have a movie starting tomorrow.

Our sweet little kitten who was nearly lost has been safely returned to us.

I may have a new friend in Dottie, eccentric as she may be.

So, then, why do I feel so afraid?

10

THRILLER

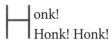onk!
Honk! Honk!
Honk!

Drying my hair in the bathroom, I think I hear a car alarm ringing on our block. Switching off the dryer, I realize Howard must be outside beeping for me. Not very gentlemanly and a little out of character with the Howard I know and love. I throw on my sweater, grab my bag, and kiss my sleepy husband and cat goodbye.

"Hey!" I say as I open the passenger door of his yellow Karmann Ghia. "What's with the honking? Why didn't you come to the door? I could have introduced you to Orlando."

"I'll meet lover boy another time. If we don't leave now, you'll be late."

"Okay. I just want you to love him as much as I do."

"Really? That much?"

"You know what I mean." I feel sulky on the subject of Orlando and opt to pick a new one. "Nice car, Howard."

"I think it strikes the right note of effortless glamour. Old money in an LA kind of way."

"I don't know, Howard, sounds like you're trying pretty hard."

"I always try hard, Kitten, but no one is supposed to know it."

"Where are we going?"

"To a conference room on the Paramount lot. You'll do all your rehearsals there. Most of the filming will be done on a soundstage, but you'll shoot exteriors in Echo Park. That's the neighborhood where they made Michael Jackson's 'Thriller' video."

"That sounds like fun."

"Carroll Avenue is pretty gentrified. My gay compatriots are restoring all the big old Victorian houses down there. The one that John Landis used in that video is still a wreck, but the one they're using for this film is spectacular. I've seen pictures of it."

"I haven't even read the script."

"Reach over the back seat and you'll find your copy, along with today's call sheet."

I do just that and discover that Howard, my love of an agent, has placed my copy in a soft brown leather binder. "How did you have time to do this?"

"Well, look closely and you'll see that it's not monogrammed or anything. I just popped it into a leather binder I already had. Don't think you're that special."

"I know how special I am to you, Howard."

"Well, let's not get maudlin." Howard reaches over to touch my hand. "Just be a good girl and take care of yourself. This will be a demanding shoot and you need to have your stamina and your wits about you."

"What *is* the story?"

"It's a modern treatment of the Hitchcock film, *Rebecca*. Based on the Daphne du Maurier book. They're just calling it *Untitled Gothic* for now."

"I loved *Rebecca*! Actually, I liked the book better than the movie. Joan Fontaine was a little snively for my taste."

"Well, I think that's why they hired you, Kitten. You have that frail Joan Fontaine quality. Minus the snivel."

"No, I don't!"

"The producers think you do. Just do me a favor and have it, okay? Play ball?" Howard turns to look meaningfully at me. Then he turns back to the road. "Anyway, I haven't actually read it yet, either. They've been keeping the script under wraps. This draft was just messengered to my house at seven this morning. I think it's *Rebecca* but scarier."

I decide to ignore Howard's insinuations and keep it light. "Who plays Max de Winter? Who plays Mrs. Danvers?"

Just then, we pull up to the beautiful gates of Paramount Pictures— my first film studio in LA—and the sense of Old Hollywood overwhelms me. "Oh Howard! I wish I had a camera!"

Howard gives my name at the gate and is directed to the appropriate corner of the lot. He continues, "Look, I don't think this is a literal remake of *Rebecca*. It's more of an homage to the spirit of the thing. You're definitely the young bride of an older aristocratic man. There's a housekeeper, but I don't think she's called Mrs. Danvers. But this goes to a darker place than the original. They're trying to compete for an audience used to special effects and gore. I mean, they've seen *Aliens* and *Friday the Thirteenth*!"

"So I'm doing a horror movie?"

"They've sticking with the descriptor of gothic, but not your grandmother's gothic. You'll start to get a feel for it in rehearsal today. They've all been rehearsing for a week already, so they know each other."

"Oh god! I forgot that part. I'm replacing Meg Ryan. I'm walking into a group that's already formed. They probably all loved Meg."

"I guess they didn't *all* love Meg, because Meg isn't there anymore."

"Who plays the husband?"

"Ben Cross. Brit. *Chariots of Fire*."

"Oh, wow. Who plays the Mrs. Danvers person?"

"Julie Walters. *Educating Rita*."

"What a cast! I can't believe they picked me."

"They said when you walked into the room, they just knew they were looking at Lavinia. At least this character has a name. The Joan Fontaine part in *Rebecca* never had one.

"No," I say, reflecting on my discussion of names with Dottie yesterday. Was that only yesterday? It feels like a decade ago—a vague and hazy memory. "We never knew her name."

"Here we are!" Howard announces brightly, trying—I suppose—to fortify my courage with his enthusiasm. "Knock 'em dead!"

11

DOUBLE INDEMNITY

"Bye, Howard. Thanks for the lift." I drag myself out of the Karmann Ghia that evening after work and cross around to the driver's side, leaning in to kiss his cheek. "I appreciate you driving me to and from work. I appreciate all you do for me."

"What's an agent for? Anyway, it's easy for me to go by your house on the way to my office. I'm happy it went well today."

"Me too. They're all so nice."

"Why wouldn't they be nice to you, lovely girl that you are? Get some rest. Today was a short day but once you start shooting, you know how long the workday is. We don't want you getting overtired."

"I'm not that fragile, Howard. But I promise I will. See you in the morning."

Howard pulls off down the road and I turn to face Rose Cottage. The flowers are all in their usual state of riotous bloom, the chintz-covered chairs sit ready on the porch. For a moment, the chairs appear to move, to rock just a little. But the air is still, no breeze at all. Maybe it is an effect of light? The sun is setting, and it hits the porch in just such a way to bounce back from the glass paneled doors to show an elongated version of myself back to me. I feel a sharp pang of anxiety at the thought of crossing the threshold. Simultaneously, I bat the sensation away. Why would I be scared to go home? Clearly, the spooky quality of my new film is already permeating my psyche. I must be attentive to that particular pitfall and not let the movie influence my life.

To come clean, that was really what happened to me on *The Finger of Fate*. After the first fabulous year on the show, my storyline took a turn into dark territory. In fact, it became so bizarre that it started to engulf me. My character embarked on an epic battle with the main character of the show. The two characters were sisters. Sylvia, the star, played—well, she still plays—Nikki Wales, one of the most popular characters in soap opera history. I, the newbie, played her much younger sister, Tiffany. Well, half-sister, to be precise.

I don't know what the writers were up to, but the storyline got stranger and stranger. The two sisters started off warmly but ended up in a death spiral of competition. Because she was the star, Sylvia always came off as the better person. I know it's just make-believe, just a part, and an actor needs to play it to the hilt, but soap opera fans can be so literal. Some of them believe you are who you play on that little screen. Maybe because you enter their living room five days a week, and because you are known only as your character—unlike a movie star who is known as herself— the viewers come to believe you *are* that character.

I received letters from fans who were irate with me. One woman, who explained that her two daughters fought in the same way that Nikki and Tiffany did, suggested that I seek psychotherapy. I considered writing her back to clarify that I was not Tiffany; that Tiffany was not, in fact, even a real person. But, of course, I didn't.

I got letters from prisons. Hardened criminals gave me advice on how to straighten out my life, correct my twisted motives, and take better control of my actions. After a while, reality and fiction started to blur. It became difficult to shake off the darkness that was Tiffany. Tiffany was jealous and conniving. Tiffany plotted against Nikki. Tiffany was obsessed with bedding Nikki's husband and eventually succeeded. That, too, was a Pyrrhic victory for Tiffany because Rand—Nikki's husband—never stopped loving Nikki and told Tiffany that she was a poor substitute for her older sister—not nearly as beautiful or as worthy by half.

Taken all together, it was impossible not to feel the weight of it. Not to feel the spider web of depression encroaching upon me. My character was bad to the bone, unloved, a loser that people wanted to lose. Tiffany went from being *Ingénue of the Year* to *The Villainess Fans Loved to Hate*.

And I went with her.

I played that character twelve hours a day, five days a week, fifty-two weeks a year. I spent my evenings and weekends reading scripts and studying lines for that character. I began to lose sight of the fact that I was not, in fact, that character. Bit by bit, I felt a return of my troubles—old, childhood demons—and I felt myself slipping south of reality.

Is that really so puzzling?

I shake off the memory and any trepidation I am feeling and stride toward my front door. This is my house, the cottage I share with Orlando, my husband. There is no reason whatsoever to be afraid of entering it.

12

DARK SHADOWS

"Good evening, Eleanor."

Orlando is sitting in an overstuffed chair in front of a crackling fire when I walk in. His legs are crossed, he has a drink on the table next to him, and he holds B Bel on his lap. The tableau makes the perfect picture of home and hearth. "I've made dinner for you as a special surprise."

I turn my head and see the table set with my grandmother's old Spode blue-and-white transferware. Orlando has replaced the candles that had dripped to nothing with new, creamy-white columns and arranged a cluster of those incredible roses from the garden. It is all just so lovely I think I might cry.

"Wow! It's beautiful! What a great surprise! Thank you!" I cross the room and drop to my knees to hug him where he sits. Though he puts his arms around me, his embrace is reserved. "Orlando?" I scan his face. "What's wrong?"

"What on earth could be wrong, my poppet?"

"I don't know." Maybe I am imagining it.

"You said it yourself last night. We're newlyweds. And I made a little dinner for my bride."

"Is this about last night?"

"Darling. Let's not rehash things."

Make mental note to self to quit while you're ahead. "I'm sorry. How was your day?"

"My day could not have been better. I met with a contractor to talk about modifying the space and we've made great progress on the concept."

"Oh. You need to do construction? I didn't know that."

"These spaces come raw and you have to build them out."

"Sure." It should be fine now that I'm working. We should be able to cover the costs. "I can't wait to see it."

"I can't wait for you to see it, either. I'll just pop off to the kitchen and get dinner on the table."

He leaves the room and I reach over to stroke Bel's glossy fur, which gleams green and blue in the light of the flickering fire, with some red and gold mixed in. Bel moves closer to me where I am kneeling, and rubs his back on my nose. It tickles and makes me laugh. What a sweet, sweet kitty he is. I say a little prayer of thanks to God and to Dottie for the delivery of Bel.

"Come." Orlando is back. "Sit and let's have a good long talk."

"I'd like that." I get up from the floor to join him. "What's for dinner?"

Orlando has placed a covered tureen on the table. It's a pretty one, part of my grandmother's dishes as well. "Hey!" I burst out with a little too much enthusiasm. "I think this pattern is called Blue Italian. Isn't that perfect, since we were married in Italy?"

"Perfect. Just like you."

"Well, hardly."

"Really? What would you say is a less-than-perfect feature about my wife?"

"I don't know. I'm just like anyone. Good and bad, mixed together."

"Is that so? I suppose you're right. We're all a mix of good and bad qualities. I suppose I would agree with that."

"Orlando, this is getting kind of weird. You sound strange. What's going on?"

"I sound strange?"

"Yes, you do. You're parroting back everything I say and you're talking like a robot or something."

"Parroting back?"

"Like that! What's wrong with you?"

"What's wrong with me?"

"*Orlando!*"

"Because I am going to ask you the same thing about yourself. I am going to show you this casserole I lovingly prepared for our dinner." He lifts the lid. It looks like a cheesy, baked thing. "And I am going to ask you a question."

"You're kind of freaking me out." Has he poisoned dinner? Why would I even think something like that?

"*Eleanor!*" He spits out my name in such a way that I jump in my seat. I am starting to feel sick as I sense where this is going.

"Orlando." I feel tears spring up in my eyes. "Stop it. Please. You're scaring me."

"*I* am scaring *you*? How do you think *I* felt when I saw this?" He reaches behind him, to the seat of his chair and grabs something in his hand. Slowly—the seconds it takes to bring his arm back around his body with the thing he is holding seem to stretch to infinity—he places a book on the table.

But I know it is not an ordinary book. In fact, I know what this book is. I am the one, after all, who has carried this book around with me for most of my life. I am the one who has hidden this book under the Spode tureen.

"Please explain this to me, Eleanor."

I stare at the scrapbook my mother created with the newspaper clippings surrounding the event of my father's desertion. Headlines emblazoned with the sordid tale of my silent shame. The smoking-gun story of a childhood I had meant to tell my husband about, when the right time appeared.

I know my time is up.

Ding, ding, ding—the bell on the gameshow of life is ringing and I did not do what I should have done at the moment I should have done it. My time for that confession has passed and I have crossed into a new territory—a territory of blame and recrimination and—what else? Desertion again? Will Orlando now leave me because I have been a complete and total liar about my life? Or, will a miracle happen and will he understand? Will he comfort me and love me and work to make me feel that I am not a worthless zero who could not even hold on to the hand of her own father?

"*Eleanor!*" He practically shouts it now and then his voice gets horribly quiet. "Or, should I say Ruby? That's who you are, isn't it? That's you there, in those papers, in black and white? Eleanor Ruby Russell?"

"Yes," I say, but I don't think he can hear the word that barely leaves my mouth.

"Why didn't you ever tell me this? Why did you lie?"

"I…I was afraid you wouldn't understand."

"Is that what you really think of me? That I wouldn't understand that you were the sad child victim of a horrible desertion by an evil man? Why wouldn't I understand that? What kind of a monster do you think I am?"

My head feels fuzzy. Why did he call my father evil? "I don't think you're a monster! I don't! I just didn't want to lose you."

"Eleanor. I am appalled that you would think so little of me. I would have understood, naturally. But now I am confronted with a liar. A fraud. You are not the person I thought you were."

"I *am!* Please, Orlando! I *am!* Just listen. I didn't tell you because I was ashamed. I *meant* to tell you. I was still going to tell you. I just hadn't found the moment."

"The moment?" He stands up. "The fucking *moment?*"

Orlando moves with a sudden lunge in my direction and I flinch in anticipation.

"What the fuck, Eleanor? Did you just wince when I came near you?"

"No! I mean, I don't know." I start to cry. Really cry. Snotty, heaving, ugly-cry. "I'm sorry. Orlando. Please."

"Please what? Just let this all go after what you've done?"

"I didn't do it to us! Please, Orlando? Please?"

Please, please, please, God, give me another chance to make this right. A do-over. A retake. One more. All I need is one more. I can do it right. I can!

"I can't even look at you," he says as he once more walks out the door.

I feel myself slipping. Out of the chair. Out of the house.

Out of myself.

13

THE WOMAN IN WHITE

"Eleanor? How're you doing?" Frank Walders, my director, leans over me where I sit, off to the right of the set. "Ready to shoot this thing?"

"Yes, Frank. I'm ready." I am dressed in a delicate and gossamer wedding gown. White lace and ruffles bedeck it from top to bottom. A pale pink ribbon ties around the neck and wrists and the sleeves drop down over my hands, showing my fingers through intricate patterns of lace. My hair—a deeper auburn now—is curling down to the middle of my back, extended with the aid of Ziggy, the wig maker. My face is pale, my lips barely tinted and I look like a ghost in a director's chair.

"All right. Good. This is it," Frank begins his *technique for preparing the actor.* "You were only married today but your husband immediately changed. He has frightened you. He has threatened you. He has locked you in your room.

"You've managed to get out when you found the little passage through the closet, and in this scene, you are moving through the dark house. You need to get out. It is your only chance to live. Your husband is somewhere in the house, as is the housekeeper. They both are a grave danger to you. You must not be discovered.

"I'm shooting it handheld, so the image will be uneven. Michael, the DP, will be waking backward in front of you. Remember to keep your pace steady, no matter how afraid you get. You don't want to bump into Michael.

"Keep your fear acute. Keep your senses open. You're listening for your husband and Mrs. Dalton. They could be anywhere. Next to you, behind you, popping out of any door you pass."

"Okay." My heart is racing. "Let's do it."

I traverse the soundstage and enter the cross section of the house that has been built inside it. I stand still, tugging a little on the wedding dress that has become stained and tattered in the five days in which we've already been shooting this sequence.

"Quiet on the set!" Scott, the AD, calls out and all eyes turn to me. "Picture's up."

"Smoke!" he yells, and the smoke machines are opened.

"Roll sound!" he calls.

"Rolling," the PA replies as the sound recorders engage.

"Sound speed!" the sound guy says.

"Camera speed!" the first AC says.

And clap—the slate is smacked together right next to my face.

"Action!" Frank says softly, and I feel my adrenaline soar beyond its already-amplified level.

I start to place my bare feet, one in front of the other, on the floor-boards of the hall. Heel first, then gently and silently rolling the foot to its toes. Step by step I go, inch by inch. It is difficult to see through the thickening fog blown in by the machines.

The cinematographer, Michael, moves backward in front of me, flanked by two assistants who will keep him from falling over. The 35-millimeter camera is heavily belted around his middle, weighted down for stability and some minor mitigation from the jarring effect of being handheld.

"Breathe," Frank whispers. "Let me *hear* you breathing."

I begin to draw more ragged breaths.

"Now fight against the sound of your breath," he further adds. "Breathe heavily but, at the same time, try to quiet your breathing. The interest is always in the struggle."

I follow his instruction and the act of it ratchets up my terror.

"I'm going to stop talking now, Eleanor. It will just be you, alone in the house, except for your husband and Mrs. Dalton. Look for them. Remember they are looking for you. Try to still your breathing, which is racing out of control. Try to quiet your heart, which you are certain the others can hear beating. Get out of the house. Get out *now*, Eleanor."

And that is it. He says no more.

I continue walking and breathing, conscious of the beating of my heart. Thump, gasp, tread. Heel to toe. Heel to toe. Breathing. Beating. *Quiet them,* I say to myself. *Quiet down. Look left. Look right. Squint your eyes and try to see. It is so hard to see. Don't look behind you. Don't do it. Get out. Get out. Get out.*

"Ruby."

I spin around.

"Ruby?"

"Who's doing that? It's not funny!" I start to move in the opposite direction of the camera.

"Ruby!"

"Daddy!"

"*Ruby!*"

I gasp and start to run. Blindly, I push past Frank and barrel toward my dressing room. I need to get out. I have to find him. I need to get out. I have to find him!

"Cut!" Frank yells. "What the fuck? Eleanor? Someone follow her, please. See what the hell's going on!"

That would be aimed at Scott, the assistant director, who dutifully trots off behind me. I can hear him coming and I won't slow down one iota.

I need to get out.

14

THROUGH A GLASS DARKLY

I shove my way out of the small, pedestrian door of the soundstage and blink at the startling glare of an LA day. Not stopping to allow my eyes to adjust, I blindly round the corner of the building and weave through the grid of hangar-like structures as I make my way through the Paramount lot. I don't allow myself to look back until I near the North Gower gate. There, I give a good long stare in all directions and determine that no one is following me.

I think I have gotten away cleanly.

Out on the streets of Hollywood, I walk as fast as I can without running in the general direction of the Hollywood sign, which looms like a beacon above me. I might appear strange—barefooted in a filthy wedding gown—but at the moment, I don't care. Anyway, I am sure I don't look all that distinguishable from the lost souls who surround me. The homeless push shopping carts or sleep on tiny patches of grass. All of them are dressed in the cast-offs of past glory—theirs or someone else's. And, all of them were probably aspiring actors back in the day. I look just like another one of them—Baby Janes, all of us.

I need to clear my head. That is really all it is. I just need to walk around a bit and shake myself loose of whatever it was that grabbed hold of me on the set. Ruby. I heard it as clearly as I hear the honking traffic of Santa Monica Boulevard as I cross it. Was it a man's voice? My father's? Or a woman's, like Dottie's the other day? That is what I can't figure out. I think if I just walk for a while it will straighten itself out in my brain.

The idea comes to me to keep going—to walk all the way home and find some comfort there. Little Bel will be there, and time spent with him will make me feel better. Orlando will be at his new shop, which is just as well. I don't even know how I would begin to explain to him this breakdown in my day.

Ruby.

I heard it. I haven't heard it for years and now I've heard it how many times this week? Dottie said it. She said it more than once. She knows it's my name. She meant it for me. She was lying when she said it was Bel's name. That is not what she had in mind at all. Why was she so disingenuous? She asked me to be truthful, but she wasn't really honest herself.

I continue to plod northward, finding a slim toehold in equilibrium at the prospect of getting myself home. I will feel better tomorrow and be right back on set bright and early in my makeup chair. That is what the studios have insurance for, after all. They can shoot second unit or use a body double or something for the rest of the afternoon. We were only supposed to work for three more hours, so I haven't done that much damage.

Damage.

The thought of it ricochets me back to the soap opera and everything that went wrong there. Damn it. I cannot afford to fall apart again. Howard warned me about it in his own gentle way. He won't, of course, come out and say directly to me that I need to keep my shit together— shit that he knows damned well was strewn all over the floor in those last awful weeks on *The Finger of Fate*.

And they *will* call Howard. Of course, they will. They always do. He's the person who stands between me and the world. Sometimes, I think he's the only thing that stands between me and the abyss.

Where am I?

I am spinning. It is happening to me again. My head starts to whirl and my thoughts bounce around like pinballs. I need to get my bearings. I look around and see that I am directly in front of an enormous building made entirely of cubes. Squares and rectangles of stone and glass sit side by side and on top of each other. *Dedicated to the Memory of Frances Howard Goldwyn Devoted Library User* a little gold plaque reads.

Is this a library?

The perfection of the universe is revealed to me anew. I *need* to go to the library. It is exactly where I am destined to be, and I've been led here without even knowing it! I have to resume my research into my father's disappearance. My psychiatrist had discouraged me from this line of inquiry but I'm not really seeing her anymore. So I can do what I want. I can walk in that door. I *will* walk in that door. I will find out, once and for all, what happened to my father.

Inside, I pause to orient myself and see an older woman at the reception table who is bent over a task in front of her. I approach her to ask for help.

"Good afternoon," I say as regally as I can, in an effort to rise above my wardrobe. "Can you tell me where you have your books on the Kennedy assassination?"

"Yes," she says without looking up. "We have a shelf toward the left in the back. Just keep walking straight and turn left when you hit the end."

I know the voice. And now, I recognize the silver curls. It is my neighbor, Dottie Robinson, but she is dressed in proper clothes—a tweed suit and pearls—and she looks less ancient that she did when I met her.

"Dottie?" I say.

"Ruby," she replies as she lifts her gaze.

"Please stop calling me that."

"Of course, dear. What would you like me to call you?"

"Eleanor. That's my name. Or you can call me Ellie. Just don't call me Ruby."

"All right, Ellie."

"What are you doing here?"

"I volunteer here twice a week. What are you doing here, my dear? And, what are you wearing?"

"I…well, I left work…I'm an actress…and I guess I just didn't remember to change." I look at her unblinking eyes. "Into my street clothes, I mean."

"The Kennedy assassination is very interesting, isn't it? So many theories about who actually did it. Did Lee Harvey Oswald act alone? And what about Jack Ruby? What forces were behind him when he shot Oswald?"

"Excuse me," I say as I bolt for the shelves that might hold the answers.

* * *

I sit amid a pile of books and riffle through words and images. If my father had been involved with the assassination of the president, that would surely be the reason he disappeared from the cave. If someone had been on to him—the FBI or the CIA or some other governmental organization—perhaps he got word that they were closing in on him. Or maybe it was the Russians? If the Russians knew that either of the American agencies was about to arrest my father, they would have followed him into the cave to silence him. What better place to grab hold of him? Down in the cave in the middle of a crowd of people but utterly invisible in the dark. Who would suspect that anything like that would—could—happen in the United States of America?

Yet things like that do happen. They happen all the time. People do disappear. But there is always a reason. You just have to find the reason. And, for me, for my father, for what happened to us, I think the clue lies in my name. I think he called me Ruby because he wanted to leave a trail—a breadcrumb trail that would lead me back to him. If I can untangle the threads—separate out one filament from the other, like links on a delicate gold chain, when you have to lay it down on the table and use two safety pins to tease one loop away from the others—the confusing parts will become clear. I will laugh when I see the whole story, amazed that it took me so long to sort it out.

"But how could your father have known that Jack Ruby would shoot Lee Harvey Oswald, Eleanor?" Thus spoke Nina Blanchard, my formidable psychiatric guide. "You were born in 1961. The assassinations took place in 1963. Two years later. Does it make sense that your father would have named you Ruby as some sort of presage of what was to come? And how would that information, if it were true, lead you to find your father now?"

"Shut up," I say to the air. I am not crazy. I know I am sitting in a library in Hollywood, California, all by my lonesome. I know Dr. Blanchard is not here talking to me now. I know I am just remembering what she said to me long ago, as I pore through the stacks of books that surround me. Books that enumerate what everyone thinks actually happened to Kennedy that fateful day.

But what if my father knew Jack Ruby? And Oswald. What if he was involved with them? What if they had come into his antique shop? Or he had met them on the street? Or on a bus? Or in a diner? And then, maybe, he just liked the name, Ruby. He heard it and retained it and he wanted to call me Ruby. And then his involvement grew. He liked Cuba, my dad. What if the Cubans got to him? Or the Teamsters or the AFL-CIO? It could have happened. It *could* have. There might be a clue in all this that will lead me to find my father in whatever distress he has been living in all these years.

"Ruby?"

I look up, expecting to see my father, and am surprised to see Dottie again. "Yes, Dottie. Please stop calling me that."

"The library is closing. May I drive you home?"

"You can drive?"

"I'm just old, dear, not incapacitated."

She is really very funny. "Yes. I'd like that," I answer.

Outside it is dark. That's another odd thing about Los Angeles. Hot days at home signaled summer. In the north, that means the days are very long indeed. Hot days in LA don't mean anything. The sun sets early, even if it's been eighty degrees all day long.

We traverse the parking lot together, Dottie in her tweed and I in my wedding finery. I am glad I am with Dottie. She doesn't make me feel like a freak.

"There's my car!" she announces and points to an old Country Squire station wagon with fake wood panels on the sides. It must be from the 1960s, but, this being California, has not an inch of rust.

"Wow! That's old." I say in admiration.

"Not half as old as I am, dear. But it works just as well as I do."

We settle into seats that are scratched, cracked, and smelly—in that noxious way of old cars—and show no indication of ever having been graced with safety belts. Dottie peers over the dashboard, disconcertingly close to her eye level, and turns to address me as she reverses out of her parking spot. "Are you ready to talk yet?"

"I don't know what you mean," I say. I can't help but crane my neck to peer behind us. "Don't you think you should look where you're going, Dottie?"

"Don't you worry about me! I know perfectly well where I'm going, my dear. I also know where I've been."

"Yeah, well, I don't mean metaphorically. I mean, literally right now. Look out!" I scream as she approaches a red Ferrari. What the hell is a Ferrari doing parked at a downtown Hollywood public library?

Dottie brakes hard. "Scared ya!" She laughs like a four-year-old.

"Dottie! You did that on purpose?"

She pulls another ratty tissue from her sleeve to wipe her eyes. "Sometimes, I crack myself up," she chuckles. "But, seriously, are you ready to talk now?"

"About what?"

"Your father."

"What do you know about my father?"

"What do you want to tell me?"

"It seems like whatever I tell you might be redundant. You seem to know everything about me already."

"Not everything, dear. Just the things you tell me."

"I haven't told you anything!"

"Oh, but you have. When you were walking in my garden, the name *Ruby* was playing like a broken record in your head. And thoughts of your father. And, maybe, thoughts of a problem with your husband."

"You can hear all that?"

"Everyone can. They just don't listen."

"That's not true. If it were true, I would know what happened to my dad. I've been trying to find him, to figure out what happened to him for the past twenty years, and I don't come up with anything."

"All you hear is the strain of your own desires."

"What does that mean?"

"It means you're trying too hard. It's the way most folks pray. Gimme, gimme, gimme."

"That's not a very nice thing to say."

"God will give you everything. He has *already* given you everything. But you're too busy looking."

We arrive at the front of my house where a parking spot is miraculously open. Dottie pulls over and shifts the car into park. "Look, Ruby, there are no accidents. You did not move to this house by accident. You did not wander onto my property by accident. You did not walk into the library today by accident. You and I, my darling girl, have a date with destiny. I think you know that. I think you recognize that every word I say is true. I think you recognized me when you saw me, just as I recognized you."

"I…I…I have to go."

I open the heavy car door and place a foot on the pavement. Then I turn back to Dottie. "I don't know if you're totally crazy, but thank you for everything. Thank you for my cat. And thank you for being there today. Even if it all was an accident. I feel so much better. Better than I've felt in a long time."

"Well." She pats my knee. "You know where to find me."

I enter my gate and walk up the path to face the consequences of my meltdown on set. Howard will surely have been looking for me. Orlando will not necessarily know what happened, if he hasn't checked the answering machine. I can still save this situation. I can make everything all right. I can pull myself together.

Tomorrow, as Scarlett O'Hara so famously said, is another day.

15

GASLIGHT

I ease open the front door and see with a sickening jolt that Orlando's shoes are next to it and his car keys are on the table. He is home, I acknowledge, and my stomach drops even further. How have we gotten to the point where his presence fills me with dread?

My husband of three short months.

How long has he been here? Has he spoken to Howard? Does he know yet what I have done? And what would he make of it if he did? These questions flutter in my mind as I consider which way to run.

The familiar hamster wheel is cranking to life in my brain. With a rusty squeak, it starts, and around and around it goes.

Stealthily, I cross to the answering machine where I see the red light flashing. Good. At least, I think it's good. I hope it means Orlando hasn't heard any of the messages. But what if he has? What if he has listened to whatever calls had come in before he returned home himself? And then what about the others that came in after that? Has he talked to anyone?

First, I lower the volume to zero. Then I click the button to play. From there, I slide the sound up to the point where I can just barely hear it as I lean over the machine and pray that it is inaudible at a greater distance.

"Kitten..." I hit erase.

"Kitten…" I punch it again.

"Kitten…" How many times will Howard call me? He knows I skipped out of work in what I am sure he's characterizing as a renewal of my difficulties. But what is the good of calling my house over and over again? Does he think I'm just sitting by the phone choosing which call to answer?

"Kitten…" Click.

"Kitten…" Howard, please!

"Kitten…" This time I decide to listen. "It's me, my love. I'd like to come over and talk with you. Everything is okay. You don't need to worry. You won't be fired. I've fixed it up. So let me come by, okay? Make you some cocoa? Huh? Come on, Ellie, pick up the damn phone."

Well, it's official. Howard is worried about me. When he gets all soothing and calm, I know he is in a full-blown state of panic. Should I call him back now? What if he just drives over here? I can't have him meet Orlando under these circumstances.

It is then that I remember my dress. I need to get out of it immediately, before Orlando comes into the room! I sprint to the bathroom and lock myself inside. Finding no alternative, I strip it off and stuff it into the back of the cabinet under the sink, working to hide it with some rolls of toilet paper. I run the shower hot, stand under the spray, and attempt to collect my thoughts. The shampoo, the soap, and the heat of the water start to make me feel better. I envision the makeup, the hair spray, the dirt—and my troubles—swirling down the drain.

Oddly, I realize I've been in here some time and Orlando hasn't knocked on the door. He must be home. The presence of his shoes and keys all point in that direction. Why haven't I seen him yet? And then it hits me that I haven't seen Bel either, and panic rises like bile.

I shut off the water and towel off quickly, throw on a robe, and crack the door open a smidgen.

"Orlando?"

I listen for a response. Nothing.

"Bel?" I walk into the bedroom.

"Bel?" I go into the spare room, the living room, the kitchen.

"Bel?" I circle the house again and end up back in the kitchen.

From the window, I see that the light is on in the office. That must be where everyone is! I breathe in deeply, do it once more, and walk outside to meet my family.

I hear a man's voice—a man with an American accent—before I round the corner to the office doors. "Frank, it's Otto," he says.

Instinctively, I pause to listen without revealing my presence. Who could Orlando have with him in there? Do I detect a slight southern lilt?

"I'm goin' through the piece and I can't find anythin'," the voice of Otto continues. "She says it's got compartments, but she won't say more. I can't find it. Yup. Yup."

This Otto must be talking on the phone because I hear his voice and no one else's. What is Otto looking for? And where is Orlando? I shrink back and hit my heel on a flowerpot, which wobbles before righting itself. I hold my breath and listen harder.

"I'll call you back," the voice of Otto says. "I hear somethin'."

Silence.

I consider which way to flee.

Just as I turn to run back to the house, Orlando comes around the corner.

"Poppet!" he says, in just the way he would have in the past. "When did you get home?"

I feel my head tilt slightly, as I work to ascertain his mood. He does not appear to know what happened today. He also doesn't seem to be mad at me anymore. He is warm and friendly, like the man I married.

"Hi," I say. "Who's in there with you?"

"What do you mean, darling? There's no one here."

"But, I…" An icy clamp of fear grabs ahold of me. He is lying. I'm not the only liar in this family. Orlando does not want me to know about whoever it was he was talking to. The man who must still be in the office.

Otto.

I put on a mask of cheer. "How was your day?"

"Fantastic! I sold a Karakuri chest to a couple from Beverly Hills."

"What's that?" I ask, straining for a note of breeziness.

"It's a piece of furniture from Japan that has drawers all over it and some of them are hidden. They were created for security in the days when people didn't have safes at home. Similar to your mother's secretary. That has secret compartments, right?"

"You've asked me that already."

"Ellie? Is something wrong?"

"Who were you talking to in the office? Who's Otto?"

Orlando studies me and then he smiles. "Otto is a client. I had him on speakerphone. He's not in the office at all. Come, my love." Orlando says it nicely, but he brusquely takes me by the arm and pulls me in the direction of the office. "Look around and see if you can find him. Be sure to look under the furniture to see if he's hiding."

"Stop it, Orlando. You're hurting me."

"My fragile little poppet," he says.

"Who's Frank?"

"Frank?"

"Otto was talking to Frank. He said 'Frank.' I heard him."

"Ellie." Orlando feels my head like a parent would a feverish child. "There is no Frank. Maybe he used the word, frankly. As in, 'Frankly, this is getting to be dull. You are frankly becoming a bore.'"

The tears come without warning. His words are delivered with a smile, but their meaning is sharp as a knife.

"Where's my cat?" It's all I can think to say. "What have you done with my cat?"

"What are you talking about now? We've gone from Otto to Frank to the cat. What are you imagining is going on here, Ellie? Do you think I'm murdering men and cats and stuffing them into the furniture? What an active fantasy life you have, my darling. The mark of a true actress."

"I...I don't know." I need to get my bearings. I have to get away from him. I must find my cat.

"Bel?" I shout as I move through the house.

"Bel!" I push through the front gate and run as fast as I can to Dottie's.

16

THE RED SHOES

Across the street I fly in search of Dottie and little Bel. Dottie is the only person who will be able to help me now. With her laser-like extra-sensory perception, she will understand exactly what is going on—just what the matter *is* with Orlando and why I am feeling confused. She'll utter one of her cryptic little sayings that will set everything to rights, yanking us back from whatever brink we are standing on. Presto. She'll do it just like that.

I let myself into her gate and latch it firmly behind me. Not that I think Orlando would follow me over here, but I need a few moments without him to pull myself together. I realize as I pick my way up the pitch-dark path that I have never told him about Dottie, so why would he look for me here?

Of course, that's another lie I could be caught in. I can't seem to help myself.

But what about Orlando's lies? I'm certain he was hiding something back in the office. Let's say it's true that he was on speakerphone with someone named Otto. And let's accept that Otto used the expression "frankly." And I misunderstood him to say "Frank." Okay, fine. It could all be true, but that doesn't mean Orlando is not concealing something.

And why does he keep asking about my desk? None of it makes much sense. He is not acting at all like himself.

Of course, how do I *really* know what he is like? I've known him a quarter of a year.

I hasten up the path toward the warmth and the comfort of Dottie. Light shines from under her blinds, which relieves me to know I won't be waking her. She's old, after all. She may go to bed very early.

"Dottie?" I push open the front door a tiny crack. "Dottie?"

"Come in, my dear, and have some soup. I find that, under duress, there is nothing so curative as chicken soup. Not a very original thought, but I think it, nonetheless."

She has set up a table for two and is already seated there.

"Did you know I was coming?" I ask as I slump into the opposite chair.

"Like you said, my dear, I know a lot. Keep getting older and you'll know more and more." She gets up and goes to the kitchen and returns with two bowls of steaming-hot soup.

"I don't know how much I'll ever know about anything. I just mess things up over and over again."

"That's good, dear."

"No, I mean it. I really mess things up."

"Well, in that case, let me amend what I said. It is really good, then."

"Life is not a self-help book, Dottie. Wow, this soup is amazing."

"What would you say life is then, my dear? I think you came here for some wisdom with your soup, and now you're about to toss it away."

"I had another fight with Orlando. There are things I've lied about. Well, not exactly lied, but omitted. I didn't tell him about my father's disappearance and the terrible publicity that surrounded it. I was just waiting for the right time. We married so quickly, and everything was so lovely, and I didn't want to spoil it. Anyway, you might have gotten mad at me, too, if I didn't tell you and you found out later. You happened to know by reading my mind, so that doesn't count. It doesn't get me off the liar hook."

"He must have treated you so tenderly once he heard what happened to you."

"Well, I'm sure he would have, if I'd told him honestly. But he found this scrapbook where my mother kept all the newspaper articles and that's why he got so angry. Because I had kept it a secret. As though I didn't trust him. He said it meant I thought poorly of him."

"Of him?"

"I know where you're going with this. I agree that it sounds self-centered, but I also understand why it would cause him to question my truthfulness. And my trust in him. By the way, is Bel here? I couldn't find him."

"No, dear, he's not."

"Really? I was certain he was here. I need to find him." I rise from the table and start for the door.

"Ruby," she says firmly. "Eat the soup while it's hot and we'll find your kitty after. Then, why don't you lie down for a bit on the sofa? Maybe spend the night. You need some sleep."

"I do." I start to cry again. "I'm so very tired."

"You just sit there and finish that soup and I'll go find Mr. Bel."

"Thank you." I'm crying harder now. "Thank you so much. You're so kind to me."

"Of course I'm kind to you, my dear. Kindness is the basic launching point for all human exchange."

"Not everyone feels that way."

"Oh." She brushes away the concept with her hand. "People are good. Your father was good. You know that, right?"

"It's what I believe. Orlando said he was evil."

"But you know it isn't true?"

"Yes. I think so. I mean, he just left me. It was dark—I can't even tell you how dark it was. Utterly, completely black. No visibility at all. I was already so afraid, and I was holding onto his hand, and he just let go."

I look around this room in Dottie's cottage. The walls are soft yellow, the lamps are covered in mica shades that deepen the amber glow. Her sofa and chairs are covered in mismatched, faded upholstery and afghans are strewn about. Cats of all sizes and shapes are curled up on every soft surface. Dottie's house is like being submerged in sunshine—the complete opposite of a cold, dark cave.

"That's not exactly how it happened," I whisper, for the first time in my life about to acknowledge the final bit of the story. The bit I am too ashamed to have told anyone, including Dr. Blanchard. Not even my mother. "I haven't been fully honest. I mean, I just left out a small part."

Dottie says nothing and allows me to find my courage.

Slowly, I set my soup spoon on the rim of my plate, making the tiniest chink of metal against china, and continue before I lose my nerve. "My father and I went to the cave together that day. He woke me up early in the morning and told me to get dressed quickly. I remember I picked my own clothes. Normally, my mother would choose my outfits. She always put them together perfectly. That day, I wore my red Keds with pink and green flowered shorts. My mother would have had me wear white tennis shoes with those shorts. But I loved those red Keds." I look up at Dottie.

"Ah," Dottie sighs dreamily. "Red shoes."

"I was going to wear a purple T-shirt, but I knew my mother would say it was one color too many. So I chose a white eyelet blouse and white socks."

"You must have looked lovely."

"Then why did my father leave me?"

"Why don't you tell me?"

"I don't know, Dottie! That's the problem." I look up at her and see her sitting with the most benign expression. It gives me confidence to go on. "Well…we got into his car and he let me bring my breakfast with me. I was supposed to have a hot breakfast everyday—my mother thought it was good for me—but he let me bring a Pop-Tart in the car. My aunt had bought them. Strawberry. It was my favorite.

"He didn't say where we were going. My mother had been just waking up when we left the house and so had Aunt Hazel. He left them a note. I saw him write it and fold it and leave it on the kitchen counter. I don't know what it said. We drove around for a while. It seemed like we were driving in circles. Maybe he went straight to the cave, I don't know. It just felt like we drove for a long time through those winding mountain roads. You can feed bears there, you know."

"I've never fed a bear."

"You're not supposed to, but people do. Especially up in Gatlinburg. My dad said that a baby bear always indicates the presence of a mama bear."

"Your father sounds like a wise man."

"It's written on every sign in the Smoky Mountains. I don't think he knew it on his own."

"Nevertheless, it takes some wisdom to read the signs put before you."

"Oh, Dottie. You sound like Confucius."

"I'll take that as a compliment. Go on."

"It gets fuzzy. I don't remember parking or going into Ruby Falls. That was the name of the place, if you can believe it. I do remember going down an elevator. We'd visited a lot of caves in Kentucky and Tennessee over the years—they're everywhere—but at most of them we just entered the side of a mountain. This one required that we descend an elevator. That was scary to start with.

"Then we had to walk down a corridor—more like a tunnel. The other caves I remember were spacious, had underground lakes and that kind of thing. This one was narrow and cramped. This tour guide—a woman—kept talking about the original guy who discovered it and how he had to crawl on his belly in the dark. I mean, why on earth would you do that? What could make you go down there and crawl into a hole with no visibility whatsoever? It's like being buried alive!"

"It doesn't sound terribly appealing to me, either," Dottie says.

"We walked that way for a while. There were lots of other people with us. We came into a bigger room. And that's when they turned off the lights. I became aware of the sound of water. The woman kept talking. She said it was a waterfall that fed a lake. She told us the divers they sent down couldn't find the bottom of it. The sound echoed all around me. I was terrified to move. I was clutching my father's hand and I think I started to cry. And that's when he did it."

I have been avoiding her eyes, but I finally look at Dottie. I could stop now, leave this story where it always has been, sealed and neat and clean. As clean as my father's unsavory actions could ever possibly be. Dottie smiles at me and I resolve to go on.

"But it wasn't exactly like I've always said. My father didn't just let go. He had to make an effort to disconnect from me. He had to reach over, with his other hand, and hold onto my wrist while he pulled his first hand away from me. And it wasn't easy. I tried so hard to hold on. I even dug in my fingernails. But he was too strong for me. As hard as I tried to hold on to him, he worked harder to get rid of me."

Again, I look at Dottie, as though the map to this old trail lies webbed in the wrinkles of her face. "He *knew* what he was doing, didn't he? He *planned* to leave me there. Why didn't he just get up in the morning and go? Why bring me to the cave? Why leave me with that memory for the rest of my life?"

"I cannot tell you that."

"Why? Because you don't know? Or you don't want to?"

"I see what's in you, Ruby, and when I look at you now, I see the same darkness you describe."

"I don't get it. Why can't you see everything? Isn't that what clairvoyance is? The ability to see past and future? The whole nine yards?"

"Not exactly. Let me put it this way. We're all connected, every single one of us. You experience it yourself all the time and you might call it a feeling. Or an instinct. Or a hunch. Right?"

"I don't know. I'm so muddled most of the time I don't know what I feel. I was talking to my therapist once and telling her a story about something that happened to me as a child. 'That must have made you angry,' she said."

"And did it?" Dottie asks.

"The weird part was that I couldn't even answer her. I didn't know if I could have gotten angry in the situation—if I was permitted to be angry—because I didn't know if I was right. 'Anger is an emotion,' she said. 'It has nothing to do with being right or wrong.'"

"That surprised you?"

"It was like a light bulb going off. I mean, the concept that I was entitled to feelings irrespective of any moral standing was a new one to me. I think I'm emotionally backward."

"You're like 99.9 percent of human beings in that regard. People mix it all up, the moral, the emotional, the spiritual, in a big muddy pie. Muddled, like you said."

"What about Orlando? What's going on with him now? He's changed. We married pretty quickly. We met on a plane from Zurich to Rome and were married six weeks later. He was just so attentive and loving and—well, kind—to use your word. He was kind. I don't know. He doesn't seem very kind lately. Can you see what's going to happen there?"

"No, my dear. I don't know what's going to happen with Orlando." Dottie stands up. "I think we've done enough talking for one night. Thank you for sharing your story with me. Let me go call for your kitty. I think he'll come now. I think he's had his adventure and I'll just bet he's waiting to see you."

She moves toward the door and I rise to go sit on the couch. My fatigue has become Olympic. I need to wedge myself between a calico and a tabby to secure an inch of space, but neither of them appears to mind.

Dottie is back in a flash and she holds little Bel in her arms. "Here you go. Just like I thought. He was out mousing on a dark night."

I take him in my arms.

Dottie shuffles around the room, turning off lights.

"I'll just leave a night-light on in case you need to go to the bathroom," she says. "I always do."

The room is pleasantly—but not fully—dark. Bel's purring acts as a sedative and calms my weary nerves. I close my eyes.

17

THE DAY OF THE LOCUST

A familiar noise tickles at my ears and teases me from sleep. My legs are leaden, and I shift to the right to relieve them. The act of turning nearly topples me off of the narrow surface I'm lying on and the weight jumps off my legs.

Bel.

Which means I'm in Los Angeles. But I am definitely not in my bed. The facts start to reassemble, and I remember that I have fallen asleep on Dottie's sofa.

I look around. Out of the darkness rise up the shapes and forms of my own living room. I sit up to see better and confirm that I am, indeed, at home. How did I get here? I thought I was at Dottie's.

What is going on?

And what exactly am I hearing? I concentrate to decipher the sound.

Rain! It is the whispery splash of rain as it hits the leaves in my garden. It is a sound that's always comforted me, but it is a first for me in LA. I've been here for months and it has never been so much as cloudy.

I switch on a lamp and think back over the evening. I'm sure I went to Dottie's. I am certain of it.

As I stand up, I feel my bathrobe twisting around me, and that unpleasant sensation jogs my memory of the entirety of the day before: my meltdown at work, my flight off the set, my suspicions about my husband, and my dash across the street in my robe.

I am falling apart again.

My perceptions of reality and reality itself are failing to meet eye-to-eye. I actually thought I heard my father on the set yesterday. I thought Orlando was plotting against me with someone named Otto, and another someone named Frank. I thought Orlando had hurt my cat. I even thought he'd killed the cat! I did. I thought all these things—experienced them as though they were real.

But they are *not* real.

That is what Nina Blanchard would tell me. It is what my mother would tell me. I don't need to actually talk to my mother or my shrink because I know *exactly* what they would say. I have heard it so many times. Sweetly, gently, in a calm, kind way—so as not to disturb me or further unhinge my hinges—they would talk me off the ledge. *Ellie,* they'd say, *let's go back to what happened that day. The day in the cave with your father and the trauma it caused you as a child.*

It must have made you sad? He must have been a cad! Dad the Cad, Ruby the Sad, and now Ellie the Mad and the Bad. I could write poems for them.

How did you *feel,* they would ask? What *did* it make you feel? Like newscasters at natural disasters, shoving their microphones into the faces of the distraught and the bereaved. How do you feel, they all ask, as the people stare back at them blankly.

How *do* we feel?

How do *I* feel?

I feel like I lost my father. I feel like I lost my rudder. I feel like I lost myself. I feel like I lost my ability to trust *anything* I feel. Mostly, I just feel lost. I feel like my feelings are illusions that slip like fog along the ground.

My mother has been calling me. She's left five messages this week. She always knows when I am in trouble—has a sixth sense for my state of mind. What is the point of calling her back? Or of calling Howard back?

Of talking to anyone, really? I know the problem lies in me. I know the problem *is* me. It is all me, always me, and always has been me. No one can help me. They never could.

I need to make up with Orlando. I have done him a disservice. Distrusted him based on demons and devils in my mind. He is my husband and he loves me. It is to him that I must cling in my current state of imbalance.

I walk into the kitchen first to pour out some kibble for Bel. As he eats, I take a few deep breaths, fill a glass of water from the tap, and drink it down completely.

As composed as I am ever going to get, I walk toward the bedroom to make things right with my husband.

18

MORNING GLORY

Birdsong percolates up into my consciousness. Can you call birdsong to mind? The sweet and gentle way a bird sings in the early morning as it rouses you from slumber? It is what dances around my head just now. I picture the little birds in the animated version of *Snow White*, twittering around her head while she laughs and reaches out to touch them. I take a moment, savoring the sensations, and then I open my eyes.

I am in my bedroom on Primrose Avenue. It is just as I left it yesterday. Or whenever it was that I crawled back into bed next to Orlando. Bel is at my feet and Orlando is lying next to me, his arm flung across my chest. They both are sound asleep. I turn my head to look at the face of my husband. His long jet-black hair—stovepipe black my mother would call it—is pushed back on the pillow just now, revealing his widow's peak, which is slightly off center. If I were to trace the point of it with my finger down the length of his forehead, I would hit a spot that is a millimeter closer to the left eyebrow than the right. I know because I've done it. I won't do it now, though. I don't yet want to wake him.

Watching him like this, his sleeping face serene, I am reminded that I know so little about him. About his family. Granted, he doesn't know much about mine. Well, he didn't until he found the scrapbook. And then, there it all was, spelled out in lurid black and white. Although that book does not contain the real story of my family. My mother's laugh. My grandmother's beef stew. My father's way of tossing me up in the air when I was small enough to do so. I guess I was always small enough to do it in the time my father knew me.

I consider that concept, which is not a new one for me. I have often thought about it. The fact is, my father does not know me now. He doesn't know what I look like. He might not even recognize me. I've dyed my hair red, after all, and he knew me as a towhead. Though my hair is the least of what has changed about me.

We get used to the physical aging of our loved ones, bit by bit, as we travel along the same path with them. If we are apart for any length of time, however, the sight of them often startles us. I even find that, when I see my mother after six months apart, her face surprises me a little. It is older. But I couldn't really say less beautiful. Maybe that is the surprising part. My mother is aging well, yes, but would my father recognize her? I would have to guess that he would. My mother has that kind of face. Always lovely, no matter the lines on it, and always essentially the same. The kind of face that you could caricature. Her bones and brows are strong enough to respond to an illustrator's pen.

Of course, she has been painted, and often over the years. My parents' art-world friends frequently used my mother as their subject. I wonder if anyone still does. Her life became much smaller once they left New York and moved to Michigan. And again when my father was gone. Once again when my grandmother died and yet again, when I left the house. She exists in a shrinking universe.

What of Orlando's family? I possess a smattering of facts. His mother left China during the war. She traveled on foot, hitched rides, made her way south on the Burma Road, peeling west into India. Why did she do it alone? And, how on earth did she manage it? It's not your average trip. Were there bandits on the road? Soldiers? Renegades? Was she ever in danger? Did she come to any harm? I find myself looking forward to meeting her with hope and a little fear. When that meeting finally happens, I'm not sure I will have the courage to ask her any of these questions.

And what about his father? A soldier stationed in India, he was literally part of the Raj—that Victorian-sounding institution. Who was he? He is dead now, like my father. Or not like my father. I, of course, don't know if my father is alive or dead. He is simply absent. Without leave, I might add.

His parents married in India, before they returned to England. His English father, Reginald. His Chinese mother, Chen. Reginald's friends were not supportive. Chen, a refugee, had none. I wonder if she made any in England, once they settled there? Orlando was born in Cornwall in 1955, which makes him six years my senior. He says they lived on the Cornish coast, far away from London, where it was milder than in the rest of the country. He came to love the sea there. He talks about the Gulf Stream and the fact that they even had palm trees.

I'd like to go visit his mother when my film is wrapped, when Orlando has the gallery up and running, when we get on our feet. We won't have to visit mine. I am sure she will come here, soon. Thanksgiving is almost upon us. In fact, it is next week. I will have four days off in a row. My mother is hinting at coming, but I need to talk to my husband. This is our first Thanksgiving together, after all. His first Thanksgiving ever, I imagine, considering the fact that he's British.

"Hey." Orlando is awake and props himself up on one elbow.

"Hey," I answer back.

"Ellie, my love," he says as he reaches out to touch my face. "I'm sorry we quarreled."

"Oh! I am, too!" I could scream with relief. "I'm so sorry I've been nervous and difficult lately."

"Don't worry, my darling. Shall I make some breakfast? Bring you some tea?"

"I don't really have time. I need to get to the set."

"Ah, yes. Your job. Always your job."

"Seriously, I need to get going. Listen, before I go, there's something I've been meaning to ask you. Thanksgiving is next week, and my mother is letting me know she'd like to come and stay with us."

Orlando's face makes the slightest wince. "Normally that would be lovely," he says. "But our first Thanksgiving I'd love to have alone with you."

"Okay. Sure. But a turkey is kind of large. Usually, Thanksgiving is a big dinner with family and friends and everyone saying what they're grateful for."

"You're all the family and friends I need this year." Orlando slides his hands up my nightgown, along my legs, over my stomach and upwards, dragging the gown up with them. "I'm grateful for you."

"Orlando!" I laugh. "I just told you I have to go. I need to shower before work and I'll be late if I don't get moving. Are you sure about Thanksgiving, though? I think my mom will be hurt if I tell her not to come."

"Say that you need to work."

"I already told her I don't."

"Why do you tell your mother so much?"

"It was just the two of us for a long while—besides my grandmother. I guess I'm in the habit. Would you rather I tell her less?"

"I'd like it to be the two of *us* now, who come first to each other. Don't you want that, too?"

"Of course, I do. It's just—well, she's my mother. That's kind of a special category. It doesn't compete with husband, but…"

"I hope it doesn't compete with husband." Orlando extracts his hands from my nightgown, leaving it hoisted up to my neck, takes hold of my shoulders and flips me onto my back. "And now, my darling wife, I'd like my matrimonial rewards."

"I can't!" I laugh again. "Really. Not now."

"Really, you can. And absolutely now." Just then, the doorbell rings. It has to be Howard. I gave him such a hard time for honking from the car that he has come to the door to meet Orlando. "Orlando, I need to answer that. I have to go to work."

"Get your priorities straight, my dearest wife." Orlando lowers his pajama bottoms and does what he intends to do. The doorbell rings again—several more times—but Orlando won't stop until he comes to a loud and lengthy climax. I am certain that Howard can hear him, and I am embarrassed and aroused together.

Sweaty, spent and flushed—without the benefit of bathing—I dash outside to find Howard at the curb, opening the door of his car.

"Howard! Wait!" I call, running after him.

Howard turns to assess me. Correctly, I might add. "If I weren't so worried about you, I'd be mad as hell right now. Where's the hubby? Is he coming out to meet me?"

"I'm sorry. He's still sleeping."

"Yeah, right. And I've got a bridge for sale. Okay, let's go then. You can't say I didn't try."

I get in the car, my tail between my legs.

It is only when we are pulling onto the lot that I remember the dress that I left crammed under the bathroom sink. Damn it.

"Howard, listen, I did something really stupid. Well, on top of all the other stupid things I'm doing. I've left my wardrobe at home. I have to go get it."

Howard turns to study me.

"I'm fine!" I say. "I just forgot my dress. I was in a hurry this morning."

"Could've fooled me."

"Come on, Howard, I really can't walk in without it."

"Look," he says. "I'm meeting with the producer to discuss production cost losses from your—what shall we call it?—your early departure yesterday. Don't they have a back-up dress?"

"Yes, but it doesn't have the right stains."

"Can't the script girl whip out her Polaroids for continuity?"

"Don't you think I should get it? Do you really think I should just waltz in there after yesterday and not bring the dress back with me?"

"Fine! Take my car, I'll go meet him, and swear to me you'll get back here pronto! Is that a promise?"

"Yes, of course. I promise. I'll be back before you know I'm gone."

Howard gets out at the gate, the guard lets me circle around his little hut, and I drive toward the Hollywood Hills.

19

THE POSTMAN ALWAYS RINGS TWICE

I run up our garden path. After our morning of lovemaking—Orlando's tender words and touches—I doubt myself for doubting him. I don't know what is wrong with me, but I need to focus on reality. Shake off my overactive imagination, which, incidentally, never serves me well. Like Dottie said—or something like it—everything really *is* all right.

Well, maybe she said something about listening to my instincts, but she clearly has no idea how off-base my instincts are. I blow everything out of proportion and make mountains out of molehills. Everyone has always told me that and I should probably start listening. What was that saying my dad had? *If one person says you're a horse, he's crazy. Two people say you're a horse, it's a conspiracy. Three people say you're a horse, then maybe you ought to buy a saddle.*

I'm not sure who the horse is in this scenario, but I suspect it's probably me.

I grab the handle to open the door and am surprised to find it locked. I know I left it open when I left here twenty minutes ago. Orlando must have gotten up and latched the front door. I ring the bell and wait.

I ring it again and wait a bit longer. Orlando has to be home; our car is parked in front. Besides, it is much earlier than the time he normally leaves for the gallery. I try the bell once more. And once more, nothing. He must be in the shower.

I walk over to the edge of the porch and tip up the pot of geraniums. We keep one extra house key hidden here for situations such as this one. I left my purse in my trailer yesterday and my keys are in it. The flower-pot key comes in handy. If I don't hurry now, I will be officially late and further exacerbate the trouble I caused on the set yesterday. I shove the key into the lock, turn the tumbler, and push on the door until it comes to a jerking halt. Now that is odd. Orlando has fastened the chain bolt.

"Orlando?" I call through the small wedge of open door. Bel saunters over from wherever he was and answers me. *Meow.* I kneel down on the porch and reach my fingers through the door to rub the top of his head. "Orlando?" I call again.

Increasingly worried about time, I decide to walk around the house and enter through the back. The key should work in that door, too, if it's locked. "See you, Bel, in just a minute." I gently close the door and move to the side of the house.

Entering the wooden gate that closes off the backyard, I go first to the door of the office. Maybe Orlando is in there catching up on work before he goes to the gallery. At least I can say a quick hello. The lights are off and the double doors are closed. It doesn't appear that he has been out here this morning.

Spontaneously—ignoring my need for haste—I slip inside the office and stealthily close the doors behind me. We have set up a couple of folding card tables where we have spread out our various papers. I run my fingers along the stacks—all neatly laid out and separated—of bills, receipts, and so on. Farther on, Orlando has piled some books on early American furniture. *Field Guide to American Antique Furniture* and other volumes like it. I pick up one, then another. They were all checked out from the Hollywood Public Library. Odd. American is not his specialty, so they strike me as a little unusual. I also wonder when he borrowed these.

I shake off my worries and move deeper into the room. There is nothing of concern here. What on earth am I even thinking? What *would* be of concern here?

I go all the way back to where my Georgian secretary majestically stands. It really is a handsome piece, more than two hundred years old and almost all that time owned by my family. It is worthy of the living room. We should move it in there and get it out of the back of this converted garage. The air must be better inside the house, although we don't have air conditioning anywhere.

I kneel in front of it and run my hands along the sides. I scoot myself in very close, under the writing table part that has been left hinged open and resting on its support brackets.

What has Orlando been looking for in my desk? Is it something specific to me or does he always check for hidden drawers on antiques? It is his profession, after all. He told me about the Japanese piece he just sold, I can't remember what it was called. Kara something. He said it had secret compartments.

I slip my hands downward, feeling the whorls of the wood. I loved doing this as a little girl. The wood feels both glassy and rough at the same time. The varnish adheres unevenly, and little scratchy bits of wood protrude from under its surface. I think my father said they used fish glue to attach the veneer. My hands alight on the molding that runs from back to front at the bottom of both sides. It has an extra length of this trim—above the bottom edge, which is cut into an elevated arch, with points and dips to give it elegance. Like that, the four corners of the piece look like legs, though they aren't actually separated from the molding.

I lower myself farther to reach my left hand around and under. I need to lie down now, because my arm won't bend at such an angle. I really only need to check the left side. The right side conceals nothing. Leaning and stretching, my head down on the floor, I feel under the secretary, running my hand over the unwaxed wood. And, just like that, I find it. A tiny spot that feels cooler than the rest of the surface. Because it is made of metal. Brass, I suspect. Although I've never actually seen it on the bottom the desk.

I press my finger into it and am able to feel the keyhole. A tiny little hole made for a tiny little key. One that I keep with me at all times, nestled in my makeup bag in the hollow bottom of a compact. All times except for this one. My purse is in my trailer on the set.

But if I had that key with me right now, I could spin it around to the right. I could make a drawer spring open. A seamless drawer invisible to the naked eye, that pops off the entire strip of molding. That is why no one can find it. The full length of the trim opens up, there are no seams to betray it. You could run your hands over it all year, and you would never know it hid a drawer.

Even if Orlando were to lie on the floor and fondle the underside of the secretary, he still would not have the key. Which is the most unusual part. Most desks like this rely on spring action alone. The use of a locking key is an extra-special element that my father said was rarely employed. When I was little, he taught me how to use it.

"Poppet." Orlando's voice startles me.

I jerk up my head, banging it hard into the bottom of the open desk. Red-faced, I rise and turn to him. He is standing in the doorway in his pajama bottoms without a shirt. "Orlando," I say. "Hi!"

"What are you doing here?"

"I live here."

"That's a strange thing to say, Ellie. You left for work."

"You locked me out."

"What?"

"You put the chain on the front door."

"What are you talking about? You left here half an hour ago for work. I locked the door to shower."

"Then why are you still wearing your pajamas?"

"Ellie? This is beginning to feel like an interrogation, and I don't quite know what you're asking. What's going on in that little mind of yours?"

"Why are you always asking me about my desk? That's one of my questions. And why did you latch the door with the chain this morning? That's another question I have."

"I just told you. You certainly are an inquisitive girl this morning."

"Maybe I should be more inquisitive!"

And then—as though cued by the word inquisitive—Mindy, the stunning real estate agent, rounds the corner with two coffee mugs in her hands. "Orlando, I couldn't find the…oh." She stops walking to look at me. "Hello, Ellie."

Just like that she says it, without even raising her voice.

"Darling." Orlando seamlessly enters the fray. "You remember Mindy? The lady who found us the house?"

"Yes, I…" I what? What am I going to say? "I…I have to go to work!"

"Wait a minute. Mindy just stopped by to have us sign a paper that we overlooked."

"Uh…you sign for the both of us."

"Shall I walk you to the door?"

What the hell is he doing standing there in only his pajamas bottoms, offering to escort me to the door like I am a visiting guest? And Mindy with the coffee mugs in her hands, like she is the lady of the house! What is going on here? I cannot, cannot, cannot go down this rabbit hole. I must go to work. I must get out of here. And I must do it now.

"I'm fine!" I shout and bolt past the two of them, posed in our garden like husband and wife.

20

THE SUBLIME
AND THE BEAUTIFUL

It is only when I greet the guard at the gate that I remember I have once again forgotten the dress. Ugh! Well, it is too late now. I can still make it through hair and make-up and get onto the set with minimal disruption of another day. I will, indeed, need to ask the wardrobe mistress for the back-up dress and promise her I will return the missing one tomorrow. There is a chance that she won't tell the producer. I park Howard's car, throw his keys into the glove box, and speed-walk toward my dressing room.

I can and will compartmentalize what happened this morning. I don't even understand what happened, but I can lock it into a tidy box and go on with my day. I can talk with Orlando about it after work. For now, I am going to assume that Orlando's perfectly logical—and palat-able—explanation is true for why Mindy was at our house making coffee and Orlando was not wearing a shirt. Or actual pants, for that matter, but I will not go down that mental path right now.

Howard, Frank, the director, and Daniel Marks, the producer, are all standing outside my trailer when I come around the corner on foot. They are in the middle of a conversation which loses steam at my approach.

"Hi," I say, out of breath. "I know I'm a little late. I'll just dash into hair and make-up and I'll be on the set in no time."

They examine me like a specimen.

"Don't worry, Ellie," Frank says. "You okay?"

"Yes. I'm fine. I'm sorry about yesterday."

"It's all right." Frank graciously forgives me.

"Look." Daniel jumps in. "We've gone through one actress on this production already. We need some assurance that you're able to do this job."

"I told you," says Howard. "She's more than able. Ellie saw her doctor yesterday who will send you a detailed letter. She had a pretty severe flu right before beginning the film and yesterday was a little flare-up. He's prescribed vitamin B shots and it won't happen again. Her doctor is certain of it."

I narrow my eyes at Howard.

What a quick liar he is. Had he thought up that story earlier or did he make it up on the spot? It sounds so preposterous—some weird flu flashback—that I wonder if it will fly. I also wonder from whom he will procure this doctor's note. We all stand around looking at each other for a moment when Daniel finally speaks. "The flu. Fine. Get me that letter. I need it for insurance."

"Forthwith," answers Howard jauntily. "Let me walk you into your trailer," he says to me. We turn away from them and climb the rickety stairs of my honeywagon, where Howard changes his tone as soon as we are shut inside. "Kitten. Consider yourself officially warned."

"Daniel seemed to believe your story about the flu."

"Don't be ridiculous. He didn't believe it for a minute. He needs an excuse for the insurers, and I will provide one. That's the deal."

"Oh."

Howard looks at my empty hands. "Did you get the dress?"

"Look, Howard, just give me some space. Please. It's a long story that I don't want to go into right now. I'm exhausted and I have to go to work and I have to do it now."

Howard chews on what I just said for a minute and appears to decide not to challenge me. Instead, he says, "You're right. You have to go to work. Work is the important thing. At the end of the day, work is what keeps us strong. C'mon. I'll walk with you. Where are you headed first?"

"Uh, I guess wardrobe. I'll let them know about the dress and ask them not to tell Daniel."

"Roger that." We walk for a while in silence. Howard finally says, "Tell me about this husband of yours."

"Orlando?"

"No, Kitten, Fred," Howard teases. "Of course, I mean Orlando. Do you have other husbands you haven't mentioned?"

"What do you want to know about him?"

"I guess I want to know if you're happy. If he's good to you."

We arrive at the costume shop. "Howard, this is a long subject. Too long for now. The short answer is yes, I'm happy and yes, he's good. I'm going in there now. I left your keys in the car. I'll see you later?"

"Sure. I'll pick you up."

"We're shooting late. I'll call a taxi. Or I'll call my husband. Orlando." I wink at him. "That one."

Howard grabs my shoulders and kisses me on the forehead, which makes tears spring up in my eyes. "Because, if he's not good to you, he has me to answer to. Hey, what are you doing for Thanksgiving? Want to come over? Todd and I are cooking and we have a fun group."

"Thanks. But Orlando wants to spend it just the two of us. I think he's right. I'm working now and he has the gallery and we don't have enough time together."

"Okay, remember what I said?"

"I will. Love you."

"Love you, too."

He turns and strides off toward the parking lot and I turn to face the music.

21

TENDER MERCIES

"Why in heaven's name is it so large?" Orlando asks as he sips his tea and watches me rinse off the turkey in the sink. Bel jumps up on the counter to offer me assistance in extracting the giblets.

"This one really isn't that big. Don't you have turkeys in England?"

"We do. My family ate goose, however, and they're considerably smaller."

"Well, can you give me a hand and pass that roasting pan over here?" I pat the bird dry, place it in the pan, and proceed to stuff it with the dressing I made this morning. Apples, chestnuts, bacon, and home-made croutons. Onions and celery, of course. I hope Orlando likes it. "You're right, though, it's a lot of food for the two of us. You know, I've met a neighbor. An older woman called Dottie. She lives alone with about three hundred cats. I could invite her to join us."

"Darling, we talked about this."

"I just feel so bad at the thought of her spending Thanksgiving alone."

"Doesn't she have family? Friends?"

"I don't actually know. We haven't talked about that. I just thought we could offer."

"But she might take us up on it. And then I wouldn't have the Thanksgiving I've envisioned. Alone with my beautiful wife. Who, by the way, works all the time now and I hardly get a moment to see."

"Okay. You're right. I'm sure she has someone. Hey! Have you heard of the Macy's Parade?"

"The one from that movie?"

"Yes! *Miracle on 34th Street*. Want to watch it? It'll be on TV right now. If you put it on in the living room, I can walk in and out from the kitchen."

"Actually, darling, I need to do some work. I'll be out in the office."

"But…? You just said you wanted to be with me."

"I do. And I will be. After I work." Orlando sets his cup on the counter. "See you in a few hours."

And he walks out the door. Bel and I look at each other.

"Shall I cook this for you?" I point at the giblets. Bel meows his assent and I place them in a pot with water and a little salt. "How about a pie now, Bel? Want to make a pumpkin pie?"

I hoist the turkey into the oven after I cover it with foil. I set the baster on the stove, wash my hands, and get busy with the other dishes. I filmed up until ten last night, so I couldn't really start early on this meal. Normally, I would have made the pie and the cranberries the day before. Well, it's not as if I have anything else to do today.

As if on cue, the phone rings. I know it will be my mother. I have been ignoring her and she is worried. She knows me and I know her.

"Hi, Mom," I say as I pick up the receiver while simultaneously removing spice jars from the cupboard—ginger, nutmeg, cinnamon, and cloves. "Happy Thanksgiving."

"How did you know it was me?"

"You have your very own ring. I thought you paid extra for that."

"Very funny, Ellie. What are you doing today?"

"Like I told you, I'm cooking the dinner I'll have alone with my husband."

"If you ask me, it's odd."

"I didn't ask you."

"It's still odd. Who has Thanksgiving alone?"

"Where will you have Thanksgiving?"

"Since you wouldn't have me, I have to go break bread with the Kowalskis."

"You're kidding! You have lots of friends. I can't believe you're going to their house. How is Dickie Kowalski?"

"They are the only ones who invited me when I hinted around at such a late date. I thought I was coming to you. Dickie's fine. He'll be running the bank soon."

"It figures. He always had ambition."

"How is your husband's gallery doing?"

"I think it's doing well. He sold an important piece last week. It was a big sale. You know how that business is, feast or famine."

"I do."

"Listen, Mom, I've gotta go concentrate on what I'm doing here. I don't want to put the turkey neck into the pumpkin pie."

"How are you doing, my love?" She finally comes to the real point of her call. "Are you okay?"

"Me? Of course, I'm okay. I'm doing a big studio film! I'm tired but I'm good."

"And married life? Is everything all right?"

"Yes! Everything is great! Love you, Mom! Gotta go!" I say as I hang up the phone.

It rings again almost immediately.

"What else?" I ask as I pick up, sure that my mother is calling back for one more tidbit she needs to share with me. Probably something about the Kowalskis.

"Kitten?"

"Oh, hi, Howard. Happy Thanksgiving!"

"I just wanted to remind you that we're starting with oysters at two. Todd bakes them á la Rockefeller, so we eat them when they're nice and hot. Don't be late!"

"Howard," I begin, completely confused by what he is saying. "I told you I can't come."

"No you didn't."

"I did! I distinctly remember telling you that I couldn't come. I'm sorry but I'm already cooking here now."

Very audibly, Howard takes a deep breath.

"All right, Kitten. You'll be missed," he says, and he hangs up the phone.

I, too, replace the receiver. That was really weird. I know I told him we weren't joining them. What is the matter with him?

I shake off those thoughts and return my attention to the meal. I grab my rolling pin, plop the chilled dough into a well of flour on the counter, and press down extra hard as I roll out my pie crust.

* * *

Hours later, the turkey is perfectly browned and the pie is cooling. Cranberries, Brussels sprouts, stuffing, sweet potatoes, mashed potatoes, and gravy are all cooked, ready and waiting. The table is set, the candles are lit, a fire is crackling in the fireplace, and I've changed into a dress. Bel has even had an early dinner of liver and gizzards. This is my first Thanksgiving foray into doing it all myself and, I must say, I feel rather proud.

"Orlando!" I shout out the open kitchen window, hoping he hears me in the office. "Dinner is ready!"

I hustle back to the turkey to carve it. I'm not really sure Orlando knows how and, growing up in a household of competent women and no father, I learned early to perform most domestic tasks.

"Hi there," Orlando says from the doorway. He is wearing jeans and a starched white button-down shirt—a very good look for him—and carrying a bouquet of roses.

"Orlando! Where did you get those flowers?"

"I'll never tell. Now, you toddle off and put these in some water and allow me to carve that bird."

In no time, we fill our plates from the platters arranged on the kitchen counter and sit at the table together. Orlando pours wine into our glasses.

"Wait. Before we eat or drink, can we say grace?" I ask.

"Sure." Orlando sets his glass on the table. "Would you like to say it?"

"You do it."

"All right. Not sure I'm quite up to it. We weren't a grace-saying kind of family. Right then. Um…thank you for this food and drink, so beautifully prepared by my bride. And the fire, and the candles, and the cat—the cat I did not want—brought into our home by my bride. And on that note, God, thank you for said bride. Well, how was that?"

"Good," I laugh. "Strange but good."

"And now may I propose a toast to the beautiful bride I was just chatting about with God?" Orlando raises his glass. "To you, Ellie."

I blush and look at my husband, in his crisp, white shirt, his black hair pulled back off his face. He is extraordinarily handsome, and I can't quite believe we are married.

"Thank you," I say, raising my own glass. "To you, Orlando. May we have a lifetime of Thanksgivings together."

On that note, we clink our glasses together and commence to eat the feast.

"This is delicious. Who taught you to cook?"

"Both my mother and my grandmother. My mother was the pie person and my grandmother was the leader of the gravy. But they both could really cook anything."

"And clearly they taught it to you."

"Thank you," I say, feeling myself blush.

"I'm glad we're having this holiday together, just us. I hope it makes up for the fact that I can't be here for Christmas."

I place my knife and fork on my plate and work to choke down the food that is already in my mouth. "What?"

"Didn't I tell you?"

"No! You didn't tell me. What are you talking about?"

"I have to fly to Japan. There is an estate that needs to be packed up for shipping and it has to happen then. It was the only time it could be done, and I really need to oversee it. And I know you only have a few days off from your movie. Maybe your mother can come then?"

I am starting to feel like I'm on a seesaw with Orlando. One day up, the next day down. I can't get stable footing. I push my plate away from me. "But Christmas is so important."

"I thought you liked Thanksgiving. You told me it was your favorite holiday."

"It is! But do I only get one?" I sound like such a whiner.

"Darling, I'll be home before New Year's Eve and we can go out dancing."

"I don't want to go out dancing! I want Christmas with my husband. Our first Christmas!"

"Ellie, please don't be so dramatic."

"Why do you need to go to Japan for Christmas? That doesn't even make any sense!"

"Ellie, it is *you* not making sense. I have to go for a few days. I'll be back. Your mother can come. We have this day together. Please don't ruin it."

"I…"

"Maybe you shouldn't begin so many sentences with the word 'I.' Anyone might think you're a narcissist."

Of course, I cry. I feel hurt and confused and sit in my chair wondering if I am, in fact, a narcissist. Orlando resumes eating. The tape of Christmas carols that I had put in the machine comes to an end, on the rousing final notes of *Joy to the World*. The room is plunged into silence, other than the sound of Orlando's knife and fork as he works his way across his plate.

22

DIAL M

The month of December begins. I enter the fourth week of filming and the specter of Christmas looms. I imagine a desk calendar, one day to a page and—just like in an old movie—each page magically ripping off from the rest and flying through the air into obscurity.

Orlando and I have had an uneventful weekend after the bomb he dropped on Thanksgiving. He went to the gallery on Friday and Saturday. I spent the days quietly—studying my lines, taking long baths—and kept myself even and calm. I had thought of visiting Orlando at the gallery but, once he'd left with the car, I couldn't muster the energy to call a taxi to get there. I am anxious to see what he has made of the space, but I find myself feeling tired. And tired and I don't mix well. I am heeding Howard's advice and pampering myself a little.

I considered Christmas shopping, but it will have to wait. I don't have many people to shop for—Orlando, of course. My mother. Dottie. Howard. Bel. I should probably get something for my director. And makeup, hair, and wardrobe. Do I need to buy for the rest of the crew? Maybe send a big basket, something to enjoy on the set? I could have it delivered to set on the 23rd. Of course, none of the actors will want to eat from a basket of food. It is all we can do the keep ourselves slim in the face of omnipresent craft services. But a basket it will have to be. I can't very well buy individual gifts for everyone. I don't even have a car.

I mean I don't have an automobile at my disposal. We're waiting to purchase a second car. Just until we get on our feet after the expense of the house, the gallery setup, the first car, and so on. It is definitely inconvenient, though, life in LA without wheels. Maybe that little market in Beachwood Canyon can organize the basket for me. At least I can get there on my bike.

We have a couple more weeks of interiors on the lot. Then we transition to night shooting on location in Echo Park. I've never actually done night shoots. On the soap, we shot everything indoors. Once in a blue moon, they did some location work—which always looked weird in video—but it never involved my storyline. I am a little nervous about it. Orlando works during the day. Our schedules may not be perfectly aligned but at least we cross over somewhat. When I go to night shoots, we'll become like two ships passing for a while. I must relax and remind myself that it is only for a few weeks.

I am sitting in my dressing room now, rereading the novel, *Rebecca*. Why are these gothic heroines always so blind to the facts that surround them? And why is she nameless? Did Daphne du Maurier think it would be easier for the reader to insert herself (probably not very often *him*self) into the shoes of the protagonist if she didn't give her a name? Or did she feel that it rendered the character more vulnerable and perhaps less consequential as a human being if she failed to name her? All of the above, I'm guessing.

What *is* in a name, after all? Not an original question, I know. Would my life have been different had I lived it as Ruby Russell? It sounds like a tap dancer in a big old Hollywood musical. Like the studio made it up. Whereas Eleanor Russell is elegant. It has a gravitas that Ruby Russell does not. Would Orlando have fallen in love with me had he been introduced to me as Ruby?

And then I wonder what I should never, ever wonder: did Orlando fall in love with me at all? Was it real? Did he mean it? It was all so frenetic and rushed. If I look at it one way, I could imagine that he was doing the rushing. That he was the one who pushed me to move faster than I was comfortable moving. But if I look at it from a slightly different angle, it is clear that I was in it as much as he was. Would I have married him in that little church in Italy if he hadn't come up with the concept? But it is a ridiculous question, after all, because it is usually the man who proposes.

I admit I was surprised that he had his mother's ring with him in Italy. We met on the plane. Literally seated next to each other traveling from Zurich to Rome. I struggled to place my carry-on bag in the overhead compartment and he gallantly came to my rescue. And then, he was right there next to me. Normally, I sleep when I fly, but we ended up talking the entire flight. I was traveling alone. After all that had occurred, I needed to get out of town. He was traveling alone, as well.

He asked me where I was staying. The Hotel d'Inghilterra. In a crazy coincidence, he was staying there too. We shared a taxi. I checked into my room. There was some trouble with his reservation, so—I can't even explain why I did it—I offered him the sofa in my suite. And that was really it. We have never been apart since then. Here we are in December, and we met in July. That means we have known each other five months. Not even half a year.

* * *

These lags on film sets are endless. You sit in your trailer for hours while they move all the lights and equipment. Our director shoots in the classical way, I am told. One master shot, one over the shoulder from Character A to Character B and then one close-up on Character B. Then, the whole operation is flipped around to shoot over the shoulder from Character B to Character A, ending up with a close-up on Character A. And the lights and camera need to be reset for every angle. If we get through two pages in a day, it is a lot.

They say Alfred Hitchcock didn't do that. That he was so well prepared and could envision exactly how he would cut the footage together, he didn't need to shoot all that coverage. He was more specific about

115

precisely what was required and filmed only that. On the other hand, they say he was a strange one. Particularly to Tippi Hedren. At least my director, Frank, is a nice guy. With everything else going on in my life right now, I don't think I could cope with a Hitchcock.

A knock at the door breaks my reverie.

"Come in," I call out.

"Miss Russell?" A P.A. opens the door. The baby-faced one. Kevin, I think.

"Ready for me?" I ask. "Kevin, right?"

"Uh, yes. Kevin. And no. It's going to be a while. Do you need to do anything on the lot? Go make phone calls or anything else?"

"Actually, yes. I do need to make a call."

"There's a payphone over near the commissary. Would you like me to drive you there in a golf cart?"

"No, I could use the walk, if you don't mind."

"Well…" Kevin looks fearful of another disappearance.

"Fine," I say, feeling compassion for the difficulty of his position. "Why don't you drive me there?"

"Great!" he says, visibly relieved that he won't lose me on his watch. "The golf cart is right outside!"

We follow the grid of the Paramount lot, a little fantasy city. People walk the roads, some with scripts, some pushing clothes racks, some in costumes, and some in clusters so deep in conversation that they don't see the world around them. We pull up to the payphone and I hop out and enter the little booth. In a futile attempt at privacy, I close the glass door behind me.

I pull out my SAG card, drop in my coins, and dial the number on the reverse. After a good thirty rings, a woman answers, "Screen Actors Guild. How may I direct your call?"

"I have a question about my medical insurance. I was married a few months ago and I'd like to add my husband to my policy."

She connects me to the appropriate extension and I pose the question again.

"Just send or bring in a copy of your marriage certificate," the second woman tells me. "It needs to have the raised seal of the state for us to process the request. A copy of each of your driver's licenses and a notarized letter from you. That's all we need."

I hadn't even considered this. "Well, what if I was married in another country?"

"You need a marriage certificate from one of the fifty states of the U. S. of A. You'll need to go to city hall to show your records from that other country and get your certificate there."

"I see." I don't see at all. "I—we—um, we were married in a little church in Italy. We don't have any papers."

"What do you mean, you don't have papers? Didn't you sign anything? Didn't the priest give you something?"

I am feeling woozy. "Um, no. I just, I guess, I…" I sit down on the bench in the booth. It reeks of smoke in here and the little counter is edged in caterpillar-like burns from years of cigarettes left there to smolder. It feels thirty degrees hotter than the air outside. I wrench the glass door open and bend forward, fearing I might throw up. "I don't have any papers," I whisper. "What am I supposed to do?" I hope to co-opt her into my secret. I will her to help me.

"You need to get yourself—and this fella of yours—to city hall and do it there."

"Do what?"

"Get married! You're not really married in the eyes of the law of the great state of California."

I don't hear any more. I drop the receiver and let it swing in the hot air of the booth. I walk out into the sunshine and am not sure where I am going. My trusty P.A. guard isn't about to let me go, however. Kevin has his eye on me. He jumps up from the golf cart, runs over and grabs my arm, and guides me back to the vehicle. He places me in the front seat, right next to him, and starts the cart moving as fast as he can. He probably figures the speed will keep me from jumping overboard.

23

THE SHADOW OF
THE WIND

Somehow I get through the day. I say my words. I hit my marks. I find my light. There is really no reason to worry. Orlando and I can easily fix this. A trip to City Hall, maybe a boozy lunch afterwards to celebrate, and married we shall be. We can even bring a camera and document it. Frame it for the grandchildren. We can invite our mothers. Howard. Maybe Dottie.

No. That might slow things down and I think it is best to proceed without delay. Why didn't it cross my mind that we needed official paperwork? Well, I've never been married before, for starters. And that would surely be the explanation for Orlando's lack of consciousness, as well.

A tiny seed of doubt enters my mind. What if Orlando refuses to go forward? But why would he do that? Because I'm a pain-in-the-ass, that's why. I'm difficult and I'm high-strung. High-maintenance, in modern parlance. He was not aware of that fact in Italy when we married. He saw the first glimpse of it when we tried to visit the Catacombs. He did not know me at all.

Of course, I didn't know him either. He has turned out to be some-what different from the man I met on the plane. He is moody and mercurial and sometimes even unkind. And, as it has become more than evident, I am not the only secret-keeper in this family.

The most important thing now is to think clearly, proceed with a well-formed strategy. I never do well when I just say the first thing that comes to mind. Should I tell Orlando over dinner tonight? He said he had to work late at the gallery, which would render that option unwise. Over coffee tomorrow morning? Maybe. Actually, maybe not. Too rushed. Perhaps I should wait for the weekend. That seems to make the most sense. Our time will be more leisurely then. I can segue from some topic that seems like a logical transition. But what topic would that be?

I can take time to figure it out. As soon as I tell him, though, he will ask me when I found out. He will ask me why I didn't tell him immedi-ately. He will say that I am withholding information, perhaps even lying again. Sins of omission are as bad as commission.

Sins of commission, of course, are those we commit by doing what we should not do. Murder. Adultery. Theft. But sins of omission are just as serious. When we leave undone those things which we ought to have done—when we do not help someone, are not generous to those in need, fail to tell our husband the whole truth and nothing but the truth, so help us God—we are no less guilty. And that is where my husband will get me, will trip me up and trap me. Of course, the argument could be made that he isn't really my husband. But, that line of reasoning serves no purpose other than to lead me to despair.

Howard picks me up after work and on the drive to my house I am silent.

"What's wrong, Kitten?"

"Nothing. Tough day. Tired." I lack the energy to form full sentences.

"Oookaaay…" Howard drags out the word.

I don't rise to the bait and continue to stare out the window.

"Come for dinner on Saturday." Howard throws out a salvo.

"We can't."

"Talk to your husband. Ask him to come to dinner on Saturday. Todd and I would like to have dinner with you and your husband."

"But we can't."

"You haven't even talked to him! What are you doing that keeps you from coming to our house?"

"I…" I hedge. "We have plans."

"What plans?"

"Dinner with friends."

"What friends?"

"Stop it, Howard!"

"You don't have friends. You two never see anyone. You're always holed up in that house and it isn't good for you. Come for dinner. It'll make you both feel better."

"We feel fine."

"You don't look fine."

"I'm working like a dog on this movie, Howard! I'm even doing some of my own stunts!"

"I know that, Kitten. That's why I want to cook for you and your handsome hubby."

"Okay, fine."

"You'll come?"

"I'll ask Orlando," I say as we finally arrive at my house. I practically jump out of the moving car. "Bye, Howard. Thanks."

Howard watches me closely as I run up the path to my door. I don't need to see him doing it. I feel his eyes on my back.

Once inside, I call out for Orlando. I know he is not here, but I need to make sure. Bel saunters out of the bedroom where he's clearly been napping. He yawns and sits to clean his face.

"Hi, Bel," I lean down to stroke him then poke my head into each room to confirm that Orlando is not home. I cross through the kitchen, out the back door, and over toward the office. I let myself in and close the door behind me. Quickly, I walk to the secretary and crouch down on the floor. I rifle through my tote, find my little makeup bag, and feel around in it. Once I have my powder compact, I squeeze its sides together, which pops the bottom off. And, voilà, I extract the key.

I lie down and reach under the desk. This is the trickiest part. Find the keyhole and insert the key, all from a prone position with no actual visibility. It was easier to do when I was little.

I slide the key in at just the right angle and turn it one circle around. I allow the key to drop into my palm and slide my arm out again. I set the key aside and reach back under the desk to press the little latch. The panel pops open to my touch. Now I reach into the cubby, still with my palm facing up. I lean in a little farther to get my hand in all the way to the back.

And—finally—there it is! I feel it. A tiny piece of paper, taped to the roof of the compartment. I do not dislodge it. I do not wish to see it. Not now. Not yet.

I only wish to confirm that it is there.

Gently, as gently as I entered, I withdraw my hand from the drawer. I pick up the key and repeat the entire operation, turning it the opposite way. I listen for the little click that tells me that everything is in its proper alignment. I remove the key, put it back in the compact, close it up, zip it in the cosmetics bag and drop it all in my purse. I press the molding back.

Wait.

I should change my pattern.

I remove the key from its compact hiding place and look around the room. My eye falls on the box of stationery Orlando gave me. I take my little key and slip it into the bottom of the box, underneath the tissue paper that keeps the cards from moving. The perfection of it pleases me.

Then I go back to the secretary and take the sleeve of my sweater to dust off my fingerprints. I decide to wipe the entire piece of furniture, so there is no tell-tale line—one side dusty and one side clean—that would hint to Orlando where to look for the hidden compartment.

I stand up and move toward the door. My sleeve, I see, is filthy. I quickly remove my sweater and, once in the house, throw it into the washing machine. I can't leave it in the basket. The dirty sleeve might arouse suspicion. Actually, washing a single sweater might prompt questions. I run to the bedroom, grab a pile of underwear from my drawer, and throw it into the machine as well. That is why I washed the sweater, I will explain. I needed to do my undergarments and it had been hot on the set. So the sweater needed washing, as well. My story is airtight.

Relieved, I go back to the bedroom. I'll just lie down a little. I won't unmake the bed. I'll lie on top of the covers and pull a throw on top of me. I need it now that I have no sweater. I'll just close my eyes for a moment, secure in the knowledge that everything is exactly where it is supposed to be.

24

BELL, BOOK AND CANDLE

On Saturday morning, I decide to sleep late. Orlando has gone to his shop to make room for the shipment from Japan. He is planning a party—a delayed opening celebration to introduce the gallery—for some time in January, after he returns from his trip. He'll do it when the new items arrive. He can't really give me a date, as yet, because everything is coming by boat and shipping schedules are unreliable. In any case, I'll be finished with the film by then. We wrap on New Year's Eve. Martini shot on a champagne night.

Orlando and I have not had a chance to talk. That is to say, I have not found the moment to tell him my little news flash about the wrinkle in our marital status. Lack of status, I should say. I'll cook dinner tonight and get him in a good mood. But for now, I will sleep. I am very, very tired. That is all that is wrong with me. Bel is curled up next to me. He can sleep anytime, anywhere. I pull a pillow over my head to block out any light and burrow my face into the clean sheets.

Eyes closed, I allow myself to drift. I imagine clouds billowing overhead and myself floating along with them. My right arm is getting tingly, so I flip to my other side. Back to the images of the sky I go, working for the feeling of buoyancy. I find I'm not comfortable on this side, either, so

I roll over on my back. This puts the pillow directly on my face, covering my nose and mouth. Not only can I not sleep, I can't even breathe. I toss the pillow to the other side of the bed and endeavor to resume my relaxation exercise. Doctor Blanchard is the one who taught it to me.

Bel is getting annoyed with my tossing and turning, and he makes a little huff and readjusts his position, as well. "Sorry," I offer and flop over to lie on my stomach. I grab the extra pillow again and press it to my ear. Clouds. Sky. Floating. Butterflies. Birds. Me. Just as I feel myself slip down into the belly of a cloud, the blackness of Ruby Falls rears up and engulfs me into the void. I sit up with a start and heave the pillow across the room. Bel has had enough of me and loudly jumps to the floor. No one is getting any sleep around here this morning.

Just then the doorbell rings. I am unused to the sound of it—we don't get many visitors—and my anxiety spikes. I jump up from the bed. Tying my bathrobe closed, I come around the corner to see Dottie peering in the mullioned-glass doors.

"Hi," I say as I open them.

"Let's go," she cheerily commands.

"Go where?"

"Christmas shopping! Have you done any?"

"Actually, no. That would be amazing. It's like you read my mind, Dottie," I tease.

"Funny that. C'mon. Get dressed. I'll drive. You might want to have some coffee first, though."

"How did you know?"

"Lucky guess."

I pour a cup for each of us and take mine into the bedroom to dress. "Where are we going?" I shout to her in the living room. "I hear the Beverly Center is nice."

"Heavens, dear. I never go anywhere like that! I have friends who still have shops on Hollywood Boulevard."

"Isn't that kind of run down?"

"You just have to know where to look."

I step back into the living room, fully clothed. "I'm ready."

"Don't you look lovely!"

I am wearing a floral cotton shirtwaist that belonged to my mother in the '60s and her old huarache sandals. "Thanks, Dottie. This was my mother's dress. Her shoes, too."

"And they suit you perfectly. I'll bet she's as pretty as you."

"Prettier."

"C'mon. Let's go. Got your wallet?"

"Yep."

I carefully close the front doors, making sure Bel hasn't snuck out behind me. We walk to the curb, through my perfect picket fence covered with those perfectly strange roses.

"Dottie," I say, touching one. "You have these roses at your house too. I've never seen any like them. Do you know what they're called?"

"Oh, my father messed around with grafting. He created them. Planted them for all the neighbors. They don't really have a name."

"Like me," I say as I consider the perfection of the placement of these nameless blossoms. "Like the heroine in *Rebecca*."

"You have a name," she says as she climbs into her old station wagon. "Maybe we should name these roses after you!"

Dottie points her car downhill and we leave the hills for the city. She turns onto Hollywood Boulevard and the world springs to life in the form of teeming humankind. Hookers in short shorts and heels. Bums pushing grocery carts. Tourists pressing their hands into the prints of the stars. Scientologists in ersatz military uniforms. An infinite spectrum of humanity passes us by.

"Aren't they all beautiful?" Dottie asks me. "See the light shining from them?"

"All of them?"

"All of them."

"That's a nice way to look at the world, Dottie."

"It's the way the world is." She touches my hand and for an electrifying moment, I see it. Colored lights dance around each one of them. The beams expand and contract, almost with a pulse, and they reach toward the lights of the others. It is a vivid dance of luminescence that moves

125

from person to person and I see the interconnectedness of us all. I pull my hand away and the vision goes with it.

"I can't see it," I fib.

"Hmm," she replies and keeps driving.

"Lookie there!" she suddenly shouts. "My parking angel is at it again!"

Dottie deftly parallel parks and we both get out of the car.

"I thought parking angels were a joke. I mean, if you're working your favors from the beyond, shouldn't you go for bigger ticket items than parking spots? Why waste?"

"You're measuring grace with a teaspoon, Ruby."

"Don't call me that."

"And don't you be so parsimonious. God is not. You can have your parking spot *and* everything else you've ever dreamed of. You don't have to pick. What's that game show? *Let's Make a Deal*? You don't have to do that."

"I would make a deal. I would give something up in order to have my father back."

"But you don't have to."

"Dottie. I have longed and prayed to know what happened to him for the past twenty years. Are you going to stand there and tell me that he *will* come back?"

"C'mon." She grabs my arm and we walk a few paces, picking our way through a cluster of teenagers huddled around a single boom box, which is currently playing at depth-charge decibels. We arrive at a tiny store, fronted by huge plates of glass that bend to curve around the corners. It makes me think of a 1940s jewelry store. In the display cases sits an array of dusty objects, most of which I cannot identify.

On closer inspection, I recognize candles. Crystals. Decks of cards. I also see jars of powders and gnarled roots, none of which are familiar to me. *Eduardo's Emporium of Elixirs and Esoterica* is written above the door in deeply engraved gold letters lined in black. Under it are the words *Liniments, Tonics, Potions, Cures*. And under that, in the middle of the door, the single word, *Enter*.

"Shall we?" she says.

126

"I guess so." And I fear there is no turning back.

Once the door closes behind us, the sounds of the street disappear. I find this a little hard to believe, given the volume at which the music was blasting on the sidewalk right outside. Inside, it is dimly lit. The floor is tiled in a pattern of small, black-and-white hexagons. The ceiling is a vivid, mid-range blue—cadet blue, my mother would call it—with tiny gold stars painted everywhere. Iron lanterns hang down on chains and appear to be illuminated by real candles, though I know that would be ridiculous. I squint my eyes to see better.

The walls are lined entirely in dark wooden shelves with glass doors, which rise from floor to ceiling. Inside the cabinets rests an expanded version of what was in the window. Crystals and candles. Bolts of jewel-colored fabrics. Funny hats—I think I see Napoleon's bicorn. Endless jars of powders, roots, and liquids of iridescent sheen. Books. Papers. Cards. Jewelry, even—I peer in at a fanciful collection of Egyptian-looking necklaces and bracelets.

"C'mon," Dottie says again, as she urges me farther in.

"Dottie, are those real candles burning?" I point at the chandeliers above us.

"Nice, huh?"

"Is that allowed?"

"By whom?"

"I don't know. The City of Hollywood? Isn't that a fire hazard?"

"Oh, this place has been here so long, they barely know it exists." With that cryptic remark, she continues at a brisk pace toward the back of the store.

Seeing little alternative, I follow.

After a distance that seems impossibly long, behind a glass and wood counter filled with more of the same, we come upon a white-haired old man asleep in an upholstered chair. The chair is green velvet and is splitting at the seams. Little tufts of stuffing pop out here and there. The man wears wool trousers, a checked shirt, and a knitted wool vest—all in tones of earth and grass. A bow tie of sparkling yellow is perfectly tied at his neck. His glasses have slipped down his nose and a cat is wedged in beside him. An orange and white tabby.

"Eddie!" Dottie shouts, causing all three of us—Eddie, the cat, and me—to jump three feet in the air.

"What?" he yells as the cat scurries behind a cabinet. "Who are you and how did you know my name?" he directs at me.

"I didn't," I defend myself. "She spoke. Not me." I point to Dottie.

Eddie turns his head. "Well," he says, turning back to me. "Why didn't you say so?"

"I…uh…" I can't think of what to say.

"Eddie, I brought you someone. She needs gifts."

"Gifts?" he asks. "What does she mean by gifts?"

I look from one to the other.

Dottie studies me. "She's not entirely certain."

"Would she like a coconut patty?" He directs this question to Dottie while pointing a finger at me.

Dottie shrugs, allowing me to answer for myself.

"Um, sure," I say.

Eddie—the Eduardo of the sign?—reaches his hand under the chair and slides out a yellow box of coconut patties. The chocolate-dipped kind my father used to buy for me at souvenir shops in Florida. "Here," he says. "Have one. You too, Dottie." He proffers the box to her.

Together, we take our patties. She unwraps and eats hers right away. I unwrap mine and take a bite. It is stiff and stale. Like a relic from an old family vacation.

"Eat up!" he commands, and I chew.

"What are you looking for, kid?" he asks me.

I've just taken a sticky bite and struggle to answer him. "Well, I need something for my husband. My mother. A few other people." I wink and surreptitiously nod my head in the direction of Dottie.

"Are they all in distress?"

"What?"

"What do you need to help them get through?"

"Get through?" I look to Dottie to save me. "I want Christmas presents."

Eddie looks back at Dottie. "Did you tell her who I am?"

"It says plain as day on the door, Eddie."

"She doesn't know what it means."

"She does. She's just out of practice."

"I don't know what you two are talking about. Dottie? You said we were going Christmas shopping."

"We are!" Dottie smiles reassuringly. "But wouldn't you like more? Not less?"

"I'm really not following."

"Eddie." Dottie turns back to him. "Give her *her* gifts and then give her *your* gifts."

"Suit yourself," he says as he rouses himself from the chair. "Who'd you say? Husband? Mr. O?"

"Yes!" I guess he is clairvoyant, too. "Orlando is my husband."

"Nope," Eddie says.

"Yes," I insist, with a sinking awareness that he must be psychically picking up on my sham Italian marriage. "He is. I mean, yes, there is a little glitch in the process. But he is my husband."

"That's not his name."

Didn't he just call him Mr. O? Suddenly, I think of the name Otto and feel dizzy. There is incense burning in this store. I failed to identify it on arriving, but I am acutely aware of it now. It is sweet and viscous, like the coconut patty. Which I really cannot finish now, because I think I'm going to throw up.

"Eddie," Dottie makes a cutting gesture across her neck, signaling him to change the subject. "She's a little touchy about names."

"It's best to call a thing by its name, girlie," Eddie says to me. "You'll never see anything clearly if you can't call a spade a spade."

"Cut her some slack." Dottie grabs my arm and shoves me down into Eddie's chair. "You look like you're going to pass out. Eddie, do you have any water?"

Eddie shuffles over to one of the cabinets and, after much deliberation, selects one of the jars of liquid. It most certainly does not contain water. The fluid inside is a vivid yellow. In fact, it matches Eddie's tie.

"Drink some of this!" he bursts out with a ghoulish, horror-film laugh.

"Eddie," Dottie says. "She doesn't think that's funny."

"Well, that's what's wrong with her. She has no sense of humor."

"I do have a sense of humor!"

"Fine." Eddie shambles to the back to an old glass watercooler. He takes a paper cone cup from a little dispenser and bubbles some water into it. He totters back and gallantly offers me the cup.

"Thank you," I say and take a sip and then another, surprised at how refreshing it tastes. "It's very good. I feel better already."

"Are you a bit of a drama queen, girlie?" Eddie asks.

"Eddie!" Dottie reprimands. "That's not very polite."

"Well, look at her. You say one little thing and she gets all woozy. Not very rugged, if you ask me."

He is clearly using reverse psychology—I've been shrunk by the best of shrinks—but I decide to take the bait. "All right," I say. "What do you mean that Orlando is not my husband's name?"

"I just don't see it," Eddie replies. "And if I can't see it, it's usually not there."

"Dottie?" I turn to her for backup. "Do you see it? Do you see the name, Orlando? You said you saw Ruby. You must see Orlando."

"Well," she equivocates. "I'm not quite sure. I don't exactly see it, but that's not to say it's not there."

"I don't understand."

"You know," Dottie brightens up. "This might be a little too much for a Christmas shopping trip. What do you have in the gift line, Eddie?"

"Like what?" He looks at me.

"Um," I begin, struggling to collect my thoughts. "My husband likes to read."

Eddie makes his way over to the cabinets again. He picks up books, flips through them, sets them back on the shelves. He moves toward the front of the store, repeating the exercise several times over. "This one!" he says in a eureka moment. "This one's for you."

He walks back to me and repeats, "For you." He hands me a paperback book. I'm surprised that he has anything so modern. *Emmanuel's Book*, it is called, and is subtitled, *A Manual for Living Comfortably in the Cosmos*.

"You need this," he adds. "You are living about as uncomfortably as I've seen. And that, girlie, is my gift to you. The only one you're getting today. Well?" He stares at me. "Aren't you going to open it? Open it up and read."

Obediently, I open it to the prologue. I clear my throat and begin:

> *"The gifts I wish to give you*
> *are my deepest love,*
> *the safety of truth,*
> *the wisdom of the universe,*
> *and the reality of God."*

I look up at him. "Should I go on?"

"Jump down to the bottom, why don't you?"

"Okay." I find my place on the page and continue:

> *"My friends, let me impress upon you*
> *how solidly*
> *you are planted in eternity,*
> *how brilliantly*
> *you can shine in your own physical world,*
> *how possible*
> *it all is,*
> *how beautifully*
> *the Plan is designed.*
> *In God's Plan, no soul is alone.*
> *No soul is ever lost."*

I look up at him again. "Why is this for me?"

"It's from your father, Ruby," he says. "Happy birthday."

25

SUSPICION

Today *is* my birthday. I am not sure if Orlando knows it. I had actually forgotten it, myself, until Eddie blurted it out. I'm not even going to consider how he knew.

When I returned from shopping—if you can call that surreal expedition shopping—I found messages from my mother and Howard on the answering machine. Then, flowers arrived at the door. Howard sent yellow roses, my mother, pink.

"What do you make of that, Ellie?" Nina Blanchard would have said. "Why do you suppose you've forgotten your birthday? What number is it this year?"

"I don't know," I would answer.

"You don't know how old you are?" She knows perfectly well what I mean.

"I don't know why I've forgotten. I'm twenty-six today. Twenty-six years old. And, before you ask, I have no idea what significance that number holds."

"Well, let's think."

"I'm already thinking," I snap. "And I can see that you are, too."

"How old was your father when he left you in the cave?"

"Nice try, but he was thirty-five. There is no resemblance between the number twenty-six and the number thirty-five."

"Isn't there, Ellie?"

"I don't see it, Dr. Blanchard."

"You do, Ellie. You're the one who forgot your birthday. You see it. I know you do."

"Shut up, Dr. Blanchard!" I am imagining this conversation, so I am allowed to say things like that. In fact, I say it often to Dr. Blanchard in my mind.

"What do two and six add up to? What do three and five add up to?"

"Shut up, I said!"

"Eight, Ellie! Eight! Eight! Eight!"

Now you see why I stopped seeing Dr. Blanchard. She is rather obnoxious. I mean, who cares about the number eight? I could find the number eight anywhere if I performed long division or multiplication or any other type of mathematical formula. It is everywhere. Just like four and seven and one. Two. Three. Everything is everywhere. So? Who cares? Why would I forget my birthday because of a stupid number? I am just *tired*, I keep saying! And *no one* is listening!

I shove the flowers in vases and leave them on various tables in the living room, which makes the house look funereal. Then, I practically crawl into bed. I'm too tired to cook. Too tired to do anything. I will sleep and when Orlando comes home, maybe we can go out to dinner. It's my birthday, after all.

* * *

"Ruby."

I hear the voice from a great distance. My father's voice.

"Ruby."

I open my eyes. Orlando is sitting on the side of the bed, smiling. He has a hand on my arm. He has called me Ruby. I am certain of it.

But am I? A nauseating swirl like the spinning house in *The Wizard of Oz* competes for my vision. It is filled with flitting images of Dr.

Blanchard and Sylvia Long and Dottie and that storekeeper Eddie with the dried-up candy and the Hallmark quotations and dozens of cats and roses and, yes, my father. Always my father.

"What did you call me?" I whisper, but Orlando does not seem to hear me.

He knows about that name; it's no secret anymore. He found the scrapbook. But why would he call me that? He will deny it, I know. If I ask him why he called me Ruby, he will say he didn't. So, I will try a new tack and not ask him at all. Two can play at his game. I do not need to reveal everything. I can conceal as well as the next person.

"Happy birthday," he says.

"How did you know?" I ask.

"How could I not know?" He leans over to brush his lips by my cheek. Not even a real kiss. "Darling, we're married!"

"We're not." I hoist myself to my elbows.

"Not what?" He looks so innocent.

"Married." There, just like that, I've announced it.

"What are you talking about? Bad dream?"

"Don't make this about me, Orlando," I say with a sharpness that I can see surprises him. I decide to keep going down this provocative path and add, "Or, whatever your name is."

"Ellie?"

"Is that what you're going to call me now?"

"Darling, I think you've had another dream. Shall I make some tea like last time?"

Last time. That feels like years and years ago. Another lifetime. The dream he says I had when I heard that screaming. He said it was me. Maybe it wasn't me and Orlando is trying to make me think I am losing my mind. We are changing movies now—going from *Rebecca* to *Gaslight*—but I have seen them all. He won't come up with one that I have not seen. I can guess the endings to whatever scenario he stages. And I can play my cards very close to the vest. That is precisely what I will do from now on.

"We are not legally married," I say. "I called SAG to add you to my insurance policy and it turns out that we need real paperwork to be considered married. Which we don't have."

I pause and wait for some sort of reaction, but his face is a blank. A beautiful blank. *The Inscrutable East,* I think as I lose my nerve.

"We need to go to City Hall," I say, trying for a more conciliatory note. "To get the papers completed. And they're only open Monday to Friday from nine to five. Maybe we can go when I'm doing night shoots before you leave for Japan? Otherwise, it'll be next year when you return."

"I see," he says. Coolly, he stands up and walks to the window. He parts the curtains and looks outside. I can see that he is not going to make this any easier.

"You won't find any answers there," I quip.

Orlando turns to look at me, still with that hard-to-read, vacant look on his face. "Why are you angry with me, Ellie?"

"Why do you think I'd be angry with you? Let me ask a better question. Who *are* you, Orlando? I don't even know you."

"Wow. Where did all this come from?"

"You know everything about me, and I know nothing about you!"

"Eleanor, I would say we know an equal amount about one another."

"Well then, you'd be wrong! You probably don't want to even marry me now."

"Is that what you're trying to provoke here?"

"What is that supposed to mean?"

"You're being terribly combative. I came home to take you out to dinner to celebrate your birthday. I entered this room and you've been aggressive and argumentative and confrontational from the moment I did so. Are you trying to provoke something, I ask you *again*." It doesn't sound like a question to me, at all.

"No, I..." I feel myself relenting. Doing the old female slip and slide. Off the ledge. Off my point. Off my confidence. A few words, firmly said, by him to me, and he wins. He has won. He always wins. "I'm sorry," I say.

"Good," he replies. "I should hope you're sorry. What a way to talk on your birthday!" I feel like a four-year-old, chastised by Daddy for her tantrum. "You're clearly tired."

Well, at least he got that one right.

"I'll go pick up some food and we can eat at home."

"Oh! I'd like to go out," I plead. Now I regret my outburst and feel I am being punished for my naughtiness.

"No. It will only fatigue you. I'll be back soon."

And that, as they say, folks, is that. He walks out of the bedroom, out of the house, and it crosses my mind that he might not come back.

26

THE TURN OF THE SCREW

Orlando closes the front door gently. Click. That is all I hear. Nothing afterwards. One would assume he has left the house. But what if he has not? I mean, come on! I'm not really up on my horror bona fides if I haven't considered that a person doesn't always go out the door when he says he is going out the door. People surprise you. Period. Over. Out.

I get up from the bed in serious stealth mode. I can be quiet, too. The trouble here is Bel. He, a cat, the quietest of animals, drops to the floor with a thud and starts to rub around my ankles, all the while purring like an ocean liner.

"Sshh," I say as I pick him up. I move to the bedroom door—which Orlando has left fully open—and press my body against it. Standing like this, if Orlando is still in the living room, I would have my back to him. Maybe he is pressing against the wall on the other side. Picture the cinematic shot. The two of us—leaning almost against each other—only plaster and wood between us. Like a tender lovers' embrace. Spooning. But this is not a love scene. Just exactly what kind of scene it is remains to be seen.

As I ease toward the opening, I suddenly realize that Bel is my secret weapon. If I toss him ever so gently into the hallway, there is a fifty-fifty chance of which way he will go. If Orlando is hiding in the living room, Bel will certainly know it. He is a cat and has a heightened sense of smell, sight, everything. Bel might walk to me, yes. But he might also walk in the direction of Orlando. And then I would *know*.

But what would I know, precisely? That Orlando is a fraud? That he means me harm? That he is secretly waiting on the other side of the wall to deliver such harm? What would be the point? What does he want from me?

He wants what is in the desk, for starters. It is then that I know where Orlando is and that I must confront him now. I toss Bel forward and he, of course, lands on his feet. He gives a little shudder, looks back at me in indignation, and sashays into the living room. I listen as hard as I can.

In a moment, I hear tiny crunches. Bel is in the kitchen at his food bowl and is enjoying a little kibble. Orlando must not be in the living room. Bel would have acknowledged him, stopped, meowed, purred a little louder. Orlando said he was getting food but I'm sure he's in the office.

And that is where I am headed.

I poke my head around the corner and allow my eyes to slowly travel the living room. It is empty. There is no sign of someone recently passing through. The curtains do not rustle. The air hangs still. Other than the little sounds of Bel biting into the dry food, it is silent. I enter the room. Happily, I am still in my mother's dress from earlier today. I won't have to play this out in my nightgown. There is something unprotected about confrontation when you're not properly dressed. You have the disadvantage.

I cross through the room and traverse the kitchen. As slowly as I can, I turn the handle to the back door. Bel looks up hopefully. A night of mousing would suit him. I slip out the door and close it quickly behind me. On top of everything, I do not intend to lose my cat.

Outside, it is already dark. I must have slept for hours this afternoon before Orlando woke me. On feet of air, I cross the garden toward the open doors of the office. Odd. Surely, he must be in there. We never leave the doors gaping open, especially not at night.

I stop when I get to the side of the building. What will I say to him? It doesn't matter. I'll figure it out as I go along. From where I am standing, I can see that the lights are off in the office. There is not a glimmer peeping out. Maybe he is waiting for me there in the dark. Maybe he plans to kill me. Maybe this is it, the final moment. Actually, I am ready to face anything to put myself out of the misery in which I have been living. I cannot go on with it. Each day of suspicion, fear, argument—the unknowingness of it all—has worn me to a nub. It must be resolved, and tonight is as good as any. My birthday, after all.

I square my shoulders and stand up tall. I walk around the open door and stand facing into the dark room.

"Orlando?" I call.

He does not answer. No matter. I will go in. I survived the cave. I can survive this office. There is nothing on earth as dark as that cave. Nothing. This level of darkness is practically daytime. In fact, there is a little shimmer from the streetlight as it hits the glass of the French door and reflects forward into the room. You think this is dark? You ain't seen nothin', mister. I'll show you dark. Dark and I know each other. Intimately, I might add.

"Orlando," I say, but this time I don't pose a question. He is in there. I know it in my bones. His presence is palpable to me in the same way I felt my father's absence on that day so long ago. Like a photograph and its own negative—the images are part of a pair. Like Orlando and me. My father, Sonny, and my beautiful mother, Peggy. We go together. Fit. But we split apart so well. Look at a negative. It has its own beauty. You can peel it away from the positive image and dissolve it back together. Rather than two separate images, they are just layers of one complete whole. Yet, no human bonds can hold them. Can't stop a dad when he wants to dump you.

I take a step forward and I hear shuffling in the back of the room. Is he really such a coward or is he simply trying to lure me back there? I see the lamp on the table and decide to shed some light.

I take three short strides and flip the switch. "Orlando!" I say with conviction.

Orlando does not answer.

I cast my eyes around the room and discover the source of the noise, but it takes me a moment to recognize what it is. A tiny possum is cowering in the middle of the floor, terrified by my presence. He must have entered through the open doors. I am grateful that I kept Bel indoors, avoiding an ugly confrontation. He's had his rabies shots, but still.

"Shoo," I say to the creature. He backs up even farther. Maybe if I move around him to the side, it will encourage him to head for the door. I tread carefully to make a wide circle to the left of the animal. He begins to emit a growl and opens his mouth wide. I wish I had some of Bel's kibble—maybe I could toss it into his general direction and cheer him up a little. Of course, it might have the opposite effect and only serve to annoy him.

He stands stock-still, mouth open, making that guttural sound as I walk ever so slowly to the far-left corner of the room. Then, I begin to narrow the gap between us. His eyes have been fixed on me, but I see him shift his gaze to take the measure of the distance to the doorway. I think my plan is working. Possums surely don't attack, do they? I mean, playing possum is called precisely that for a reason, right?

I take one more step and he starts to move away. Slowly, he makes an exaggerated creep toward the door. I wait while he takes his time. Just then, Orlando rounds the corner and says my name. Loudly. "Eleanor," he barks, like he has caught me up to no good. "Orlando," I whisper. "Stay where you are."

But he takes no orders from me. Into the room he stomps, which causes my possum (we have bonded enough for me to consider him mine) to freeze.

"Orlando," I stage-whisper, a little bit louder. "There is a possum in the middle of the room."

"A what?"

"A possum."

"Are you sure? It looks like a rat."

"Yes, I'm certain."

"I think it's a rat."

"It's not!" I feel defensive of the little guy.

"Well, how are you going to get out?" He doesn't offer any assistance.

"Um, I think you need to go back into the house and let him walk out the door. I can follow along."

"That's it? Should I bash it with a shovel?"

"No!" I knew he had a murderous side. "He's just trying to get out. Leave him alone, Orlando!"

"Fine. Would you like me to let the cat out?"

"Certainly not. Just go back inside and I'll be right there."

"Well," he smiles. "If you say so. I brought back some birthday dinner. Please come in soon."

I look at him long and hard. I don't know. Maybe I am overreacting. Maybe I am a little off balance. He looks pretty normal. He looks like the man I married. Not just in facial features, but also in the warmth I see there right now. Maybe I'm working too hard. Maybe I'm obsessing too much. Maybe it's me. It usually is.

"I'll be right in. Why don't you light some candles? There's another bottle of the Chianti." This could be a good birthday after all. I am twenty-six years old. That should be a pretty good year.

"All right," he says dubiously. "If you're not in the house in five minutes, I am coming back with the shovel. And the cat."

"I'll be there."

Orlando spins on his heel and heads for the house.

The possum gives him about three minutes clearance then exits after him.

That leaves me two minutes before Orlando returns.

I shut the doors, grab the box of stationery, retrieve the key, drop to the floor, unlock the compartment, pop it open, and reach for the piece of paper.

There it is, the code that I know so well: 839938*863392591291115*181.

See how easy it is to find the number eight?

27

SNAKE PIT

"Good morning." She looked up from her ultramodern desk in her glass and chrome office and blasted me with a toothy smile. Good orthodontia in her youth, I reflected. "I'm Nina Blanchard. You're free to just call me Nina. Keep things informal."

Oh, please. There was not one informal aspect to her *or* her office. "Chanel?" I asked and pointed to her suit. Navy bouclé with gold buttons, epaulettes, and a little fringe at the edge of the skirt. She wore spectator pumps, too, off-white with navy toe and heel. An elegant and under-stated choice. My grandmother would have approved.

Dr. Blanchard was very attractive. Slim, chestnut pageboy, pearls. Not at her most beautiful stage of life—that would have been in her thir-ties, according to my mother—but at the full apotheosis of her power look. I pegged her at about forty-five. Maybe even fifty. That magical age for a woman's face when she has completely lost the baby fat and the angles and bones stand sharp. Faint lines around the eyes and mouth, but the sag of the jowls and the creeping of the neck haven't happened yet.

"Chanel's a little rich for my blood," she said, laughing. "This is just St. John."

Just St. John? I'd be careful where I said that. Might come off as elitist. Instead of answering her, I looked around the office. I didn't believe that Chanel was too rich for her blood, at all. I considered her desk. It was sleek, made of a medium-toned wood. Highly polished. Beautiful grain. Not cherry. There was no red in it.

"Walnut?" I indicated the desk.

"Yes!" She seemed surprised. "You have a good eye." She narrowed hers, ever so slightly. Most people might not have perceived her doing it—it was the subtlest of motions—but I saw it.

"Why don't you take a seat?" She gestured toward the artful grouping staged to the left of the room. Everything was upholstered in shades of taupe, white, and gray. The coffee table was glass. The end tables were steel. Even the orchid was white. There was not a spot of color. Not even the requisite decorator's touch of red. Chanel was not too rich for her blood. Too warm for her blood, maybe. She was definitely a cold fish.

I glanced at the bookshelves. All her books were covered in white paper. Someone had written the names of the books in black ink on the spines and it looked like they'd used a ruler. The books all looked the same and the lettering was straight and symmetrical. I wasn't sure which one of us was in need of a psychiatrist.

"That must have been quite a project," I said. "Did you do it yourself?"

"No," she answered as she walked over to the cluster of chairs, offering no further explanation. "Do you have a preference? I usually sit here." She gestured to a chair upholstered in off-white. There was not a stain on it. Clearly, she never slurped take-out Chinese in that chair.

"Any chair works for me," I said, but I was not ready to sit. I couldn't quite process the books. It was like a junior high school girl who covered her textbooks with wrapping paper, but Nina Blanchard's paper was all the same blank white. I tore my eyes away from them and looked at my seating options. What would she do if I sat in her chair? If I hauled a bag of chips out of my bag and settled in to eat them there? She seemed to sense what I was thinking and quickly slid her butt onto the chair in question.

"I was about to pick that one," I deadpanned.

This time her smile was strained. She half-raised herself up and offered to cede the chair to me. I lost interest in this game and went to plop on a different one.

"Shall we begin?" she asked. "May I call you Ellie?"

She seemed anxious to get on a first-name basis.

"Nowadays, most people call me Miss Russell," I answered. "Since I've been starring on a soap opera."

"Is that what you'd like me to call you? It seems rather formal."

"That's what I like about it."

"Mmm hmm…" she said as she made a little note in the steno pad she had carried over from her desk. "Tell me about that."

"I just did."

She looked up from her pad. "What did your parents call you?" she asked.

Now, lady—Nina, Dr. Blanchard, whoever you are or whatever I choose to call you—that's a tricky question.

"They called me by my name," I said. "They also used terms of endearment, like most parents, I imagine. Honey. Sweetie. Darling. Sugar. One of them called me Sugar."

"Which one?"

I got up and crossed to the window. It was one of those disgusting spring days in New York. Rain and damp that got into your bones. It felt colder than winter. At least in winter, you wore the right coat. I had come out today in a trench coat and I wished I'd been wearing a parka. I glanced across at a digital clock that beamed through the raindrops from the top of a building nearby. I didn't like to wear a watch, so I'd memorized the locations of clocks like this one. Two thirteen, it projected in red numbers. That would have been a good red for Nina Blanchard to add to this whitewashed room. "My father called me Sugar sometimes," I finally responded.

"Please do tell me what you'd prefer that I call you. I'd like to respect your wishes and I'd like to start off on the right foot."

I could have continued teasing her and said I'd already told her she could start by calling me Miss Russell. But I was tired. Too tired to continue playing. That was why I was here, after all. It had been two months since I'd left my show and I could hardly get out of bed. My mother wanted me to come back to Michigan. When I refused, she flew here instead. She was sitting out in the vestibule right now, my mother. It was she who had picked Nina Blanchard. It was she who had accompanied me here. And it would be she who would block me from exiting, if I tried to escape from this session.

I gave in. "Ellie is fine."

"Wonderful." She couldn't help but let out a little sigh of victory. "So. Ellie. Please. Sit." That was how she said it. Every word completed with a full stop. "I understand you've had a difficult time of late."

Had I had a difficult time of late? Had my time—of late, as she put it—been any more difficult than other times I'd had? I could not have said with any certainty. "I've been very tired."

"I understand you're not working at the moment, Ellie?" It was incredible how she phrased these things. She opted not to say that my mother had told her this. Instead, she told me that she understood it, like it had come to her through some intuitive ability. Like she had divined it out of the pouring rain.

"No." I gave her as much on that subject as she had given me on the question of the white books.

"Why aren't you working, Ellie?"

"I was fired."

"Why were you fired, Ellie?"

"Well. I guess I wasn't doing a satisfactory job anymore. Isn't that why people normally get fired?"

"People are terminated from their employment for a variety of reasons, Ellie."

"Did you take a Dale Carnegie course?"

Dr. Blanchard blushed beet red. Finally! Some color in the room.

"You keep saying my name," I continued. "Isn't that what they teach you, in *How to Win Friends and Influence People*? What's the most pleasing word in any language?" I looked straight at her.

"The other person's name," she conceded.

145

"Yes. It's a good way to increase your popularity, they say. Although it makes me feel a little manipulated."

Dr. Blanchard looked away. I had made her mad. Mad enough to throw out a bold question: "Did you take Miss Long's wig, Ellie? Did you soak it in water and hide it in the green room freezer?"

What the hell kind of psychiatrist was she? She was going straight for the jugular, just like that?

"Miss Long?" I asked.

"Sylvia Long. You played her sister." Nina Blanchard came at me with both barrels blazing. "The star of the show."

"I know who she is," I said and smiled sweetly. "I'm not crazy. It's just that you're calling her Miss Long when you want to call me Ellie. Not Miss Russell. It seems unequal."

"I'm not sitting in the same room with her and having a conversation. I've never met her. I'm referring to her in the third person and I've used her more formal title. Pretty standard protocol."

"Yes. I understand. And, yes. That's what they tell me I did."

"You don't remember doing it?"

"No. In fact, I don't even know how I could have done it because I was unaware of the fact that she wore a wig. Miss Long, I mean. So, if you follow that line of thought, how would I have known to wet her wig if I didn't know she had one? It doesn't make sense, now does it?"

"No, Ellie, it doesn't." She went back to using my name.

"Dr. Blanchard." I used her name, too, but I was not about to get too cozy. "Is this really what you think is the most important thing for us to talk about today?"

"What do you think is most important, Ellie?" She must have memorized that damned Dale Carnegie course.

"I can't get out of bed! I sleep all the time. I think that is depression, Dr. Blanchard?" I took my voice up at the end of my sentence so that I didn't appear to be telling her what her job was. But, really, I thought I *did* need to educate her on the nature of her job. I was suffering from a serious case of depression and all she wanted to talk about was some wig that got wet and frozen. It wasn't like someone was murdered or anything. Who really cared about some dumb wig?

"I understand that Miss Long was considering assault charges against you, Ellie. I understand that she may have been talked out of it, but I would definitely suggest that the incident of the wig is an item worthy of our examination."

28

THE UNEXAMINED LIFE

I consider Dr. Blanchard's words to me last spring as I force myself to lie in bed today. It is Monday, the fourteenth of December, and night shooting starts in eight hours. I know I will have to work from dusk to dawn and it is my intention to sleep a little extra during the day to get myself ready. I spend a great deal of my time, it seems to me, longing for sleep, preparing to sleep, sleeping, and feeling anxious when I find myself unable to sleep. The already-thin wall between sleeping and waking grows thinner.

The studio is providing me with a driver for these final weeks of the film. I guess they're afraid I might get off work and fall asleep at the wheel, or—given my earlier behavior—maybe they're afraid I'll just keep driving off into the sunrise on Sunset Boulevard. Of course, I don't expect Howard to ferry me to Echo Park at such odd hours, given that he works during the day. For similar reasons, Orlando can't do it. He is leaving soon anyway.

I feel like I am entering a parallel universe, one in which my waking moments will occur while the rest of the world is unconscious.

It reminds me of the cave. Down there, in that complete and total blackness, no other reality continued. There were no people who lived in the light above me, who shopped in markets, or walked in parks, or diapered babies. No households of families, no hospitals of patients, no cheerleading squads, or football teams, or teachers. Nothing. While I was underground—both the time I was with my father, as we descended on the elevator, walked the passages, and stood in the dark hand in hand, and certainly the time after he left me, as I waited alone with the sound of the falls, the tour guide's voice, and the wheeze of bodies breathing—the outside world did not exist. If God had appeared from on high to tell me that this, in fact, was hell, that I, in fact, would be there forever, I would not have been surprised. In actual fact, one could say it was true. I have never fully left that cave. The cave has held on to me from the inside out.

At the end of this week, Orlando will fly to Japan. I feel as though today is the day we are officially parted, however, since our schedules will barely overlap from this point forward. He has already gone to his shop this morning and I will be picked up by my driver before he returns this evening. I am filled with a dull sense of dread. It is not a full-blown panic attack, just that pit-of-the-stomach sensation that something is about to happen.

What will not happen—what neither of us has time to pull off—is a trip to City Hall this week to cement our union in legality. The entire proceeding, it seems, requires a blood test. Which, naturally, requires a doctor's appointment and a wait for lab results. There is just not enough time to do this before he goes, so it will have to wait until he returns and the movie wraps. Next year.

Avoiding a deeper look at the ramifications of this delay, I drift back to Ruby Falls. Did I experience that same visceral awareness the morning before it happened? Had I had a premonition that my life was about to change? I have often examined this question. It is a useless exercise, I know, the most fruitless form of navel-gazing. Dottie says I should listen to my instincts, but any fool can see that my instincts are unreliable, at best.

I'll go see Dottie. There is no point in pretending any sleep will result from forcing myself flat in this bed. I throw on some jeans and a sweater and scoot out the front door. Looking both ways before crossing the street—following the crossing guard rules—I am startled to see Mindy to the left of me.

Shit. I haven't put on any makeup.

Double shit. What is Mindy doing on my block?

She appears to be taking out the garbage, wheeling a large plastic bin to the curb. My mind is immediately torn between the realization that I have forgotten to take out our own garbage, which will certainly irritate my husband, and the screaming, neon light alarm bell asking me what Mindy is doing taking out garbage for the house next door to mine.

"Ellie!" She bares her teeth at me in a sham smile. "Nice to see you. How are you feeling? Orlando says you haven't been well."

I don't even know what to say to that. There is so much jammed into her little speech that I cannot begin to unpack it. My mind homes in on the rudimentary concept of Orlando discussing my well-being—or lack thereof—with the real-estate agent, Mindy. Who is taking out the next-door trash. Who was in our garden not long ago, having coffee with my husband. Who happened to be half-dressed. It is like an elaborately set mouse trap, where one gear links to the next and the next and the next.

And I'm the element of surprise in this scenario?

Which I would appear to be, once again. Why is everyone always so surprised to see *me*? I am the one who lives here! This is my house. That was my coffee cup. And the fact that Orlando is my husband hardly needs to be added. For all I know, Mindy could be taking out *my* garbage!

I dart away from her and into the street. Simultaneously, a car screeches, fishtails to the side, and slams on the horn in a nonstop wail.

"Watch where you're fucking going, lady!" the driver screams at me from his open window. Chivalry is dead as a doornail.

I resume my bolt across the road and open Dottie's gate as quickly as I can, fumbling with shaking hands. I run up the path, dodging cats as I go, and find Dottie weeding a patch of flowers.

"Dottie!" I pant. "Do you know Mindy?"

"Hello, my dear." Dottie presses her gloved hands on both of her thighs as she works to lift herself up from her knees.

"Here." I hold out my hands. "Let me help you."

"Why, thank you," she says as she takes my support and winks at me. "Chivalry lives."

Ignoring this trespass into my thoughts, I stick to my point, "Dottie, do you know who lives next door to us? I just saw a woman taking out the garbage and I think I know her."

"Isn't that natural, given that she's your neighbor?"

"No, I mean I think she's the real estate person who sold us the house. She never said she lived next door."

"Did you ask her?"

"I'm serious. It's really weird. Really. She's very pretty and she was, now that I think of it, extremely familiar with my husband during the house hunting. And then, a couple weeks ago, she turned up in our backyard having coffee with Orlando! That's strange, isn't it?"

"If she lives next door?"

"But that's just it! Why does she live there? Since when does she live there? And, if she lives there, why didn't she say so to both of us? Why would that be some secret information imparted only to Orlando and not to me? Why wouldn't he tell me, while we're at it? So, now I'm asking you, do you know her?"

"Ruby," Dottie says softly. "Come inside. Let's have some lemonade. Remember how it made you feel better that first day we met?"

"Why is everyone so worried about how I feel?" I practically wail. "I feel fine! Let me repeat: do you know her, and does she live there?"

"Simply put: no, I don't know her. And I don't know if she lives there. You seem quite agitated about this Mindy person and about your husband's relationship with her."

"Yes, Dottie! Agitated would be a great word to describe my state of mind right now!"

"Please come inside." She stands with her hands outstretched, in a gesture of embrace. I don't know. Maybe it is the gardening gloves, but her hands look abnormally large and threatening. Can I even trust *her*? What if Dottie is in league with all of them?

My mind ricochets to a line from the movie *Breakfast at Tiffany's*. "I believe he is in league with the butcher!" is the phrase that Holly

Golightly practiced over and over when she was listening to records to learn Portuguese in preparation for her marriage to a dashing Brazilian. Which never happened, by the way!

I have to get out of here!

"Ruby. Please." Dottie interrupts my reverie. Inserts herself into my reverie, is a better way to say it. Once again, she reads my thoughts. "You can trust me," she professes.

"Get out of my head!" I scream and run back down the path. "Get out! Get out! Get out!"

It is too much. They are all closing in on me now.

29

CHRISTABEL

Orlando is gone; he left on Thursday. That would be yesterday. Night shooting continues. We are only five days into it, but I feel myself slipping further away from the land of the living and into the realm of I-know-not-what. A white heat imbues my brain and my sinews feel loose and rubbery.

They send me the same driver—no one says chauffeur anymore—late every afternoon and, miraculously, he appears every morning to whisk me back home. I don't know where he goes in between. I don't see him on the set. Bracy is his name, my knight who leads me through the forest.

Bracy ferried me home at five this morning. When we are nearing a wrap—having received some mysterious summons unknown to me—Bracy arrives to wait outside my trailer, always at a respectful distance. If he stood too close, he might hear signs of life within: a laugh, an argument, the flush of a toilet. That would cross the line into intimate awareness and Bracy seems to understand the concept of boundaries. I suspect he was trained to know how near or far to stand from a lady's dressing room. Maybe he went to chauffeur school. Then, sadly, after all his training, one day he would have been informed that he was no longer a chauffeur, he was just a plain old driver. At some recent moment in time, secretaries became assistants. Chauffeurs became drivers. Perhaps we Americans have our own version of the *Académie Française*, governing the usage of foreign words. Expelling them and replacing them with our own. Le *hot dog* becomes le *chien chaud*. Though I know it is really just a *saucisson*.

I write things down now. I noted on a slip of paper that Orlando left on Thursday, December 17, 1987. I put it in a drawer. I am having trouble holding on to the threads of tiny details such as that. Thursday versus Monday. It is hard to say. If I write it down when it happens, I can go to a drawer and reassemble the puzzle pieces later. It requires that I remember which drawer holds what specific *aide mémoire*, but I can always scrounge around. Take that expression—*aide mémoire*—going back to the idea of language. It is such a lovely phrase. Sure, you could say it in English, but it really is nowhere near as nice.

Tiny slips of paper have always had multiple uses. There is the one at the bottom of my family's old desk, certainly. That would be categorized as important paper number one in my books. The value of it far outweighs the other scraps I leave in drawers around the house—my memory ticklers.

There is another type of paper that has relevance, as well—a piece of paper that was metaphorically, not literally, pressed into my awareness when I was a young actress in New York. I had been there about a year and I was experimenting with the art of the dinner party. I didn't really have any idea how to throw one, other than what I had observed my mother doing. Sticking to her formula, I thought I could not fail.

I had not factored in the presence of Lisette.

Lisette was French. She had come to the States on a ballet tour, as a member of some third-tier *corps de ballet*, and decided to plunk herself down in New York. She was tall and lithe, as you would imagine a ballerina to be, and she was in the process of studying graphic design. Still, she continued to dance. We had met at a dance studio taking a class—one of those sweaty, second-floor spaces up creaky old stairs above Broadway. We became friendly because I spoke some French and Lisette's English, at that point, was nearly nonexistent.

A restaurant manager from one of those broad-sidewalked cafés near Lincoln Center (not Fiorello's, where I had worked, but one of the many others) had fallen under Lisette's spell and she was living with him in a railroad apartment in Hell's Kitchen. She rode a bicycle everywhere, which was terribly glamorous to me. No one rode bicycles in New York in those days, with the exception, perhaps, of messengers.

My apartment was minuscule. I had found an old wine-tasting table from Burgundy that I could tip up flat against the wall day to day. For entertaining, it folded down to hold four easily and six sitting shoulder to shoulder. That night, I opted to invite six. My mother had always stressed the conviviality of a crowded table.

Lisette arrived late and carried a wicker basket of pears. That was just the sort of thing she did. Most people bring you chocolates or flowers or wine. Lisette winnowed the gesture down to a fruit. She removed the flowers I had meticulously laid in the center of my little table and replaced them with the basket of pears. "Better, no?" she asked, in the way that French people pose a rhetorical question.

"Much," I conceded, grudgingly, as I scooped my vase from the floor where she had placed it and carried it into the kitchen. Lisette had captured the room. She laughed and ate and drank and kept everyone in her thrall. There was my boyfriend at the time, an aspiring actor named Grant. Neither one of us had landed an acting job as yet and our sights were trained less on each other and more on our separate aspirations. There was a French professor from my college and his very young wife, who had come to New York for the weekend. And there was my neighbor, Harry Schmidt. Harry was about eighty and we had bonded over cats. In my tiny apartment, I lived with Charlie, my old Siamese from childhood, and Harry had a tabby called Ginger. Each year in May, Harry traveled to the Chelsea Flower Show in London, and I took care of Ginger. When I would go away to visit my mother in Michigan, Harry would return the favor.

I came back from dumping the flowers to find the conversation had not ebbed in my absence. Just as I resettled and was about to take a bite, Lisette raised the timbre of her voice and eerily changed its tone.

A crackle went around the table, as though she had stuck her finger in a socket and we were linked to her in a chain.

"Many years will pass," she began. "You will have forgotten. You will no longer think of him every day."

Of course, even without looking, I knew she was addressing me. I stared at my *coq au vin*, suspended midair on the tines of my fork. From the corner of my eye, I could see that my dinner companions had frozen in position, as well.

"Do you know how you get a little feeling? How do you say *prémonition* in English?"

"Premonition!" the men called out in unison, like contestants on a television game show. Really, I thought, to quote my mother, the wrong one was the actress at *this* table.

"Thank you," she said, pronouncing it as "sank you," and then she went on. "If you get that feeling of him, do not open the door. Every day when you leave your house, place a little piece of paper in the door. At the level of your eyes. If you ever come home and you see that the paper has dropped, if you get that feeling of him, do not go into the house. Do not."

She precipitously stopped talking with a theatrical intake of breath and the room was plunged into silence. No one spoke. No one moved. Lisette was like a gypsy fortune teller who had total command of her audience. I looked at her, gloating across the table. What had gotten into her? I looked around the room and realized that everyone was looking at me, not at Lisette, at all. They knew she was talking *to* me and *about* me. Did they also know who the *him* was in her little vignette?

"Or what," I asked, suddenly reckless. "What if I open the door?"

Lisette looked annoyed. There was a rhythm and poetry to her performance and a delicate restraint to what she had left out of it. It was Hitchcock, her scene, where you only *imagine* the murder, not De Palma, where the gore practically gushes out from the screen. The rest of my guests pursed their lips in disappointment at me and my too on-the-nose Americanness. My old professor shook his head, letting me know I had failed this test.

But if it was my father she was referring to, why wouldn't I enter the house? I wanted to see my father again. If she'd been referring to someone else as the mysterious *him*, I needed her to tell me who it was. Could it be the person who was after my father in the cave? The KGB agent, the CIA agent, the FBI? The Cuban, the Teamster, the enforcer for the Dixie Mafia? Who?

"Who are you talking about, Lisette?" My voice had become pinched and high. "Why don't you just say?"

"I think I have ruined your little party," she said, pronouncing it, of course, as "sink." "*Je m'excuse.*"

Well, I wouldn't excuse her. And the party, thanks to her, was soon over. Everyone found a reason to leave before dessert and made their way to the door.

"Wait!" Lisette called out to them as she ran back for the basket of pears. "Take one, please." Smiling, she distributed the fruit to my friends, like the serpent with a tree full of apples. Grant escorted them down the hall to the elevator. He returned to find me sitting at the table, staring at the hole where my flowers, then the pears, had sat. He was eating his pear, the juice of which dribbled down his chin.

Grant and I broke up soon after.

So, now that Orlando is gone, I am employing Lisette's little paper plan. When I left for the set yesterday, I placed a small tab of paper in the door jamb. When I returned this morning, I found it sticking out, exactly where I had left it. It was comforting to know that my house had rested untouched, except for the night prowls of Bel, while I had been away. I will do this every day going forward.

Such important matters of life and death that rest on slips of paper. It has always been so for me—from that day so long ago—when my father changed the course of my destiny.

I picture the piece of paper taped in the hidden compartment at the bottom of the secretary in the office. I had told Dottie, when I was still speaking with her, that I was sharing the entire story of what had happened with my father in the cave. The story that I had never told my mother and never told Dr. Blanchard.

Was I telling Dottie the truth? Well yes, I was, up to a point. Another sin of omission, I'm afraid. In fact, I *had* told Dottie more of the story than I had ever told anyone else. And yet. There does remain one final bit. A bit that is about as big as a slip of paper.

Let's look at it as a quiz.

True or false?

Is it true that my father left me in the cave? Yes, we can comfortably check the true box.

Is it true that my father had to struggle to release his hand from mine? Yes, go ahead and check the true box once again.

Is it true that this extra fact is something I have only told to Dottie? Yes, add one more check in the true box.

And, is it true that this is the entirety of the story? Hmm. Not so fast. We'd better check the false box here.

Quiz finished. It tallies up to three trues and one false. On balance, anyone can see that my story is much more true than false.

But let's take a look at that false box, the one other thing that happened in the cave that morning. Let's play out the scene once more.

For most of the details, we can move through on fast forward—Ready? Get set. Go! I got up, got dressed, chose my own outfit, picked the red shoes, skipped the purple shirt, got into the car, ate the Pop-Tart, rode around the mountain, arrived at Ruby Falls, entered the lobby, descended the elevator, walked the narrow passages, noticed the stalactites, admired the stalagmites, clung to my father, entered the main room, and—when the lights clicked off—grasped even harder to my father until he wrenched his hand free from mine. There! That is the story as it is known to date and we can resume normal speed.

All of the above did happen and it happened exactly as I have recounted more than once. But then, after my father disentangled our hands, he leaned over and said something to me, softly and close to my ear. As he did so, he placed something into my hand, square on the palm, and used his hands to close my own fist around it. A little piece of paper. "Keep this, Sugar," he said. I am so glad he did not call me Ruby with the last words he uttered. "Hold on to this paper. Don't show your mama, okay? Hide it good. I'll be back, Sugar. Promise. But you may need this someday."

Then he kissed my cheek. I don't know how he knew where my cheek was in the pitch-black dark, but he found it. And before I could reach out to grab him again, he was gone.

The little slip of paper that is taped in the concealed compartment of the secretary was secreted there by me. I had held it in my fist from the moment my father put it there in the belly of that underground beast. Miraculously, I did not let go of it while I slept on the back seat of my aunt Hazel's car. Then, when we got back to her house, I hid it in my little toy wallet. Later, at the end of that excruciating summer, I transported it back to Michigan. And, finally, one day when my mother was not looking, I found the key to the secret compartment that my father had already shown me how to use. It was right where we both had left it, in a normal drawer of the desk. Had he had this scenario in mind? Had he been planning his escape all the while? Brushing that thought away, I taped the paper into the hidden compartment.

The secretary stood on the south wall of our living room as it always had. It went on standing there until my mother shipped it to me this fall. But the key? The key I had kept with me.

My mother never knew about the paper. Did she know about the key and the compartment in the desk? She has never mentioned it. For reasons that I have not yet deciphered, Orlando somehow knows about all of it. He knows the paper is in the secretary—though he has not yet found it—and he also knows its significance. If he were to find it, I fear that he would know how to decipher the code. My biggest fear—the mother of all fears—is that he will also know what to do with it.

I do not intend to let that happen.

30

THE MANCHURIAN CANDIDATE

I am going to kill my husband.

There is no other way out of the closed maze that my situation has become.

When he returns home, as is his way, he will disapprove of what I have been doing in his absence. As day follows night, it will surely play out as I envision it. That part I do not need to orchestrate.

The next part requires careful planning.

At night, I will lead him outside after an argument that I will have intentionally provoked. He will follow me in anger as I move quietly, stealthily, in bare feet through the lightless garden. I will make my way around the back cottage, along narrow paths, to a site where I have left a rake lying—ever so naturally, it would seem—upon the ground. What is strange about a rake being found outside? Nothing, I would assert.

There, the argument will continue. He will—as he often does— frighten me. My foot will alight on the rake. Not hard enough to flip it up and knock myself unconscious. That would turn this into a comedy worthy of Charlie Chaplin, and a comedy is not what this is. I will discover the rake, I will pick the rake up, and—just as quick as you can say Jack Robinson—I will bash in his handsome head.

Harder and harder I will hit him with the tines of the rake facing toward him. It will take all my strength, both physically and psychologically. And let us not forget emotionally. I have married this man, after all, in all innocence and hope. I have joined my life to his—for richer and poorer, in sickness and in health, for better or worse. But things have gotten worse than anyone could have envisaged when they wrote up those little vows. And death must us now part.

I am not talking about Orlando. I would never harm Orlando. I am talking about my husband in the movie and the scene we will play out tonight. I am working in the Method and immersing myself in my character. Or immersing my character in me. What, really, is the difference?

Howard was certainly correct when he said they were taking this film into a darker territory than the original. Everything in *Rebecca* turned out well in the end. The nameless heroine discovered that her rival—her husband's deceased first wife—had never been a threat to her at all. She discovered that her husband, Max de Winter, actually loved her all along. She discovered that the only villain in her story was the dreaded Mrs. Danvers, who conveniently burned up in a fire. Not to be overlooked, of course, was the villainy of her own mind. The heroine's mind had betrayed her into seeing demons where none existed.

My husband in this movie is called Maxim Lange, and I play his wife, Lavinia. Lavinia and Maxim Lange. Fancy-sounding names. No more pretentious, though, than Eleanor and Orlando Montague. In fact, we may have raised the level of affectation a notch or two above that of the movie. My mother had suggested, when I first told her Orlando's name, that it didn't even sound real. And Howard guffawed outright. I'll admit, it does sound like the name of the heartthrob in a bodice-ripping romance.

I miss Howard. Since we've converted to night shoots, I haven't even talked to him, much less seen him every day. I now realize I had come to rely on twice-daily doses of Howard for his humor and moral support. He has left several messages for me. I intend to call him back soon.

I miss Dottie, too. I may have—in fact, I probably *have*—misjudged her. It was just that when I saw Mindy right there on my block and Dottie acted so strangely, like she didn't want to discuss it or that I was somehow to blame, I conflated all of it together. I will reach out to her when this film is over. Invite her to the house. Apologize.

I miss my mother. We haven't talked for more than a week. She leaves me messages, too, but I haven't called her back yet. I know that her worry level is on overdrive. But because I am shooting the movie and because I am now married, she hesitates to jump on a plane and just show up. Besides, we have a plan. She will come for Christmas and that is only a few days away.

I miss Orlando. He left me a message when he first arrived in Japan, but we have not actually spoken. His voice sounded good, though. Loving and warm. Kind. The phrase, "the kindness of strangers," peeks its nose into my consciousness, but I successfully bat it away. There is no similarity between me and Blanche DuBois.

I miss my father. That needs no further elaboration.

Missing would be the word that best describes my state of mind. I am missing those I love. That is how we say it in English, anyway. I miss you. In French, it flips around to *tu me manques*. You are missing to me. You are missing *from* me. It really makes more sense since "to miss" is not a concrete action—it's not really even a feeling. It is a lack of feeling. A feeling of lack, more precisely. To be missing, that is more realistic. Like, for example, my father. He is the one who is missing. Not I. I'm right here in a honeywagon all trussed up in hair and makeup.

And ready to murder my husband.

31

MEMENTO MORI

Bracy drops me off at home at 5:45 this morning. It is still dark, and I realize that we have arrived at the moment of the winter solstice. I suppose this is why the producers scheduled our night shooting for the end of the film. To ensure maximum minutes of darkness.

Frank let me go a little early. They had one more setup to shoot before sunup, but he said he would shoot it around me. In the car ride home, I fell into a deep and dreamless sleep.

"Miss Russell?" I hear his words, but it is extremely difficult to rouse myself when Bracy tries to wake me. He stands on my street, outside my open car door saying my name. I don't know how many times he has to repeat it, but I eventually take notice and open my eyes. He never reaches down to shake my shoulder or touch me in any way. I guess that would not be permitted in the professional chauffeur handbook.

It has been a struggle to turn myself around to sleeping days and waking nights. It is like jetlag without the travel and it leaves me stupid from exhaustion. Day for night—that technique of shooting in full daylight and underexposing the film in the camera to create a creepy approximation of night—is rarely done anymore. *La nuit Américaine,* is what they call it in French. Like Truffaut's film, that homage to the illusions of cinema. Instead, we find ourselves sleepless for the greater good of the picture. But as my director, Frank, would advise, I am using it. My character, Lavinia, is a total basket case so what does it matter if I have dark circles and am stumbling from lack of sleep? It is all in the service of art.

Today, I am confident that sleep will finally come. I am so tired that nothing will get in my way. We are now one week into this and, even over the weekend, I tried to maintain the schedule, so I didn't need to restart the adjustment process all over again. It is Tuesday, the 22nd of December, 1987. I will write it down when I get into the house, just so I stay on top of things.

The one who is enjoying this schedule is Bel. Nothing is more fun to him than the midnight kitty Olympics. Every night, he runs around the house, jumps on all the furniture, and chases his ball with the bell. The very loud bell, I might add. And every morning, he burrows into the covers on my bed, ready for his sunshine snooze. These are his preferred hours and he seems happy that I am finally getting with his program.

"Thank you, Bracy," I manage to say as I get out of the car.

"You are very welcome, Miss Russell," he replies. "Would you like me to accompany you to the door?"

"I'm fine, thanks. See you tomorrow. Oops. I mean tonight."

"Certainly, Miss Russell." He closes my door and walks back around the car to the driver's side. "I'll be here for you at six p.m."

"Oh good. That'll be nice. More than twelve whole hours at home. Thank you, again," I say as I start up the path to my door, fumbling for house keys in my oversized tote.

Between my fatigue and the way that I have stuffed the bag with script, books, sweater, cosmetic bag, and who knows what all, I am having trouble walking and digging in the bag at the same time. I get through the picket fence and up the front steps and realize that I have to dump the whole thing out onto the porch if I am ever going to find the keys. I hear Bel's voice just inside the door and see his little face through the glass, eye to eye with me in my crouching position. He meows loudly to let me know that he is ready for his breakfast and I tap the glass a few times to say hello.

At least I remembered to leave the porch light on so I can see what I am doing now.

Dropping fully to my knees, I tip the bag over, scattering its contents on the porch floor. What a packrat I am. I could go on a two-week vacation with the amount of stuff I have piled into it. I sift through the rubble of personal artifacts and my hand alights on a small slip of white paper.

I freeze.

I stare at it, unable to formulate a coherent thought.

It is possible that this piece of paper was in my bag, tumbling around with the rest of my junk. I could have dropped it in there at some point when I was making those little slips to leave in the door each evening. I tore up quite a few of them—made a little pile of them—and this one could have made its way into my tote.

But, on the other hand...

What if it wasn't? What if it fell out of the door?

I know I need to look up at the door to verify the source of the paper, but my eyes are riveted downward. If I just stay like this, kneeling on the porch surrounded by the contents of my carryall, can I stop this moment from happening? Can I direct this scene and cut it off right here?

Well, it should be abundantly clear to me that I do not have now, nor have I ever had, the power to affect the course of events.

Finally, I look up. Inescapably, I see it. The paper is gone from the door. Missing. The paper is missing to me. The paper is missing from me. It is missing from the door. The fucking paper is not in the door and it is currently in my hand. I do not miss the paper. I have my hand on the paper. It has fallen out of the door and I found it resting on the floor of the porch. And there is only one way for the paper to be missing from the door. Just like Lisette said.

Someone has been in—could still be in—my house!

"Bracy!" I scream as I bolt toward the street. His car is just rounding the far corner and is immediately gone from view. Bracy cannot help me.

I stand in the street hyperventilating and assessing my next move.

Do not go into the house. That is what Lisette said. Do not. She said it just like that. But Bel is in the house. Can I leave him to whatever fate awaits me? Let him suffer my destiny? Surely, whoever is in the house would not hurt a little cat?

Dottie. I can go to Dottie! She can help me. She was always able to help me, and it was horrible of me to run from her that day. Was that only a week ago? Yes, it was just last week. All right, then. It is not so bad that I haven't gone to see her since then. It hasn't been such a long time.

I run across the still-dark street and up the path to Dottie's. Her house is completely black. There is not a light on anywhere. That seems odd to me. I remember that she had left a nightlight on when I stayed late—when was that? A month ago? A year ago? I need to write it down. On a little slip of paper.

Gently, I tap on the door and wait to hear her answer.

Nothing.

I look around the garden. From the sliver of the streetlight's beam that penetrates the dense foliage, I scan for cats. I don't see any. Of course, they must be asleep inside with Dottie.

I knock a little harder and wait once more for a response.

Again, there is no sound.

Where could Dottie be? Is she really such a heavy sleeper?

I picture Dottie in bed with her cats. Then I imagine Bel alone in my house with an intruder. This thought is alarming enough to make me pound on Dottie's door. I hope I don't scare her, but I really need her now.

"Dottie!" I call. "Dottie!" I rap on the door some more.

Still not a peep.

On impulse, I reach down to rattle the handle. It makes a full turn to the left and the door creaks slowly open. I was not anticipating this, and I stand for a moment, jolted, as I consider what to do next.

Should I walk in? I ran away from Dottie in such a dither last week that she might be angry with me. On the other hand, anger does not seem to be in Dottie's repertoire of emotions.

I cross the threshold and pause to listen. I hear the ticking of a clock and, after a few minutes like that, the creak and shift of an old house settling. I guess houses never finish settling until, one day, they fall down.

I take a few more steps into the room. "Dottie?" I call. Where is she? Where are her cats? Surely, a cat would have wandered out to greet me when I waltzed in through the front door.

"Dottie?" I say again, this time a little more forcefully. Dare I walk into her bedroom? I am paralyzed by indecision.

Finally, I just do it. Just put one foot in front of the other and open her bedroom door. "Dottie?" I lean my head in to say it.

Something is not right. The room is too quiet. There is no sound of breathing whatsoever. Not human. Not feline. Could she be gone? Could she be dead? Could the person who has entered my house also have entered Dottie's? Unable to stand another minute of this, I run my hands along the wall, find the light switch and flip it up. The room springs into brilliance. And no one else is in it. Not Dottie and not her cats. Her bed is neatly made. The entire room is tidy. There is no sign of struggle or foul play, but it is empty of all life. I cannot even fathom what is happening here. I leave her house as quickly as I can and catapult top speed down her path.

When I get to the gate, I realize that I should have checked the rest of her house. Dottie could have fallen. She could be lying unconscious somewhere. She could have broken her hip. They say that a broken hip is the worst thing for an older person, a gateway to death's door. I cannot go back, though. I am overcome with fear. I went into the house once, but I can't go in again. In my mind, her house looms like the cave.

Emerging from her gate, I look across the street and see lamplight in the living room of the house next door to mine. The house that Mindy emerged from. Out here, the sky glows subtly to the east, telling me that the sun will soon rise. It must be close to seven.

Right now, I am even willing to ask Mindy to help me. I need to act quickly.

I tiptoe—as though someone might hear me—over toward that house. It is surrounded by an unpainted wooden fence. The fence is tall so that, from the sidewalk, passersby cannot see inside, but from the vantage point of Dottie's across the street, the house was fully visible. I think if I get close enough, if I can just open the gate a little—not so much that someone inside would see me—I might be able to tell if there is anyone awake in there.

I slide my hands along the wooden slats and find the little latch. Pressing it down with my thumb, I push the gate forward just enough that I can peek through a narrow crack. I stand very still and allow my eyes to travel, to search out the illuminated room that I had noticed from across the street. There it is. The curtains are open. A lamp glows from the center of a table, like a lighthouse guiding me to safety.

But can I trust it? I remember the wreckers in *Jamaica Inn*. Another Daphne du Maurier novel. In order to retrieve marine salvage—to claim it as their own, snatch it, and sell it for huge profits—they would go to the rocky beaches of Cornwall late at night. There, they would shine lights toward passing ships to deliberately confuse them and steer them into the reefs. As the ships were sinking, the wreckers would bash the surviving sailors' heads on the rocks. All for their ill-gotten gain.

Maybe this light is just that sort of false lure?

Just then, someone walks into the room from the right. Mindy. She is talking and gesturing, I am guessing, to someone who is out of my view. She is fully dressed though it is not even dawn. She wears tight black pants and a black T-shirt. Tennis shoes. Her hair is pulled back in a ponytail. Maybe she's about to go running.

I lean back to prepare myself to flee. If she comes out the front door, I don't want to appear to be hovering. I can scoot back to the front of my house and call to her from there. "Mindy?" I can say. "I have a little problem. Maybe I can ask for your assistance?"

I mean, I did not know she lived next door and it is very strange that she neglected to tell me that fact. But that is water over the dam or under the bridge or out the fucking window, at this current moment in time. I am having a bit of an anxiety attack and I just need some other human being to help me.

Just as I start to retreat, the person that Mindy is talking to is revealed. He walks into the room, looking as beautiful as he did the last time I saw him. Before he left our house, on his way—he told me—to the airport to fly to Japan. My husband, Orlando. He emerges from what must be the bedroom. He wears the pajamas bottoms that I know so well. Nothing else. He is not in Japan at all.

Like the Sirens to Odysseus, Mindy has bewitched my husband.

Orlando approaches her. I am repulsed but I cannot tear my eyes away. He walks across the room, slowly, seductively. Tenderly, he takes her face in his two hands and kisses her full on the lips. He takes her shirt and tugs at it. He pulls the ponytail holder from her hair. He holds her hand and leads her back from where he just emerged.

The bedroom.

32

ARS MORIENDI

I stumble away, allowing the gate to sputter and slap a few times before settling into its latched position. It is so loud they may hear it. They may decide to walk out the front door to investigate what—who—may have made that noise. I don't care. They. Mindy and Orlando. How did they become a they? My mind turns around an ancient thought of Orlando and me—a he and a she—the two of us becoming a we. And now, he is part of a they. With Mindy.

I am stupefied.

I walk like the dead toward my house. Every detail of its former preciousness, currently suffused in red from the rising sun, is now garish and overdrawn. The roses are too abundant, and their scent is much too sweet. They are dying. A cloying smell arises from their rotting petals. The hollyhocks have grown leggy and are falling over themselves. Their life, too, is over. Putrescence surrounds me and I recognize the stench of death.

Through the gate and up the path I lurch. There, on the porch, is scattered the detritus of an hour ago when I had emptied out my bag. Funny. Then I was feeling afraid. Frightened that someone was in my cottage and meant to do me harm. Now, I am feeling terror. That soul-sick horror of the alone-ness that is closing in on me. Ha! If there were only someone inside my door right now, I might have a companion. As it is, I understand that I have no one. Have never had and never will have anyone.

I scrounge around the debris—random coins, a hairbrush, some dog-eared paperbacks—and find the key to my door. Not bothering to put anything away, I step over all of it to unlock and enter the house. Bel darts between my legs and runs in the direction of Dottie's. I cannot chase him now. I do not have the life force required to find a cat. He will return when he finds that Dottie's house is empty. Just like I did before him.

I relock the door and slide the chain bolt closed, securing myself inside. Whatever fate awaits me inside the walls of this cottage, I am in its possession. It can have me now. I can no longer resist it.

Once inside, I do not know what to do. That's the thing with grief. What do you do with your body? Just like in the cave, when I went all stiff and rigid, I am at a loss for how to arrange my muscles and bones. Do I go lie on the bed? That option seems to offer me more comfort than I deserve. Do I collapse on the living room floor? That option seems overly dramatic and pandering for attention. Should Orlando return home, making some excuse about his trip to Japan being cut short, what if he were to find me in a heap on the floor?

That is just the sort of thing that would make him angry. I—who have had my heart broken, my faith shattered—I, who have every right to throw myself on the fucking floor if I want to—find myself second-guessing my own intentions and looking at my motives through the prism of Orlando's demands.

Demand number one: don't ever—and I repeat *ever*—make him feel that he is to blame for anything. I mean, I could straight up accuse him of kissing the woman next door—even take a photo of him doing it—and I am certain he would turn the tables on me. Make me feel like a dirty voyeur—a Peeping Tom—for seeing what I saw with my own, two eyes.

I have always felt that everything was my fault, ever since my father left me. But how did I end up with a husband who reinforces that belief? Isn't your husband supposed to make you feel better? Contradict your baser feelings about yourself and see the good in you?

While I am at it, how did I end up with a husband who might be plotting against me? A husband who sets traps like he did with that Spode tureen? What if this is a trap right now? What if Orlando is next door with Mindy because they have some plan to get into the desk, take the code, decipher it and go claim what is waiting in store for someone. For me. My father said he would come back to me. But—here's the thing—he hesitated. I know he hesitated. I told the whole story—finally, fully—everything that happened, every word he said. But I did not punctuate it accurately. I omitted the ellipsis that would give a clearer picture of what Sonny said to Ruby in the cave. What my father said to me.

Let me try it again.

"Keep this, Sugar. Hold on to this paper. Don't show your mama, okay? Hide it good. I'll be back, Sugar. Promise." That is what he said. All exactly as before. But here is where it alters. "But…you may need this someday."

The simple addition of the ellipsis—dot, dot, dot—which I had left out of the story before, changes the meaning of that last sentence. An ellipsis, the dictionary will tell you, is a series of dots in a sentence. Generally, it indicates the intentional omission of a word, or a series of words—or a thought, I might like to add. Something that the speaker is concealing from the listener. Sins of omission, again!

So, what was Sonny thinking? Did he hesitate because he feared he would never return to me? He gave me the code, carefully printed in block numbers, because he wanted me to have it. But why?

Well, for starters, he must not have wanted to hold it on his person. If there had been someone pursuing him that day, someone who had followed us into the cave, Sonny would not have wanted that person to get the paper. There are so many things that my father could have been embroiled in. Governmental, criminal, espionage. The list is practically limitless. And I have researched them all. Delicate threads, like spun sugar, link the CIA to the FBI to the KGB to emissaries from Cuba, from Russia, from a weird Southern syndicate called the Dixie Mafia! Any one of those, or all of them together, could have been after my father. How would I know? How would my mother know?

Now, that brings me back to another point. My father did not leave the slip of paper at my aunt's house that morning. He did not hand it to my mother, hide it in a book, or stuff it in the cookie jar. Why not? Why did he have the paper with him and why did he give it to me?

Well, I believe that whatever the code was hiding was something he wished me to know. Something that might help me to solve the mystery of what happened to him should he find himself unable to return to me. He said he would be back. But then that fateful pause. Ellipsis. He feared he would not return. If he had left the paper in the proverbial cookie jar, it may have disappeared forever. Thrown away with the garbage. If he had handed it to my mother, well, I am not quite sure what would have happened. He wanted me to have it. Me.

"I'll be back, Sugar. Promise," he had said. "But…"

And then it hits me. *Today* is that day.

33

THE TELL-TALE HEART

I sprint to the office, leaving the back door of the house gaping wide. If Orlando and Mindy are plotting to take the paper, I need to retrieve it now. I don't know why I have left it in there so long. Orlando, with all his machinations, has been determined to get to it. He may have already done so. Someone was in the house last night—I know from my little paper watchdog in the front door—and it very likely was him. I wonder if he brought his consort with him.

I find the office closed, but not locked. I slip inside, shutting the doors fast behind me, and flip the lock. Normally, I would be hesitant to lock the door, knowing Orlando might accuse me of something—of engaging in secretive behavior or being, generally, up to no good. I no longer care. What can he accuse me of, now? His sins are sins of commission, way beyond my own paltry offerings. What did *I* do, after all? I did not tell him I had changed my name? I did not tell him my father had abandoned me? I did not admit to the secret drawer in the secretary? Ha! Those are all child's play! Having an affair with the next-door neighbor? Now that is big stuff—specifically forbidden in the Ten Commandments. And Orlando has broken more than one of those cardinal rules, to get right to it. Number six: Thou shalt not commit adultery. Number nine:

Thou shalt not covet thy neighbor's wife. Well, Mr. Orlando Montague? You stand on no moral high ground. I charge thee guilty and guilty!

Grabbing the key from the box, back to the secretary I slink, as though an unseen presence might be watching me in here. I drop to my knees and pop it open. Just as I lay my hands on the old and dusty paper, a cat emits a piercing yowl from somewhere just outside. My blood goes icy. Could it be Bel? I stuff both paper and key in the pocket of my jeans as I move quickly to the doors.

Quietly unlatching them, I peek my head outside. I am as still as I can be while I listen for another sound from Bel. The first cry seemed to emanate from behind the office. Our property climbs steeply up the hillside back there. There are steps carved out of stone through the remnants of what I am sure were once pretty gardens. But, frankly, they have become overgrown. The whole area is deeply shaded by a few old eucalyptus trees that are sadly in need of trimming. I like to sit on an old iron bench that pops out of the underbrush and watch their shadows dance around me. Mostly, I like to breathe them in. Their scent is clean and antiseptic.

I step outside and pick up on a sound of scratching. It is very faint and stops intermittently. I might hear another cry of a cat, too, but I can't really be sure. Whatever it is, I think it is coming from somewhere back there. Fearing that Bel has been injured, I steel myself to investigate.

I slip around the building and up the old stairs. Ice plants grow in the crevices and bloom up out of the cracks. Their thick and waxy leaves are crowned by feathery bursts of pink, yellow, and white. Why is everything so fecund here? It's like Disneyland on steroids. I loved it in those early days, when I believed that we were happy. Now, it makes me nauseous. It is as though the earth is growing toward me, sending shoots to twine around me, to close me up and seal me in...well... what? A cave, I guess. All roads lead back to a cave for me. Like a baby duck, I imprinted on that cave. And, like the proverbial duck, I will inevitably seek it out.

There! I hear it. It is most definitely scratching, and underneath it, there is the faint sound of a cat crying. It must be Bel, but where could he be? Why is his voice so muffled? Gingerly, I follow the direction of what I am hearing. I need to go off the path to do it, and deep under the eucalyptus trees. Their smell is sharp is as it hits my lungs. Acrid. Nothing here is clean anymore.

I pause to listen. The sound is coming from the property next door. Mindy's. I carefully make my way through the brush and grab onto the fence to keep from falling. The ground is loose and pebbly here. The sound is louder now. Scratching and meowing. It *is* Bel and he is somewhere beyond this fence.

As I lean in to get a better sense of exactly where he is, the thin slats of the fence collapse under my weight, sending me tumbling downhill into the neighboring yard. When I stop sliding, all I can do is lie still for a moment to take an assessment of where I might be injured. I look at my hands, which are scratched and bleeding; I reach up to touch my forehead and come away with more blood. The knees of my jeans are stained green and black. I shift position a bit to get a feel for my general condition. Other than scratches, I think I'm okay.

I hoist myself up to my elbows and pause again to listen. It seems the noises are coming from farther up the hill. I get up and work to pick my way through the foliage. It is shady and dim but at least the sun has fully risen and I can see. What time would it be? Eight a.m.? Nine? I have no idea. Suddenly, my overarching fatigue—the exhaustion that had been tempered these past few hours by the adrenaline coursing through my body—threatens to undermine me. I am so drained. So wretchedly tired. I have an aching desire to lie down right now in these brambles and let the plants grow over me. But Bel meows again—something is radically wrong, and he is in need of my assistance—and it gives me the strength to move forward.

It is then that my foot lands on something that sounds hollow. The rising ground has shifted under me. I look down. I drop to my knees. I use my hands—bloodied and scraped already—to dig at the earth. I feel something smooth. I keep clawing, pushing the dirt to the sides. And, then I see it. A wooden panel. Against all rhyme or reason, I think I have found a door. My nightmare, my biggest fear, the boogeyman that has hounded and haunted me my entire life has come calling. This is a door into an underground passage. A cave of sorts, maybe even a cave for real.

And I fear my cat is in there.

34

FATAL ATTRACTION

See a scary movie in Times Square and you will find yourself surrounded by a vocally reactive audience. Unrestricted by conventional
inhibitions, your fellow movie-goers will gleefully shout out to the room,
to the actors on celluloid—to anyone who will (or can't, in the case of the
movie actors) listen—their advice on how to behave as the plot unfolds
before them. There is a single piece of counsel that is bellowed most frequently as a character is about to do a stupid thing, and it is simply this:

"Don't open that door!"

As I crouch on the ground behind Mindy's house and consider a
small, wooden door in the hillside, I telescope myself out of my own
body in my mind, and hear those words coming at me from a darkened,
imaginary theatre. *Don't open that door!* Everyone knows it is a bad idea
to open a door that may hold horrors on the other side of it. Everyone
knows it is best to find help, seek safety, retreat in whatever way one can
without proceeding through a door that leads to…what? Where does
this door lead?

Maybe it is a shed. It could also be a shelter—some man-made escape
from the threat of an A-bomb in the 1950s. What if it is a tunnel that leads

to my house? What if Mindy and Orlando have gone to and from my house using a subterranean passage? What if Orlando has not ever spent a full night sleeping by my side but has escaped this way every night to tryst with our neighbor, Mindy?

"Why wouldn't he just use the front door?" asks a smirking Dr. Blanchard. "Or the back door, if he was being covert?"

Well, sure. He could have. That would certainly have been a more conventional choice. Then my mind jumps back to the day Mindy emerged from my kitchen with coffee for the two of them. What if she got there through a tunnel? Racking my brain, I mentally scan my house and try to envision any strange panels that might conceal a secret door.

"Ellie!" interrupts Nina Blanchard. Rudely, I might add. "Don't you think you're getting a little convoluted?"

"That would be my strong suit, Dr. Blanchard," I snap. "I'm a Byzantine thinker. It's the key to my creativity." Our dialogue is halted by a renewed sound of scratching.

"Bel?" I call softly to him, leaning in to press my ear against the wood.

"Meow." It is faint but I hear it. Bel could very well be on the other side of the door.

Once again, I set my hands to work. I brush away more earth and rocks and soon reveal a handle—a small, rusted, metal ring screwed into the wood. A wave of nausea sweeps over me. The act of opening this door is beyond my ability to perform, even for my cat. Even for little Bel. Even if it means that he will suffocate and starve and die a cruel death under the darkness of the earth. Buried alive. I don't want to let that happen to him, but I cannot open this door. I just can't go in there. *Don't open that door!* I want to save Bel, but it would mean going against every instinct in my bones and guts and brains. *And* it would mean defying the wisdom of the theatre crowd. What kind of fool would I be?

"Yooowwwwww," he cries again, in a long and plaintive wail.

The kind of fool I am.

I grab the handle and give it a sharp pull, before I have time to second-guess myself. The door does not budge. I tug at it with more force, and still it does not move. How did Bel get in there? It doesn't seem likely that he entered through this door which I am struggling to open, even with the aid of opposable thumbs. Plus, the full force of my weight, which is many times his.

Bel scratches again—could he really be on the other side of this door?—and utters a pitiful call. I haul myself up from my knees, plant both of my feet on opposite sides of the door, grab the handle with both hands and pull with all my might.

The door resists and then—all at once—bursts open. The sudden force knocks me back onto the ground. A cold, wet smell—the smell of a coffin unearthed—emanates from it and keeps me pinioned to the spot.

"Bel?" I whisper into the gaping maw. He is nowhere to be seen. I shake my head, trying to rattle away my confusion. I felt certain that he was just scratching on the back of the door. Where on earth could he be now? "Bel!" I call out even louder.

Nothing but drifts of clammy damp blow back into my face. Maybe if I sit right here and call out encouraging words, little Bel will find his way to me. It is possible that I scared him when the door crashed open. Could he have retreated farther inside? Could he have escaped unseen?

"Bel?" I call. "Kitty, kitty, kitty?" I hardly need stress that my goal is to get him to come out, rather than me going in after him.

It is strange that Bel has become suddenly silent once the door is open. It is full daylight out here. Surely, he can see that and should be trotting toward me now, meowing all the way.

"Bel?" A beam of sunlight breaks through the foliage and beats strong and steady heat onto my back. The warmth of it on my ragged bones has a soporific effect, reminding me that I still have not slept. My sole intent when I returned home what must have been hours ago was to go straight to bed. Instead, I have spent those hours stumbling around my neighborhood.

I am so tired I cannot even think straight. Maybe if I just lie down for a moment here on the ground. I am practically lying down already. It is not so pebbly here. In fact, the dirt feels warm and dry as it is baked by the same sunbeam that is lulling me to sleep.

Maybe I'll just close my eyes for a few seconds. I won't leave Bel alone. I'll stay right here. Then he will recover his courage and, before I know it, he will be purring in my ear. Just for a second. Just a tiny, little rest. Just…

35

BLUE VELVET

I am cold.

I blink my eyes open and strain to find a clock. I need to see what time it is, in order to reorient myself. The room is very dark, and I can't get a sense of my place in it. Where am I? I shift to raise myself up and my elbow strikes something sharp. A rock.

My stomach drops in a sickening awareness of exactly where I am. Damn. I've slept all day on the ground at Mindy's. Damn. I've missed my call time at work. Damn. My driver is probably long gone. Damn. My cat is nowhere to be seen. Damn. I can't see anything at all. Damn. Damn. Damn!

All of it floods back to me—my arrival home, the paper fallen from the door, the emptiness at Dottie's, discovering Orlando with Mindy, losing Bel and following his voice to this strange place. In one day, the world has tilted on its axis and no longer resembles the universe I once inhabited.

Who am I kidding? That tilt did not happen in a day. Well, it did happen in one day, but not *this* day. It happened on a July day in a cave in Tennessee when I was six-and-a-half years old.

"Get over it, Ellie!" barks Nina Blanchard. "Move on. Just move on with your life."

"Dr. Blanchard, aren't you supposed to have a little compassion?"

"Ellie." She has never gotten over her Dale Carnegie roots and still uses my name in every sentence she utters. "Ellie, you got a rotten break. But you've got to move on." Just then I hear a meow from Bel, very faint under the droning of Dr. Blanchard. "I mean, I've had bad things happen to me, too, when I was a little…"

"Shut the fuck up, Dr. Blanchard! I'm trying to save my cat here, and you won't stop talking!" My subtle suggestion works, and Dr. Blanchard puts a lid on it.

"Bel?" I call.

"Meow," he replies. I can't tell if his voice is coming from the dark hole where the door once was. Maybe it is somewhere beyond it.

"Come on, Bel. Come here. Please?"

"Meow," he says again. For whatever reason, he is not advancing toward me. He must be caught on something. Maybe this is a tool shed, cut into the side of the hill. Maybe Bel's collar is caught on a rake. Or a rope.

There is a faint hint of light that arises behind me. I turn my head and see that the streetlights have clicked on. Faint rays from the nearest one just barely reach to this spot in Mindy's backyard and fizzle and die right here. There is some visibility, but not enough. Not nearly enough for me to look into this cavern and find my cat.

I remember the flashlight in my kitchen, in a drawer near the sink, put there by Orlando in case of emergency. Just what sort of emergency he might have envisioned, I am certain was not this one. I get to my feet and set off to retrieve it.

As I make my way through the tangle, I notice that the lights in Mindy's house have been put on as well. For a moment, I pause to look. That gentle amber glow of light bulbs suffuses her kitchen—the room at the back of the house—but I don't see anyone in there. Her cabinets are just like mine, original to the house and painted glossy white. Her countertops are tiled like mine, as well. Whereas mine are aqua bordered by a band of turquoise, hers are celery green banded by a darker olive. Our houses are twins, I realize, with tasteful variations.

Who built these sister houses? They date to the 1920s, a little later than Dottie's. Was it a pair of siblings who wanted to live close by? Could it have been their father who gave them each a cottage? And now, here we are, Mindy and I, side by side, sharing an architectural footprint and sharing my husband's body. Along with his mind and, it would seem, his heart. The magnitude of it makes me gag and I turn back to my purpose.

I find the back door open, just the way I left it. I dart inside to the drawer and quickly lay my hand on the flashlight. A click of the button tells me it's working. I turn the beam in the direction of the little clock on the stove and see that it is after nine p.m. Well, I've blown another day at work. Nothing to be done about it now. My cat still needs saving and there is no one who can help me do that. It occurs to me that a knife might come in handy right about now. Whatever is hampering Bel, I might have a better chance of freeing him with a knife.

I select a big one.

Thusly armed, I turn to go back. As I do so, I see a flash of motion from the front porch. My cottage is small, and the glass front doors are visible from the kitchen, if you are standing in just the right spot. I drop to the floor without thinking and the knife slips out of my hand. Fumbling, I turn off the flashlight. Instinct has taken over and my mind takes a few seconds to catch up with my body. When it does so, it confirms the rightness of my response. Of course, I don't want to be seen. Whoever is on my front porch portends no good news. It can't be Bracy. He was meant to pick me up at six p.m., well over three hours ago. Dutiful as he is, he would have eventually gone to the set to confess the loss of his charge. I hope they don't fire him. He is a nice enough sort and it is not his fault I've gone missing.

Lying on the floor, I have a partial view of the door. The person is still there, dimly visible and backlit by the streetlight. It is most certainly a man. He jiggles the doorknob. If it is Orlando, why isn't he using his key? Wait, I remember that I fastened the chain on the door when I entered the house this morning. Unless he breaks the glass, he will not be able to get in that way. He rattles the handle again and leans in close to peer in. He lifts both his arms and I can tell, even though his face is not visible, that he is straining to see inside.

I see the knife glinting about three feet away from my hand. It has become more useful to me than ever and I must find a way to reach it. Moving as slowly as I can, I inch my hand across the linoleum. I manage to touch the tip of the hilt and, using my longest finger, tap it to spin it to where I can more easily grasp ahold of it.

I hear the key in the lock. The sound is magnified through the otherwise silent house and every ridge along the length of it connects audibly inside the tumbler. In it slides and around it turns.

Without waiting for him to push the door open and for the door's subsequent thud against the chain barrier, I grab the knife, jump to my feet, and run. As best I can without light, I dash out the back door, around the side of the office, and up the steps in the hill. I don't stop until I round the rear of the building and pause there, pressed against the wall and out of sight to anyone who might have entered the backyard.

I listen with ferocious intensity, straining to hear. The tiny bones inside of my ear—ossicles, I think they are called—practically leap outside of my ear canal to travel in search of sound waves.

Nothing.

Orlando certainly will have discovered by now that the chain is blocking his entry. And he is doubtless making his way around the house.

Stealthily, I resume my path back to Bel. There is not enough ambient light under the canopy of the eucalyptus trees for me to proceed, however. I am going to have to use the flashlight. I click it on as gently as I can—as though the sound of a flashlight button will reveal my position to my pursuer. The light comes on in a brilliant beam—it might as well be searchlights arcing over Grauman's Chinese Theatre announcing the première of a movie.

I slap my hand over the bulb to tone it down. My hand, just like it did when I was a child playing with flashlights at slumber parties, glows orange, its veins a darker hue. If I keep my hand like this, splitting my fingers a little to let out a pinpointed ray, I think I can make my way to Mindy's property without anybody seeing me.

And then I hear it!

I don't even need to make an effort—my ear receives the sound waves, loud and clear. Distinctly, from down the hill on the other side of the office—maybe fifty yards below me—I hear the chinking thud of a flowerpot as it is knocked over. Then I hear the ringing echo as it spins on the ground, around and around in a circle, before it finds its final rest.

He is in the backyard. He is coming after me.

36

THE SHINING

Time is my enemy now. If I hesitate, I am lost. If I move in the wrong direction, my fate is equally sealed. He has not come around the side of the office yet. He has not yet seen me. But it is only a matter of time. He will look for me in the office first, maybe inside the house. But neither search will take long.

Of the four basic directions I could take, three of them are impossible.

At the rear of my property is an increasingly steeper climb up the hillside that ends in a tall cyclone fence and a precipitous drop on the other side. Even if I could scramble up the hill, climb the fence, and roll in some clever way to keep myself from getting injured, Orlando—if he is, indeed, my pursuer—would surely be able to overtake me before I got very far.

Back in the direction of my house, my path is blocked by whoever that pursuer might be. That way, there is only one narrow passage around the side of the office—reversing the way I just came—and subsequently the side of the house, that would take me back to the street. If I made it that far, I could scream for help. But I would have to run right by him, which would mean running straight into his arms. He could pretty much stand still and catch me.

To the right, there is the house on the other side of mine, but whoever lives there has enclosed his backyard with a high stucco wall that is densely overgrown with bougainvillea. It is thorny and thick, and I would slice my skin to ribbons if I attempted to climb it. And, again, my follower would be upon me in no time and could pluck me out of the brambles.

There is nowhere to go but toward Bel. In that direction, the fence has collapsed so I could easily make it over the property line. Once across, I could leave Bel a bit longer where he is trapped, and I could run to the street from Mindy's. As soon as I got help, someone would be able to accompany me back to that cavern and free my little cat.

I more or less know the way and could probably find it without any light. Resolved, I click off the flashlight as I turn to make my way in the dark. It is impossible, however, to proceed in complete silence. My feet keep landing on sticks and stones that skitter down the hill as I pass. With the noise I am making, I can't hear if anyone is following me. If he is, he must be making the same level of racket with his own feet. Like that, he might not be able to hear my movements.

Before I realize that I have arrived at the edge of my land, my foot lands on the spindles of the rotten fence and they snap with a loud crack. I freeze on the spot to listen. As my own noise settles around me, I hear rustling near the office. If my sound locators are working properly, I would gauge that he has just come around that building. That would place him about forty yards away. From here, I could run to the street via Mindy's driveway. That would cause me to pass not very far to the side of him. And he certainly would see me as I dashed by.

Mindy's back porch light has been turned on and I would run straight through the illuminated circle of it, directly past my huntsman. Yes, there remains a stretch of fence separating my property from Mindy's. But, if I fell through it so easily, I am certain he could simply push his way through the part of it that is still standing.

I hear the crack of a twig.

He is closer than he was before. My situation is impossible. I can't get past him. I won't make it to the street. I still have a chance, just the tiniest chance, if I crawl into the hole that holds Bel and pull the door closed behind me. I feel myself breathing faster as my heart races wildly in my chest. This is the thing I have lived in fear of my entire life. My worst nightmare come true. They say you attract what you fear, but how could I have attracted this?

If I run toward the street, I am dead. If I slip into the hole, I am dead in a different way. I don't know if my mind can survive it. Another twig snaps. He is getting closer. I don't have any choice. Could it be that I have never had any choice? Has my entire life been leading me to this point where I willingly enclose myself under the earth? Should I just stay above ground and let him kill me? Is that better than the alternative?

"Ellie?" he calls out. It is Orlando.

Well, who else could it have been? He is coming for me. I have seen the darkness that lives in that man's soul. I have seen him look at me with dead, flat eyes. I have felt him yank my arm and squeeze my wrist, chastise and belittle me. I know he is capable of killing me. I cannot imagine any other reason he would be climbing through the brush in pursuit of me. Did I not see him inside Mindy's house when he was supposed to be in Japan? Was that only this morning?

He is a liar and a fraud of the first order. I wonder if his name is even Orlando. I wonder if any of it is true—the English father and the Chinese mother. The story of the war and the flight from China and the meeting in Calcutta and the marriage and the entire overblown spectacle that he created for my consumption!

I heard him on the phone in the office, all those weeks ago. I know I did. He tried to make me think that I did not, but I did. Otto, he said. Frank, this is Otto. He has to be someone named Otto! I have no idea who Otto is or what he wants from me. But if Otto went to the trouble of carrying out the elaborate fiction he has for so many months, he must want something very badly, indeed.

Giving myself no time for more second thoughts, I turn and run the five steps to the entrance of the hole. As I gingerly place my feet inside, I reach back and grab the wooden door. Crouching as low as I can, I grasp the edge of it and swing it over my head.

It closes on top of me. I am inside now. In the cave. In the dark. Full circle.

37

THE BLACK CAT

For a very long while, I cannot move. I am immobilized in much the same way I was in Ruby Falls so many years before. When I was a child. Another person. When I was Ruby. Before Eleanor. Do I hear the waterfall coming toward me all the way from Tennessee? Or am I closing in on it?

I don't know how much time passes in this way. I forget to listen for footsteps outside. I forget to turn on my flashlight to search for little Bel. I forget everything but the gelatinous presence of the darkness that presses in on me—a living thing with hands that stroke. Like Orlando touching Mindy. Otto touching Mindy. Orlando. Otto. Orlando. Otto.

Otto.

Can it be that simple? Can it simply be that Orlando is an imposter?

Orlando most certainly tricked me. He pretended to be someone he is not. I think back to the conversation I overheard him having on the telephone. The day I came home unexpectedly and stood outside the office. He was talking to someone named Frank. And he—Otto or who-ever it was who was speaking—had an American accent—a Southern accent—I am sure. He was talking to Frank about my desk. So, there is a Frank in on the plot. Otto and Mindy, yes, but also someone named

Frank. The three of them. But there could be more. Is it possible they have ties to whoever my father was fleeing in 1968?

The intricacies begin to form a constellation in the darkness of the space that surrounds me. I am in a planetarium, like a child on a school fieldtrip, and tiny pinpricks of light glow and swirl around me. But—unlike that child and her classmates—the power is now mine. The power to see, yes, but—more accurately—the power to understand. Only I can connect these dots that seem to be randomly strewn. Only I know that they are not haphazard at all.

Orlando arrived in Italy in possession of an engagement ring—one he claimed belonged to his mother. Yes, I found it odd at the time. But I willfully ignored my instincts. He boarded that plane in Zurich. He placed himself next to me. He came with me to my hotel. He used a false name. Could it all have been prearranged? Now I see the preposterousness of the tale of the English father and the Chinese refugee mother and her flight across the Himalayas.

He got on that plane because of me. He carried that ring because of me. He targeted me, he followed me, he married me—well, he went through a sham approximation of a marriage ceremony.

But why?

It can only be that the code my father gave me all those years ago holds information that Otto and his gang desire.

The code. 839938*863392591291115*181. Why did I keep the paper? I have memorized those numbers and I have known for years what they mean. They are not so difficult to decipher. Any fool can do it. How long did it take me?

I didn't figure it out right away. I was only six years old. I hid the paper away, in the secret compartment of the secretary. I hid the key in my toy wallet.

I would visit the paper from time to time, but it was always a little difficult to manage. As a child, I was not often home alone. Sometimes, however, on a rainy afternoon, my mother would take a nap. When she did, she would advise me to do the same. If I resisted, she would suggest that I at least lie down and read. Established that way, she in her room with an eye mask, I in mine with a book, I would wait until I heard her breathing change. It usually took about ten minutes. And then I knew I had about twenty minutes more since half an hour was the normal length of her naps.

In the first few years, I just looked. I stared and stared at those numbers. I willed them to dance off the page—like a sequence from *Fantasia*—and rearrange themselves into a meaningful picture. An understanding of what my father had meant for me to know.

By the time I was ten, I no longer needed the ruse of the nap. All I had to do was wait until my mother was sleeping at night. I trained myself to wake up spontaneously—usually at around three in the morning. It was thrilling to realize I could control my mind so easily—directing it to wake when I chose. In those years, I regarded the numbers differently. I no longer tried to make them leave the page to come to me; I worked on entering into them.

At twelve—the stage of séances and Ouija boards—like most of my peers, I naturally discovered astrology. From there, it was a very short leap to numerology. A leap I made in a day.

By then, my mother left me home alone for short periods. She, too, had been affected by my father's disappearance, so she had a strangulating need to protect me. Though we never spoke about it, I think she subscribed to the theory that my father had been abducted. I suspect she felt she could have prevented it, had she been with him when it happened. Thus, she liked to keep me in her sights. But, as most consuming emotions do, her paranoia wore thin over time. If she had a meeting of her bridge group and it was a day I was home, she grew comfortable leaving me alone.

On just such a day, I took out the piece of paper and—armed with a pencil and steno pad—copied out the code. My father had written a strange series of digits. On first pass, it could have been the combination to a lock. But what lock would have so many numbers? And why were they divided as they were? That explanation would only serve if the numbers represented numbers. If they were, in fact, what they were. But it was abundantly clear to me by then that things were hardly ever what they seemed. Hence, the digits must represent something else. The easiest thing for them to represent—I am sure you are light years ahead of where I was at that age—could only have been letters.

Numerology, as a belief, as a practice, as a way of codifying a world that was unpredictable, has been around for millennia. I did not know this at age twelve, but something in my primitive brain—some kinship with my biological antecedents—must have given me over to understand it.

I wrote out the alphabet and assigned to each letter a number. We all know there are twenty-six letters in the English alphabet. And my father spoke only English, as far as I knew at the time. Singing the alphabet song—the mnemonic device I still use today—I tried to work it out with numbers one through twenty-six.

It made no sense. The sequence of numbers amounted to gobbledygook when translated to letters. Looked at in this way, the code would reveal: HCIICH HFCCIBEIABIAAAE AHA. The only part of this that had any recognizable features to me was the aha. As though, once I figured out the first two words, my father was supplying the dialogue for my eureka moment. Aha!

What if I stuck to single digits? Like that, I would repeat the sequence of one through nine several times over. Each numeral one, for example, could signify several letters—an A, a J, or an S. The number two could mean a B, a K, or a T. And so on. Et cetera, et cetera, et cetera, as the King of Siam so wisely said to Anna.

I had to try again. First, I ran into the kitchen to check the clock on the wall. My mother had been gone two hours by then. She could safely be counted on to stay away for two hours more. Reassigning letters to numbers, I gave it several passes.

I wrote the first set and the possible corresponding letters below it:

839938

HCIICH

QLRRLQ

ZU**UZ

Nine only repeats twice, hence the blank spaces on the third round of possible letters. The number eight could represent an H, a Q, or a Z. The number three, a C, an L, or a U. Stare at it for a while, as I did that day. Allow the letters to dance around, some becoming bold, some receding from sight. Do you see it, Ruby? There it is! There is a word and the word is a place. A place I had never been, at that point in my life, and a place I had a hard time imagining my father visiting. ZURICH, it said. The place was Zurich and my father was sending me there.

Suffice it to say that I sorted it out. All of it represented a geographical location that my father wanted me to know. Presumably, a place that my father wanted me to go. The first set of numbers was the word, Zurich. The second set of digits was a word that was strange to me, a word it took some years and research at libraries to figure out. Zollikerstrasse. It is the name of a street in the city of Zurich. And the final set of numbers turned out to be just numbers. 181. The number of a building on Zollikerstrasse in the pretty town of Zurich. The address of a branch of the Rothschild Bank. A branch that opened in 1968.

The year my father disappeared.

38

HUSH...HUSH, SWEET CHARLOTTE

"Ellie?" I hear a voice on the other side of the door. It is Orlando. Oops. Otto.

I realize I am still crouching next to the door. I have not budged from this spot and I have not yet turned on my flashlight. A new sense of steeliness suffuses me. How is it possible that I have been able to tolerate such complete darkness for as long as I have and not had a total breakdown? Could it be that I am getting over it, as Dr. Blanchard advised me to do?

"Eleanor?" Even through the barrier of the door I know it's his voice, whatever accent he's using. I turn my head in the direction of it. No light seeps in from outside. That could be because it is still night, or it could be because the door is sealed. I think it is time to turn on my flashlight, to see what sort of place I inhabit. I might be in here for a while.

I reach down to the little button that I have been clicking on and off all night. I press it and point it down to my own feet. There they are in their filthy shoes. I am covered in grime. I have been sleeping on the ground, falling down hills, and digging bare-handed in dirt for a good many hours now.

196

My eyes adjust to the dim light and I see that my feet are on a surface of soil. No floor has been laid in here; it is simply pounded earth. I tilt the flashlight up and discover more of the same. The walls are just cut into the hillside. They have not been paneled or covered over in any way. So far, there is nothing else in here. A dirt floor and dirt walls. I need to move deeper inside to determine the purpose of this place.

"Ellie?"

I snap my attention to the door when I hear Mindy's voice. Has he actually brought his paramour with him to look for me? The utter outrageousness of such an act propels me backward away from the door.

Wait. I see an old rusted hook. Feeling my way gingerly, I grab it and latch the door closed. Hook in eye. Hand in glove. Man in wife.

Locked.

"Ellie?" She has the nerve to continue addressing me. I know I am on her land and that could be perceived as trespassing. But if we're talking transgressions here, she is with my husband! I back away from the door while training my flashlight on it.

She rattles the door.

"Ellie?" she practically pleads. If I weren't so afraid, I would laugh out loud. "It's not safe in there. You need to come out."

I retreat a few more paces. All at once, the ground seems to loosen beneath me and bits of it crumble away. In a flash of instinct, I drop to my knees and lurch myself forward. There is a sound of rocks dropping and a delayed plopping sound as they land in what must be water. I have lost control of the flashlight and it is lying on the ground glaring back into my eyes. I don't know where the knife is.

"Ellie?" Mindy goes on. "Listen to me. You're not safe. You need to come out right now. I am going to open this door and I want you to be prepared."

Prepared? That is a pretty tall order. I don't really know what aspect of my current situation I could have prepared myself for.

"Don't come in here," I say, and my voice comes out as a croak. I don't remember the last time I drank any water.

"Ellie, you need to come out of there now!" she states emphatically. "I don't mean to alarm you, but you're in danger in there."

Little does she know that I am in danger everywhere. I reach for the flashlight and scoot myself toward the door. As I do, I feel my leg slide across the knife. I grab it. Rolling over to sit, I hold up the light and point it in the direction of the floor that just slid away behind me.

Of course I am not surprised by what I see. Why would I be surprised? Statistically, what are the odds that my father would have abandoned me in a cave with an underground waterfall? I am not mathematical, but even I know they are infinitesimal. And, statistically, what would be the odds that I would—for the second time in my life—find myself underground with another source of water? Slim to none.

Yet. Yet. Yet. The history of the world is built upon unlikely events. You can't game this life. You can't wager it. Predict it. Draw conclusions for what might happen based on anything that has happened in the past. Why do people lock their doors? Statistically, odds are that you are not going to be robbed or intruded upon at home. Why do people lock their cars? Statistically, odds are that your car will not be stolen. Yet, it somehow makes us feel better. As though we have a degree of dominion over our circumstances. Statistically, I should not be standing in a cave talking to Mindy in the middle of the goddamn night! Statistically, I should be at work, completing my goddamn job! But there it is. My life—maybe everyone's life, I don't know—has defied statistical probabilities for a very, very long time.

"There is a well in there, Ellie!" Mindy shouts. "An old well! We closed it over years ago. You need to get out! The ground is not stable!"

No shit.

39

SCYLLA AND CHARYBDIS

And, so I find myself caught—smack dab in that awkward position between a rock and a very hard place. On the one hand, there is this well. A deep, dark pit of water accessed through an underground space. Sounds familiar. And maybe a little bit tempting, if I were to be honest with myself. On the other hand, there is Orlando—or Otto—and the next-door-neighbor, Mindy. Not so familiar to me and offering no attraction at all.

What is a girl to do? I can't very well stay here. Bel is not in here. A finger of anguish taps at me at the thought that he could have fallen in. That he could have clung to the ledge and held on for as long as he was able. I took too long to get to him. I was too busy falling asleep and running around and all the other various distractions I have entertained in the past however many hours. I have no idea how long it has been since this episode began.

I can't see how Bel got in here. This chamber seems to be exactly what Mindy described, an old well cut down into the side of the hill and boarded over long ago. The little shelf of earth on which I now sit must have been where a person would stand to lower the bucket down. Bel was never in here. There was no other way in but the way I came, and no one had passed that way before me—in recent years, at least. Bel must have been calling to me from somewhere else, and I misidentified his location.

It is my fatigue that is tricking my mind. I am so very tired. There are not words to describe the level of exhaustion that imbues my cells. I had visions of sleeping for days and days once the movie wrapped. Normally, that might have made me feel better. But how can there be any relief now?

When I step out of here, I will have to face the truth about whatever charade my life with Orlando has been. How can we repair our marriage after all this? Does he even want our marriage to be fixed? Is his infidelity with Mindy a passing whim or something he takes more seriously? And do I want to be married to him? He has become unfathomable to me—he probably always was, and I am only just now recognizing that fact—like this well, like the water in the cave of my childhood, a plumbless depth that I don't possess the tools to navigate.

I sit with the flashlight and the kitchen knife and stare at the hole in front of me. It does hold a certain appeal. It would certainly put an end to my troubles, if I allowed myself to slip. Then again, I wonder if I would fall straight to the bottom or bounce along the walls. And if it would be painful. I wonder how much water is at the bottom. Enough to drown in or just some spider-filled puddle in which I'd have to lie until I died, if I survived the impact? Considered that way, I don't think I can do it. There is no guarantee of a quick and merciful end. Why throw myself into a deeper level of suffering?

Perhaps there is actually a way that I could shove open the door with one hand, keep hold of the flashlight and knife with the other, and manage to run past Mindy and whatever my husband's name is. If I did it with force and suddenness, there is a possibility that I would have the advantage. A chance that they would react in slow motion, like Wile E. Coyote when the roadrunner passes him. Then I, like that high-speed bird, could give them the slip and make it—where? Where exactly would I make it? Into the house? Into the office?

The impossible nature of every alternative presses in on me as much as the darkness did earlier. I don't know where to go or what to do. I don't know where Bel is. I don't know where Dottie is. I do know where Orlando is, but that knowledge offers no comfort.

I circle back to the idea that Orlando must have planned this. He saw my claustrophobia in the Catacombs. He read the newspaper clippings about my father. He has learned my weaknesses well. Perhaps he knew them all along. He boarded that plane in Zurich with a feeble story about a hiking trip he'd been on in the Alps. How long had he been following me? If he was looking to get into the bank in Zurich, then why didn't he approach me there? Why wait for the plane ride to Rome?

The spiderweb of facts and figures glitters before my eyes, then merges back into darkness. I can't quite piece it all together. If Orlando knew about my father, if he followed me to Zurich, then why did he hesitate? Why did he fail to approach me there? Well, the answer to that is clear: he may have wanted to observe my movements undetected by me.

Why did he choose the plane ride to make contact?

I don't know but this is not the time to figure it out.

"I have a knife and I'm coming out!" I muster enough voice to shout out to them. "Go away! I have a knife and I know how to use it!"

I am greeted by the sound of silence. Then, a low rumbling. They are talking, discussing what I have just said, making their plans in reaction.

"I mean it! Get out! Go away!" I repeat.

There is a likelihood that they will attempt some trickery. One of them will walk away and the other will conceal him or herself in an attempt to overtake me. There is that chance, but I have to take it.

As silently as possible, I unlatch the rusty hook.

I assume my starting position. Clutching the knife and the flashlight in my right hand to leave at least one hand free, I rear back and kick the door with my full force and hear it hit something with a loud thud.

"Fucking bitch!" Orlando shouts.

The door must have hit *him*. I don't have time to stop and assess the damage I have done. I leap out and run toward the light at Mindy's. I know what I will do now. Once I get to the street, I will continue across and hide at Dottie's. Orlando does not know her. Dottie told me that she doesn't know Mindy. No one knows anybody else but me. The genius of it—the undiluted spark of divine inspiration that has come through to me just now—is so startling I almost trip.

But I do not.

"Are you all right, honey?" Mindy calls him honey! Right in earshot of me! "Do you want me to go after her?"

"Let the bitch go." Really, he should consult a dictionary and come up with some cleverer synonyms for the sentiment he's trying to convey. Well, fuck him, is what I say. No synonym required. I run like the wind, like the devil himself is chasing me.

Which, in a manner of speaking, he is.

40

THE SLEEPING CITY

I flip the latch to Dottie's gate as quietly as I can, thrust myself inside, and close it behind me. I run a short way up the path and veer to the left to hide behind some bushes. From there, I ease myself forward under cover of Dottie's jungle, so that I might observe the street.

I crawl closer to the fence in order to see in both directions. Like this, I can see the world, but the world cannot see me. If only I could remain this way indefinitely. I scan the road for a good long while and determine that it is empty. The streetlight, as it always does, casts its circle straight down. Our cottage sits just where I left it, and Mindy's is in its own spot. The inanimate objects of our block all appear to be in perfect order.

But the animate ones? Those are the ones that concern me. I settle down to watch for Orlando—Otto—and Mindy. For the first time in hours, the clench of panic loosens its hold on my insides. Mindy and he—I don't think I will use his name anymore and just refer to him in pronouns—will never think to look for me here.

Up above, the moon—in its unstoppable, endless motion—reminds me of itself when it peeks between the canopy of trees that protects me. I am suddenly illuminated by a shaft of its silver light. I scoot back into the shadows in order to conceal myself from detection. As dense as the growth is in front of Dottie's, the moon can still find a way to cut through it.

That reminds me of Dottie. Where can she have gone? She had not mentioned travel. And what about her cats? I can't really imagine a place she could go and bring all those cats along with her. I suppose she could have taken them to a kennel. But there are so many of them. And why would she leave without saying anything? Well, that would be my doing. I am the one who ran away from her and have not reached out to her since.

The headlights of a car make their way down the street. They are coming from the end of the block near Cahuenga. Someone is driving home in the middle of the night. Should I run out and ask the driver to help me? Odds are, it might be frightening to have a person covered in blood and dirt run at your car on a darkened street in the Hollywood Hills. The image of me being the scary person in this scenario is comical, but I can see that it might appear that way to a driver unaware of my situation.

The car advances and I see it is a taxi. The yellow light on the hood is dimmed to signal that there is a passenger aboard. I wonder what time it is and where this driver might be taking his charge. Just then, instead of passing, the taxi pulls to the curb in front of my cottage!

After a pause of idling—I imagine the passenger is paying the fare—a middle-aged man emerges from the driver's seat and, leaving his door open, moves around the car to open the trunk. From it, he extracts two medium sized suitcases and sets them on the curb. Next, he goes over to the passenger door curbside and opens it.

"Let me carry your bags to the door," he says to the person who has still not emerged from the vehicle. I don't hear that person's response. My curiosity is extremely high. I wonder who might be arriving and which house this person is visiting. I wonder why the person is arriving so late at night and why there is no one popping out of a front door to greet this midnight guest. As I am imagining and wondering and thinking—my usual activities of choice—the passenger gets out of the car.

It is my *mother*.

And I remember that it is Christmas and I haven't bought a tree.

41

PANDORA'S BOX

"Mom!" I stage whisper as loudly as possible, as I scramble up to my feet.

I see my mother's head swivel around to gauge the source of my voice. The driver looks confused, as well, and he glances up to the sky.

"Over here," I whisper again. I stumble through Dottie's greenery and finally emerge at the gate. By the time I am lifting the latch, both my mother and her taxi driver have located me and are staring in my direction. As if to telegraph their surprise, the driver's hands hang limply at his sides, while my mother clutches tightly to her Birkin bag.

"I...I thought your house was over here?" my mother tentatively gestures to my cottage, staring open-mouthed at my clothing.

I barrel across the street toward them.

"Do you need help?" the driver asks. "'Cause I got another fare to pick up tonight."

"I do need help," I gasp, so relieved that I could hug him. "I'm in grave danger."

"Listen, lady, I don't need no danger. I just drive the cab and carry the bags. Like I said, I got another ride tonight. You want me to carry these bags or not?"

I am trying not to look at my mother's face because I know she is assessing me, and her assessment is not good. I feel her eyes narrowing on me as she works to categorize my mental state.

"Ellie," she says sharply. "What's going on here?"

"Look, I gotta go," the driver interjects. "Bags or no bags?"

"Certainly, I need you to carry my bags," my mother says to him regally and then turns her attention to me. "Which house is yours, Eleanor?"

"Um…" I wave my arm in the direction of Dottie's. "This way." I am not really lying. I don't actually claim that Dottie's house is mine. I just indicate it as our destination.

Like a little parade, the three of us march single-file back across the street. I unlatch the gate and lead the way up the narrow path. I open the front door, flip on some lights and the two of them follow me inside.

"Can I leave these bags here?" he asks. "Or you want me to put 'em in a bedroom?"

That is an excellent question. Where should he put her bags? "Just leave them there for now," I answer.

"Okey dokey," he says as he sets her bags on Dottie's living room floor. "I'll just be going."

I don't try to stop him as he lets himself out the door. I turn to face my mother.

"Ellie?" she says, just that one word. She looks around the room—at Dottie's faded old furniture and the patchwork of quaint afghans strewn about. "Where are we?"

She knows—of course she knows—that this is not my house. That these are not my things. This is my mother, the woman who raised me. These would never be the furnishings of Peggy Russell's daughter.

"Um, this is my friend Dottie's house. She's away and I'm house sitting."

"In the middle of your movie?"

"Mom," I whisper. "I'm in a bit of a tight spot right now. Can you just cut me a little slack?"

"Eleanor, I don't know what is going on here, but you look like hell. I arrived here to find you in the bushes of a property that you say belongs

206

to someone else. Someone for whom you are house sitting. What precisely, may I ask, in this house, needs to be guarded in the absence of its owner? I should think a door lock would suffice."

"It's just...I...Orlando...I..." I don't know where to begin.

"Where is your house?"

"It's across the street."

"Why are we here? And don't give me any malarkey about house sitting. You don't have to sleep in a house to check on it. Can we just go to your house now?"

"No."

"What do you mean, no?"

"It's not safe. Mom, I...I..." I realize there is no way out of this explanation but through it. "I think I made a mistake."

"What kind of mistake?"

"When I married Orlando. We're not even really married."

"What on earth does that mean?"

"It means that we never signed any papers. We were married by an Italian village priest but there is no actual documentation."

"Well, thank heaven for small mercies." The tension in my mother's body loosens visibly—as though the problem has been fully solved. "Can we go to your house now? Put on our pajamas and have a cup of tea? Frankly, I'm exhausted, and you look like the Wreck of the Hesperus."

"Mom, that's just it. He's over there. With someone."

My mother's brow furrows, and she reaches a manicured hand up to massage her temples.

I feel bad. I know that I have been a handful for my mother, and the problem of me does not seem to be getting any easier. "I'm sorry, Mom. I don't know how I got into such a mess."

"Can you give me a full picture of exactly what the mess is? You are not married to this man. He is in your home—a house you bought with funds from your trust—and he has someone in there with him? And you are forced to be here in this..."—she struggles for the word—"...bungalow?"

That is not the word I would have chosen.

"Eleanor, it's the middle of the night. I've been delayed in a snow-storm in Detroit Metro Airport for hours and sat for even more hours on the plane. I tried to call you from the airport and only got your machine. I'm tired. You're tired. Can you come to the point and tell me what's going on? Are you having trouble again?"

Naturally, I start to cry. Standing in the middle of Dottie's living room, face-to-face with my mother, I sob as I pour out the long, sordid tale. Our meeting on a plane, our whirlwind romance, our early happi-ness in Los Angeles and its transformation into what it is now. I tell her almost everything. I don't tell her about my trip to Zurich. I don't tell her about my absences from the set.

My mother stands rigid to listen. She never sets down her purse. Again, I can see the burden I am to this woman. This constant source of worry. She has aged in a way I never thought she would. And it would be fair to say that I have aged her. Her face is more lined than the last time I saw it in April. And her chin is not as defined as it once was. My mother has gone from being a beauty to being a handsome woman. What a way to describe someone. She might as well grow a beard.

"Did you hear me, Eleanor?"

"What?"

"I asked you if that is the entire story."

"Um, yes." I know! I know I should tell her all of it, but I just can't do it right now. The Zurich episode would require so much explanation—revelations of a lifetime of hiding from her. And the work episode would just upset her more. She doesn't need to know that I am messing up again at work.

"How are things going on your film?" As usual, she cuts right to the heart of the matter.

"Fine."

"Really?"

"Yes, Mom. All good."

She looks dubious. I wonder if Howard has called her. "Do you have to work tomorrow? Shouldn't you get to bed?"

"Look, I just need to figure a few things out."

"Ellie, right now, we should call the police and remove those people from your house."

"They're probably not in my house."

"Isn't that what you just told me?"

"His friend lives next door. Mindy. She is the one who sold us the house. He is probably with her."

"Well, then, let's go home. Let's deal with them in the morning."

"Can't we just sleep here?"

"Oh, for God's sake, Eleanor. This is ridiculous."

Just then, there is a knock at the door. Three sharp raps ring out through Dottie's house, like someone has struck a tuning fork and we are stuck inside it. My mother and I both turn to stare at the offending object.

"Police!" a voice cries out. "Open up!"

42

AND THEN THERE
WERE NONE

"Good then," my mother says, as though she has telepathically summoned the cops and they've promptly responded to her thought waves.

I don't know why they are here, but I know it is not in response to Peggy Russell's telegraphed wishes. If anyone else shows up tonight, we might as well sell tickets.

"Open the door!" they shout again.

My mother finally puts down her purse. She squints at Dottie's coffee table—looking for dust, I presume—and acquiesces to place her Hermès bag upon it. Then, she sharply turns on her heel, trills, "Coming, officer," in her most welcoming hostess tone, and walks to Dottie's front door.

"Good evening, officer," she says as she swings back the door on its hinges. "Officers. Excuse me. I didn't realize there were two of you."

"Ma'am," says Officer One. "Miss," he says in my direction.

I have an instinct to show him my beautiful ring—in just the same way as I did in the Catacombs, when the tour guide mistook me for a *signorina*. Then I remember I am not wearing it, having only recently returned from the set. And I also recall that I am, in fact, not even really married.

My mother takes control of the situation. "How might we help you?"

"Well…" Officer Two walks through the door and moves over toward the coffee table.

My mother eyes her purse. It occurs to me that these might be fake cops and that my mother is thinking the same thing. I can see her think it and it relieves me to know that I am not being paranoid.

Officer Two resumes speaking. "We got a call from one of your neighbors to report suspicious activity in this house."

In this house! Suspicious activity here? What about everywhere else in this neighborhood tonight?

"Can I see some ID?" Officer Two looks from one to the other of us. His eyes linger on me. I realize I am covered in dirt and blood and must look like I snuck up here from Hollywood Boulevard to squat in Dottie's house. What I am doing here with a woman who resembles Grace Kelly has evidently got them puzzled.

"Of course," my mother says as she strides over to her purse and whips out her driver's license. Officer One takes it and gives it a once-over. "Thank you, Ma'am. How about you, Miss?"

Obviously, I don't have identification on me. With my jeans and shirt as torn as they currently are, I'm barely wearing clothes. "I, uh, I don't have mine with me."

"Right," says Officer One, letting me know he had already figured that out. "So why don't you tell us what you're doing in this house?"

"She is house sitting for her friend," my mother boldly answers. I wish she had not said it. It is not true and even I—compulsive liar that I seem to be—know that you are not supposed to lie to the police.

"Is that so?" Officer Two pipes in.

"Well, I'm not *exactly* house sitting," I backpedal. "I mean, not precisely. My friend went away and I looked in on her house tonight. I mean, earlier. And then I came back to look in on it again tonight. Later tonight."

"That sounds like house sitting to me," says Officer One.

I cut a glance over at my mother. She does not like where this is going.

"Well, she didn't exactly ask me to do it," I admit.

"I'm not surprised," says Officer Two.

This is when I wish I could disappear. Could sink down into the floor or evaporate. My mother looks at me. The cops look at me. The entire room is looking at me.

"Why is that, officer?" my mother demands.

"I'll tell you why," he retorts. "She's not house sitting for the lady who lives here because the lady who lives here is dead. She's been dead for six months. I think we can all agree that she doesn't live here anymore and she's not in need of a house sitter."

My mother is struck dumb.

Officer One picks up the narrative. "The people across the street saw the lights on tonight, and they called the precinct to ask us to investigate. So, lady," he turns to direct this question to me, "you wanna tell me what you're really doing here?"

I watch as my mother turns her head away. In pain? In disgust? In shame that she brought to life such a daughter?

"Well?" Officer Two repeats even louder into my face. "What are you doing in here?"

"You know what?" Peggy Russell finds her voice and takes charge—mama bear protecting her cub. "My daughter is in need of rest. I think we need to table these questions until we have the benefit of legal counsel. I would like to take my daughter home and put her to bed."

"It doesn't work like that." Officer One has his dander up. "You don't get to tell us when we stop asking questions. We stop asking questions when we don't have any more questions to ask. You got that?"

"I appreciate your need to do your job. Surely, you can appreciate mine. I am her mother and she needs to go to sleep."

"She's not an infant!" Officer Two asserts.

"You'd be surprised," my mother quips. She picks up her purse from the coffee table and slings it over her elbow. "Would you mind?" she asks, nodding in the direction of her suitcases. It is evident that she wants the cops to carry them for her across the street.

"Look…" begins Officer One.

"No, you look, young man." She drops the officer title. "I have tangled with greater men than you. And I am asking for your help. I would like to take my daughter home. Not to my home in Michigan. To her home across the street. A house that she owns, by the way. She is not a house robber. You can see by looking at her that she is unwell. She is a young woman in need of sleep and the care of her mother. Surely, compassion falls into the purview of your duties?"

Officer One and Officer Two look at Peggy. They look over at me. They look back at each other. "Yeah, all right," says Officer One. "This place looks fine. But you listen here," he is speaking directly to me now. "You can't just trespass on people's property. Even if they're dead. That lady across the street is the real estate agent for this house. She happened to see the lights switch on and she became concerned. Consider yourself warned. Next time, there won't be a warning. Got that?"

My mother tightens her grip on her purse and links her other arm in mine. Like this, she marches me to Dottie's door. We have to turn a bit sideways to sidle out the door like a pair of conjoined twins. Not daring to look back, I hear Officer One and Officer Two following along behind us, carrying my mother's bags.

As we walk, I struggle to process what the policemen have said about Dottie Robinson. Dottie cannot have died. And certainly not six months ago. I hadn't even arrived in Los Angeles at that point.

The fact is I know Dottie. I have spent time with her in her home and she has spent time with me in mine. I've gone shopping with her and met her at the library. I've eaten her soup and ridden in her car. I've slept on her sofa with her cats.

The cats.

I turn to face the policemen. "What happened to her cats?" I ask.

"Whose cats?"

"The lady who...Dottie."

"I don't know about any cats. I only know what the woman across the street told me."

There! Mindy is somehow behind this. Dottie is not dead at all. Where she is, I don't know, but I am certain that Mindy does.

43

ROPE

Damningly, we come across my tossed belongings strewn all over the porch as soon as we climb the steps. I don't know why it makes me feel so exposed to see it—guilty, even—like I've been caught doing something illegal.

"What happened here?" Officer One asks my mother. Clearly, I've lost all credibility in his eyes and he doesn't even bother to ask me.

"My daughter dropped her bag," my mother coolly answers as she sinks to her knees to clean up.

I can't very well let her do it alone and I fall in line to help her. The policemen watch us work. In short order—many hands make light work as my mother has so often told me—we complete our task and stand awkwardly.

"You gonna open that door?" Officer Two directs the question to me. It is then I remember that I departed by the back door earlier, having chained the inside of the front.

"I need to go to the back. I don't have my keys." I turn to make my way around the side of the house and am struck with a renewed frisson of anxiety. Orlando could still be lurking. "Um…can someone go with me?"

"Sure," says Officer Two. "I'll walk you around and my partner can wait with your mother."

It seems as good an arrangement as any and off we troop together. Of course, we find the back door wide open.

"Hang on a second." My police escort gallantly attempts to protect me. "Someone may have entered the premises."

"It was me. I left in a hurry."

"You went out by the back door?"

I know I am getting into tricky territory here and anything I say could be held against me. "I was taking out the garbage and I..." I should tell him the truth. I will, of course, tell the truth. But, I'm not quite sure that this is the proper moment. As much as I longed for police intervention earlier, it is now making me feel oppressed.

I flip on the light switch in the kitchen and am stunned to find the contents of the utensil drawer scattered across the linoleum floor.

Had I done that? Now, I am completely confused and gripped, once again, by panic. I know I came in here earlier to retrieve a flashlight and a knife, but I have no memory of spilling the entire drawer. In fact, if I were to be questioned, as I suspect I am about to be soon, I would say that I did not drop all these things on the floor. I remember grabbing the flashlight and one knife—one knife only—when I was interrupted by the person at the front door.

"What went on in here?" The policeman eyes me carefully as he asks.

"I don't really know."

Which is more or less the truth. What I don't say is what I am thinking. It must have been Orlando who did this, when he came in search of me. He must have come into the kitchen and collected a knife for himself. And dropped the drawer in his haste. And—to follow this train of thought to its logical conclusion—he must have followed me up the hillside while carrying that knife. To bring that train into the terminus, I realize that Orlando must still be armed with that blade. My knife, I suddenly recall, I left in the bushes at Dottie's when I ran out to the road to meet my mother. My flashlight is still there, as well. Our two big knives are missing. There is nothing sharper here than a potato peeler.

"You don't know? Like you don't remember?" the officer asks me. "Or you think someone came in your house while you were in the house of the dead lady?"

I detect the sarcasm in his voice and decide the best course of action for me is to remain silent. I stride through the kitchen and living room, flipping on lights as I go. As I am reaching down to turn on a table lamp, I hear Bel's voice behind me. Instantly, I whip my head around and see him emerge from the bedroom and sit to clean his face.

"Bel!" I scream as I run over to pick him up. Remembering myself, I determine not to let this police officer know that I was afraid my cat was dead. With as much detachment as I can muster under the current circumstances, I set Bel down on the floor and continue toward the front door. There, I slide back the chain to release the lock and open the door for my mother and her security detail to enter.

"Well," my mother notes, "you certainly took your time about it."

"Sorry, Mom."

"This'll only take a few minutes to get some information from you." Officer One takes out a notepad. "Names?"

"Margaret Russell and Eleanor Russell," my mother answers for both of us. "The actress," she chooses to add. I don't know what she hopes to gain by it.

We are definitely not in Kansas anymore as that remark does not warrant as much as a raised eyebrow from either of these Hollywood cops.

"Address?"

"My daughter lives here—6330 Primrose Avenue. Los Angeles. I live in Birmingham, Michigan. 835 Oakland Avenue."

"Uh huh," he says as he scribbles.

Officer Two jumps in. "Anything you wanna share about what's going on here tonight? Stuff dropped all over the place. And you seemed pretty excited to see your cat. Almost like you didn't expect to see him."

"Well, with the back door open…" I am proud to be so quick on my feet, "I was afraid he had snuck out of the house."

He narrows his eyes. "Who left the back door open? And why were you across the street?"

"I was looking for my cat." I am feeling cocky now, like I have all the answers.

My mother feels differently. "Look," she begins. "As I said earlier, you can see my daughter is exhausted. She is filming a movie—that's why she looks so disheveled." I am amazed by my mother, once again. "Why don't you give us your cards and we'll be more than happy to stop by the precinct to answer any questions you might have. With our lawyer, as I'm sure you understand."

I can see now what she is worried about. I had forgotten, briefly, in the frenzy of the evening, about the saga of Sylvia Long. What, exactly, if anything, is on my police record in New York? Sylvia was pretty upset about that wig, even though we paid for a new one. She was encouraged to drop her charges. Which, in the end, she did. I think. So does that leave any note on a person's record? I'm not about to ask these two.

Officer One hands my mother a card. "I'll be talking again to your neighbor. I'll let you know if I need to speak with you again."

"Will you at least search the house?" Of course my mother thinks of everything. They could still be hiding somewhere.

"Yes, of course."

The two policemen walk in the direction of the two small bedrooms and the tiny bath between.

I sit on the floor of the living room and Bel climbs onto my lap. I bend my head over and press my face into his fur. He smells clean. Indoorsy. Not like he's been in a cave at all. Oh God. What is happening to me?

"All clear," says Officer Two, as he strides into the living room.

"Thank you," responds my mother.

The policemen leave my house.

"Eleanor…? Let's get you in the bath. Nothing like hot water to calm the nerves. Do you have any Epsom salts?"

I don't have enough energy to utter another syllable.

She bustles around, opening closet doors, running the water of the tub, putting a kettle on to boil. I am safe now. I can sink into the cushion of my mother's presence. I don't need to worry about Orlando or Mindy or Dottie or the movie. I can let it all go, for now.

Finally, I will be able to really rest. Not some pseudo-version of sleep that plays out in netherworlds of darkness, but rest, real and restorative rest.

44

SPELLBOUND

My mother asks no questions. She makes no comment. She knows better than to try to talk to me at this point about what is going on. But when Peggy Russell restrains herself, you can be sure she is deeply worried. Panicked might even be closer to the truth, except that my mother would never reveal an emotion so florid as anxiety.

"Pretty chair," she says, making light conversation, it would seem. But, really, she is working to root me in my surroundings, to keep the ephemeral me from lifting off like the red balloon in that old French movie from childhood. She holds up a pillow—upholstered in the same cabbage-rose chintz as my curtains. "Laura Ashley?"

I nod and bump up against my original vision of creating an English room for my English husband, who may not be English, at all.

"Yes. I thought it would be. You can get something like this at Calico Corners for less." She cleverly adds a mundane note when she sees that I am teetering into a loaded subject. But really, what subject is not fraught for me at this present moment in time. Family? Work? Home? Health? I suppose we could talk about food. But, since I don't actually remember the last meal I ate, that might make me cry, as well.

"I'll make you a grilled cheese. That'll help you sleep." My mother is not psychic—not like Dottie—but her intuitive skills are pretty high when it comes to the state of her daughter. She leaves the bedroom for the kitchen, leaving me alone with my thoughts.

Dottie.

What on earth could Mindy be up to, telling the cops that Dottie is dead—and dead for six months, at that? And that she is the real estate agent for Dottie's property? Dottie did not disclose to me that she was selling her house and she told me flat out that she didn't know Mindy.

Mindy.

The tightly wound skein of her secrets unravels, at the same time revealing nothing. I sense that if I could only clear the cobwebs in my head and find the right angle from which to look, I would be able to grasp the circumstances in which I find myself. But I can't seem to locate that angle. Everywhere I look, I find surprises and I can't tie them all together. From the moment I saw Mindy taking out the garbage—even earlier, from the moment she walked into the backyard with coffee for herself and my husband—it should have been apparent to me that Mindy was at the center of whatever it is that is going on.

Orlando.

Of course, Orlando. He is in up to his eyeballs, as well. I don't even know how to begin to tell my mother everything that has happened between us. I did not tell her I was flying to Zurich last summer—she would not have known what it meant even if I had. Three months into seeing that awful Dr. Blanchard, I just had to get away. Digging up all those old stories—ones I'd thought I'd buried—it finally seemed like the right time to go. I had known for years that the code led to a bank in Zurich. What I would find there—and how I would actually gain access to it once I got there—was unclear.

Why didn't I go earlier? Life, I guess. I figured out the name and address of the bank when I was only an adolescent. But I was still a child at home. A schoolgirl. I did not have the ability to go to Switzerland by myself. Then, time passed. Years went by. On the surface of things, I had put the incident of the cave behind me. My mother didn't know about the paper and I saw no reason to alarm her.

And then there was the whirlwind of the college years. Admittedly, I did study in France in my junior year. And, if I were to be completely honest—from a ski trip to Val-d'Isère with friends—I dropped out early and made my way to Zurich. I located the bank visually. I walked the block, and, from the opposite side of the street, I watched. The building was modern, like one of those university libraries built in the era of Brutalist architecture. It looked like it could survive a bombing.

For whatever reason, at that age and stage of my life, I did not cross the street. I did not enter the bank. Maybe it was fear. Perhaps insecurity. Probably, it was more than that. Maybe I did not wish to discover what secrets my father had left there. Walking into that bank might prove to be the last frontier I'd get to explore with my father. Ever. Did I want to do it just then and have it over and done? Might it leave me with nothing to look forward to? Knowing how to find it, actually seeing it, keeping it ever-present in the Rolodex of my mind—as something on the horizon, some final step I still could take if my father never returned to me—in a way, it kept him alive. It maintained the possibility of him as a living being, retaining a placeholder for him in my heart.

If I went into the bank, I would have to give his name, give my own, show my passport and—what else? Where could it lead? Was there something in there? A safe deposit box? An account? I had no number for either. All I had was the address. He never even named the bank. That was for me to discover in my research.

Unvisited, whatever existed inside the Rothschild Bank in Zurich, Switzerland, could be anything I wanted it to be. It could be gold bullion. A formula for a scientific advancement. A cure for cancer. A treaty, a treasure, a stack of dollar bills. It could be a letter from my father to me, an explanation of what had happened to him, advice for my future, expressions of his love, anything. It could be anything.

It is like the myth of the unreleased movie. Before it comes out, you can ride high on it. Carry it into your auditions, talk about it—never boastfully, always humbly—but share with the world its potential. Once it is released, it is somehow diminished. It is, in the end, only what it is. Beforehand, it was everything it could be. That is how it was with the Rothschild Bank and whatever my father had left in it. It was, until I actually went in that door, everything it could be.

"Upsy-daisy," my mother says in her old-timey way when she returns with a tray full of food. I hearken back to the day when Orlando used that very same expression. It was here in this room. In this bed where I currently sit. It was practically the same situation. I was overwrought. I was being cared for. Then, by my husband. Now, by my mother. Maybe this is eternity for me: bedridden in the care of my minders. There could be worse alternatives. Really, all I would have to do is surrender. Stop fighting the fight and lie down. Drink the tea and eat the food as it is brought to me.

"Come on." My mother has set the tray on the dresser and engages in some fierce pillow fluffing. She manually leans me forward and shoves a few more behind my back.

"Mom, that's uncomfortable."

"Suit yourself. Just sit up and get some food into you. You need to eat. Well," she says as she grabs the tray and sets it on my lap, "at least you're clean now." She had run a bath, found the Epsom salts, and made me soak in it for twenty minutes. Twenty minutes, she says, is what it takes to absorb the magnesium in the salts. She had even helped me to wash my hair.

"Eat," she commands, and I do it. And, finally, finally, finally—the result of the magnesium in the bath or the calcium in the cheese or the presence of my mother—sleep will welcome me. I push the tray away. My mother takes it and assumes her post, on the chintz-covered chair by the window in my bedroom, in the home I share with Orlando.

Sleep comes, but it is fitful. I wake over and over and see my mother bent awkwardly in the chair. When the clock says two a.m., she is leaning her head to the left, with her knees tucked up under her. When the clock says three, she has shifted in the opposite direction. When the clock says four thirty, she has stretched her legs out straight and has crossed her arms atop her stomach. She opens her eyes and looks at me.

"Mom," I say. "There's a bed in the next room. Please, get some sleep. It's almost morning and I'm fine in here by myself."

"Are you sure?" she asks as she stiffly groans herself forward.

"Yes. Really. I'm fine. We'll both sleep better that way."

"Okay. You're right. The sun will come up soon. I guess my back could use a bed after all those hours on the plane." She braces her two hands on her thighs—just like Dottie did the last time I saw her—and pushes herself upright.

"I'll just leave both doors open," she says as she kisses my forehead. Who else but your mother can kiss you on the forehead so tenderly, when you are so completely unworthy of it? "I can be in here in two shakes of a lamb's tail."

"I know." I take hold of her hand and look at her. "Thanks, Mom."

"Ah." She brushes off my gratitude. "What's a mother for?"

And she walks out of the room.

It is almost Christmas. My mother will get a tree. She will decorate it and cook a meal. I fall asleep by keeping my mind tightly focused on the holiday. Like a mantra, like counting sheep, I circle a narrow loop of images and words. Christmas is here. My mother is here. Christmas is here. My mother is here.

And on and on it goes.

45

HOME FOR THE HOLIDAYS

one to grocery store, the note on the kitchen counter reads.
It is dark. The kitchen clock says it is 6:30 and it can only mean
p.m. I must have slept the entire day and half the night before it. Why
didn't Bracy come to get me? Why didn't my mother wake me up?

Coffee has been made, but the pot is icy cold to the touch. What
time my mother rose, what time she went out—none of it is clear. What
is apparent is that she has cleaned up the mess in the kitchen, cut roses
from the garden for a vase, and gone off to fill the larders. She is most
certainly gone. And I am here and not where I should be—at work.

How did she go to the store? Orlando left in a taxi for the airport
to fly to Japan, so our car would be on our street. But, how would she
know which one it was? Well, the keys always sit in a dish on the table
next to the door. I warm up some coffee and walk over to investigate
said table and find that the car key is missing. My mother has always
been resourceful. She would have taken that Volkswagen key and
walked the block to find the car it opened. Finding a store would pose
no challenge for her.

I also notice that my mother has already put up a little Christmas
tree, which means that she'd gone out earlier today, as well. The tree sits

atop a table and sports a fair number of ornaments. Where my mother got it and the decorations, I can only chalk up to her superpowers to wrestle a new city to her bidding.

And this reminds me that it is Thursday, the 24th of December. Christmas Eve. Of course, Bracy wouldn't come to get me because we are not working tonight. We will resume our schedule on Monday, December 28, and that will take us to our wrap date on the 31st. I have four whole days off with my mother.

Smiling, I turn to go back to the kitchen to feed Bel. As soon as I shake the kibble box, I hear his feet hit the bedroom floor. He comes around the corner, stretching and purring. I fill his bowl and decide to go out to the office to check on things. I left in such a hurry last night.

I walk across the lightless patio and over to the glass double doors. They are closed, just as they are supposed to be. I suspect that my mother was out here, as well, fussing and tidying up. Had I remembered to shut the compartment of the desk before I ran off in search of Bel? I can't remember.

I open one door and step inside. I don't wish to close it. I'll just turn on a light. When I do so, I whip my head around, having suddenly had a premonition that someone is waiting in here for me. I scan from wall to wall and back again. There is no one at all, not even a possum.

I stride over to the secretary and face it head-on. It is such a beautiful piece. It stands—as it has for two centuries in one house or another—impassive, impervious to the doings of its human cohabitants. There is no sign of a hidden drawer. Looking at it this way, it is sealed up and intact.

I took the paper last night. I put it—and the key—in the pocket of my jeans. I left them on the bathroom floor when I took a bath and then I went to bed. Damn. What did my mother do with them?

I turn to leave to go back to the house and gasp when I make eye contact with Orlando!

He is standing square in the middle of the doorway, blocking me in the office, holding the butcher knife. Knife number two—the one he took from the drawer after I had taken one of my own—knife number one—the one I left in Dottie's bushes. Orlando is wearing jeans and a white, button-down shirt—my favorite look on him—and striped espadrilles on his feet. His hair is pulled back in a ponytail and his sea green eyes are boring their way straight into my own. His expression is one I cannot read. Fear?

"What's up?" he asks. Once again, I try to pinpoint the accent he uses. Is it English or American South? Too hard to tell with only those two words. "What's up" is an odd turn of phrase for the current situation. He is holding a knife, after all. He is supposed to be in Japan, to boot. Add to that the fact that I have seen him with our neighbor, *in flagrante*, in the wee hours of yesterday morning. And let us not forget that he chased me through the bushes, up a hill, and into a cellar and then I beaned him with that same cellar door as I made my escape. "What's up" is definitely a funny thing to say.

"Not much," I reply, stalling.

"The door was open," he says.

Yes, indeed, it was. "You sound American," I say.

"I'm sorry?"

"American. As in one who is born in the United States."

"Right. Um. Well." He lifts up the knife in front of him. "I found this on the ground." He steps forward to set the knife on the long table—the one that holds all our papers—and then puts his hands in his pockets.

"We should talk," I say.

"Yes. There are things that…" he stops himself and reaches back for the knife. But he does not pick it up. He twirls it around a little, with his finger on the handle. It spins on a pile of papers and its blade flashes as it catches the beam from the lamp nearby.

"Where did you say I dropped that knife?"

"I didn't," he says, cagey as that possum.

"Where did you find it, then?"

"The patio here." As if I needed any more proof, he has just told me a bald-faced lie. Right to my face. I need to get away from him.

"Look, my mother is here. She's just gone to the store."

His eyes dart to the left in the direction of the back door.

Tentatively, I take a small step forward, hoping he will readjust his position a little farther away from the knife. "I think maybe we should table this for now."

"What are you talking about?" he asks.

"There is so much that I think we should maybe—I don't know—make an appointment to talk when we're both prepared."

"I have time now," he says as he advances into the room.

I take a step back.

"What's wrong with now?" he persists.

"Nothing," I say and shift my weight to the side. The knife is behind him now, and I could, if I moved slowly, make my way to it without his notice. I think I can, anyway.

"That was a little out of control last night, wouldn't you say?" Again, he steps toward me. "I mean, *you* were out of control."

Again, I move sideways.

"What are you doing?" he asks.

"I..."

"Jesus. What is wrong with you?"

Suddenly, I seize the moment and spring for the table and the knife. He bolts after me. We reach it at exactly the same moment and I just grab the hilt before he does. This leaves him grabbing onto the blade as I am pulling the knife away from him and the gush of blood is immediate.

"Fuck!" he yells as he retracts his hand. I see the slice, long and diagonal across the fleshy insides of his fingers. Pity will not distract me now and I brandish the knife in his direction.

"What is wrong with *you*?" I shout at him, waving the knife, backing him deeper into the room, closer to the old family secretary. "You! What are you doing to me? What do you want from me? Why are you after me?"

"Look..."

"No, you look!" I am so tired of people talking to me like I am a child. "I am not a child!"

"I didn't think you were." He takes a conciliatory tone as he continues to step back toward the desk, squeezing his bloody hand with his other one. "I just…can't you put that knife down?"

"Why? So, you can grab it? You must really think I'm an idiot."

"I came here to talk to you and picked it up from the ground. I don't really know how we got into this situation but you're acting crazy and I'm not quite sure what's going on here." He holds his bloody fingers.

"*You* don't know what's going on? Welcome to the club!"

Just then, he makes a motion toward me and—I don't know why—I lunge at him with the knife. He feints to the side and I graze his shoulder.

"What the hell?" He grabs onto my wrist as he shouts out and we start to struggle in earnest. I manage to grab onto his hand—the one that is squeezing my wrist and leaving blood all over it—and dig in to pry off his fingers. Like this, we twist and turn. He is a slender man, stronger than I am but not dramatically so. My adrenaline is so high right now that I am a match for him. I give him a kick between the legs.

"Fuck!" he cries as he reels away from me, clutching his stomach and bending in that age-old position of the man-who's-been-kicked-in-the balls.

I turn to run back to the house and find Mindy blocking my way.

Faster than I can even think, I dash behind the old secretary. Mindy charges forward but does not approach me. She goes straight to Orlando, who is making a gagging sort of sound.

My options are limited now. I am behind the tall desk at the back of this room. There is no way out but past the two of them. Orlando is inca- pacitated for the moment, but I know it is only temporary. And Mindy is a tall girl. She could take me down in a moment. I have the knife, but it is not much use to me against the two of them. They will overpower me in an instant.

"Oh my god, are you okay?" she says, clearly to Orlando and not to me. "What did she do to you?"

"She's crazy," he says, also not to me. But I know it is me he is referencing.

"Eleanor!" Mindy says in a stern, schoolmarm kind of tone. "I've had just about enough of this. I'm calling the police. C'mon," she says in a softer tone, obviously to Orlando, who is still on the opposite side of the desk. They are both there, in fact, just on the other side of the secretary. My family heirloom. The piece of furniture that Orlando has been trying to violate for months.

"Do you hear me, Eleanor? Drop that knife and come out here. Or I am calling the police right now."

Well, I can't have that, now can I? Not after Sylvia Long. Not after last night. Not now with Orlando all bloody. Not ever. I simply cannot have that. I am leaning on the fine antique specimen of my illustrious family lineage. This piece that has traveled down through the generations of my family on its westward migration from Connecticut to Michigan and, finally, now, to California. Here, in the Hollywood Hills, rests this artifact of my ancestors. It has meaning for me because of that—yes—but mainly because of the use I have made of it over the course of my life as a resting place for that secret piece of paper that was handed to me one dark day by my father. There is no real value in this desk. It is just a thing. A thing that can be disposed of, much like a little girl in a cave.

That is when I know what I will do. I lean my body against the back of the desk and inhale the smell of its wood. The reverse side of it is dry, not waxed like the wood on the front. The smell is dusty and a little bit musty at the same time. There would have been a time when this secretary encountered damp. There is the slightest tinge of mildew in my nose. I loved this object. I loved my husband. I loved my father. But all of that is in the past.

And that is all it takes.

I push. The secretary is top heavy, its glass covered cabinets rising up to the filigreed swirls of the pediment at its crown. It rocks a bit under the pressure of my hands. I realize I need to use more strength and give the thing a quick, hard shove. And down it crashes onto Orlando.

Mindy just manages to squeak to the side unscathed and she and I face each other panting. I, from my efforts to topple the desk; she from panic. A supine Orlando and the now-shattered secretary lie on the floor between us. A faint cloud of wood dust rises up from the pile. Orlando lies motionless, the bulk of the desk covering all but his head and feet. His eyes are closed, his beautiful face unscathed. If you would ask me, I'd say he was smiling.

I look up at Mindy and it is evident that she is terrified. She looks at me with a mixture of fear and, I guess I would call it, sadness. She is sad about Orlando. Well, I am not. It was clear it was going to be me or him and—even as exhausted as I am—I suppose I still have the will to live. This is a case of self-defense, if ever there was one.

I look down again at Orlando and his exposed feet. His striped espadrilles have remained on. Like this, his stripey feet sticking out from under the rubble, I am put in mind of the Wicked Witch of the West who was felled by the house of Dorothy. Or was it the Wicked Witch of the East?

East?

West?

East?

"Eleanor!"

My name rings out from the door and Mindy and I snap our heads simultaneously in the direction of the intruding sound.

There stands my mother in the company of Howard Silver, who is clutching a pile of Christmas presents.

46

FLORES PARA LOS MUERTOS

"Kitten?" Howard utters in a jagged whisper.

"She's killed him!" Mindy wails and takes a few stumbling steps in the direction of Howard and my mother, her hands outstretched as though she expects Howard to place a gift in them. I don't know why she thinks they are going to help her. They are my people. Orlando is my husband. This is my house. Mindy is the intruder here. In fact, it would be her word against mine.

Nausea overpowers me and I drop to a squat on the floor. I raise my own hands to my forehead and, in so doing, perceive that I am still gripping the knife. I try to drop it, but it is stuck to my palm with the drying fixative of Orlando's blood. This upsets me more than I can say, and I shake my hand violently to dislodge the knife from my flesh. It continues to adhere until it pops off and shoots in an arc to land next to Mindy's feet, clattering on the stone floor.

"Aaaaahhhh!" she screams as she runs for the door.

"Just a minute!" My mother deftly grabs the fleeing Mindy by the shoulders. "What exactly is going on here? Howard, call the police."

"No!" I cry out.

Everyone stares at me.

"Well, if you don't call them, I will," shouts Mindy. "Look at him! He might be dead. He might be gravely injured! She knocked that desk over on top of him!"

"I'll call. I'll use the phone in the kitchen," Howard sighs, and he turns to go to the house.

"Let's check his vital signs," my mother—ever practical—says. She lets go of Mindy and strides across the room to Orlando, Mindy and I staring at her as she goes. Gingerly, she picks up Orlando's arm and checks his pulse and listens. We wait.

"He's alive," she finally tells us, and we both exhale audibly.

"Eleanor, what is happening here?" my mother demands.

"I…uh…" I don't know where to begin.

Howard comes around the corner, minus the stack of gifts. "They'll be here momentarily. Is he…?"

"He's alive," my mother repeats.

"No thanks to her," Mindy says with a gasping breath as she, too, slumps to the floor and leans back against the wall. She starts to cry. A heaving, gulping sob. Tears run down her face, making black mascara rivulets. It makes her look ugly and I am unashamedly glad of it.

"Eleanor?" my mother repeats. I see that she fears the worst. That my own mother thinks this is all somehow my fault. Suddenly, she—like Mindy and I did before her—sinks onto the floor. Howard is the last man standing.

This is the scene that the police come upon. They take about three seconds to study the picture we make—Orlando flat on his back, partly covered by the blanket of broken desk, me crouched to one side of him, my mother on the other, Mindy on the floor near the door, and Howard standing not far from her. It is the same two cops from last night.

Officer One grabs his radio and checks on the arrival of the ambulance.

Officer Two walks over to Orlando and checks his pulse. "He's alive."

Officer Two looks straight at me. "You wanna tell me what happened here?"

"She killed him!" Mindy blurts.

"He's not dead," my mother counters.

"The paramedics are on the way," Officer One says. "Now, until they get here, let's take this real slow and somebody tell me what's going on around here. How about you, Miss Russell? That's your name, right?"

"Uh, yes. Um, I…"

"Did you push this desk onto this man? Who is this man?"

"My husband."

"Who said that?" The policeman spins around.

"I did."

The strange thing is that two of us are speaking at once. I am answering the officer. But Mindy is saying the same thing at the exact same moment. Like a myna bird, she copies my words.

"Wait a second. Whose husband is this guy?" Officer One looks from one to the other of us, as does everyone else in the room.

Just then, the paramedics bump in the door with a stretcher on wheels and order us all to step away from Orlando. "What happened?" the first paramedic asks.

"The desk fell on him," answers Officer One.

The room falls silent as the paramedics work to stabilize Orlando. They pick the pieces of my antique desk off his torso, slip a blood pressure cuff around his arm, press and prod him gently, lift up his eyelids to look at his pupils with a flashlight, slip him onto a board, raise him up to the gurney, attach a fluid drip to his other arm, and wheel him out the door. It takes about, I don't know, ten minutes? In that time, my superhuman adrenaline force deserts me and my fatigue returns with a vengeance.

When Orlando and the paramedics are gone, the cops order us all to walk into the house. They will ask each of us some questions, they announce. Privately, they add. They wish to divide us up and conquer us. As we start to troop into the house, they hold back Mindy.

"You," they say. "Let's start with you."

I know this is a bad sign, but there is no way out of it, now that it has begun. I trudge into my house with my mother and Howard. In the living room, my mother had already turned on the Christmas tree lights—probably when she passed through earlier with Howard—along with several lamps. The room has a warm and cozy glow, but it offers no comfort to any of us.

We neither speak to nor look at each other.

One by one, the policemen call us back to the office. I am the last to go. First, of course, was Mindy. After they're finished with her, they don't let her return home but herd her into my living room to sit with the rest of us there. Then they call in Howard. And then my mother. I don't know how long they spend with each of them. It could be an hour. It could be ten years. Bel sits on my lap on the living room sofa and I stare at the Christmas tree lights.

When my mother returns to the room, Officer Two trailing behind her, I rise to take my turn.

"Please let me go in with my daughter," my mother entreats in a pathetic, small voice. I feel sorrow and remorse that I have brought my proud mother to begging.

Officer Two shakes his head.

"Can Mr. Silver go with her? He's her agent but he's also an attorney," my mother says.

They can't say no to a lawyer.

Back we go, through the kitchen, across the patio and into the office, where the carcass of the secretary lies in splinters. All that we have back here in the way of seating would be a couple of folding chairs. Our budget—Orlando's and mine—had not quite opened up enough yet to enable us to buy upholstered furniture for this room.

"Take a seat," the officer says to the two of us, turning on a tape recorder.

"So. Miss Russell. Let me begin by saying that we are just gathering some information here and nobody is being charged with any crime at this point. Is that clear?"

"Yes."

"But, having said that, you do have the right to an attorney. Anything you say can be held against you. Do you understand all of that?"

I look at Howard. He nods.

My mind briefly travels to an image of Mindy sitting inside my house while I am out here. It unsettles me beyond my already-unsettled condition.

"As I was saying," Officer Two resumes. "You have the right to remain silent. Anything you say can and will be held against you in a court of law. You have the right to an attorney. If you cannot afford an attorney, one will be provided for you. So. May I go on?"

"Yes."

"All right, then. Your mother and your agent—both say you had some trouble last winter and on into the spring. Right about when you received some bad news. Would that be a good assessment, Miss Russell?"

Bad news? Why are we even discussing the news I received last winter? What does it even matter?

"Miss Russell?" he prods.

"Yes."

"Would you mind telling me—in your own words—what news you received last winter?"

"You may answer the question," Howard says.

I telescope in my mind back to the cave. Not to the moment when my father abandoned me but to the period just before that. Before the lights were turned off. When I was just a little girl out for the day with her dad.

If I can conjure up now whatever I was feeling then, I am certain it was not fear. I was not afraid at all. I have wondered over the years if I had had a premonition of what was about to happen, but I can see clearly now that I did not. Right before it happened, I felt peace. I felt serenity. I felt a joyful and easy sense of companionship with my father. I felt safe. I felt protected. I felt loved. I felt full from the strawberry Pop-Tart. It is the last time in this life that I have ever felt any of those things or all of those things in a package. Did I feel safe with Orlando? Did I ever feel loved or protected or at ease? I rack my brain over these past months to try to remember how I felt and when I felt it.

"Miss Russell?" The eyes of the room are on me.

If my mother were here, she would reach out to take my hand in hers. I do feel loved and protected by my mother. It would be unfair to suggest that I do not. But, that father-shaped hole in my insides is a hard one to fill. My mother has tried—and tried mightily—but I don't seem to be able to let her do it.

"Miss Russell?"

"Um. Yes. I received some bad news. It was hard for me to perform my duties at work after that. I had some...problems."

"What was that news, Miss Russell?"

I do not wish to say it. I do not wish to make it true. I have not said it and I don't know if I can.

"Miss Russell?"

"It's okay, Kitten," Howard says as he squeezes my hand.

Howard wants me to say it. My mother wants it, too. I open my mouth and close it again. Howard presses once more on my hand. And I decide to jump. I cannot resist any more.

"My father died. I received news that my father had died." There. I have said it.

Howard squeezes my hand even harder.

"I see," says the cop, unemotional. "I understand that may have been difficult for you."

He could not possibly understand the level of difficulty that bit of news presented for me. Here we sit, in some kind of law-enforcement-group-therapy, but I am the only patient. I am the only one who is being dragged into these lurid admissions in front of the room. They want admissions? Fine. I will admit.

"I had been estranged from my father for years. Since I was little. He left me in a cave. Maybe you read about it?" I look up at both cops. They don't register any recognition at the mention of my ugly past. "Ruby Falls?"

They look blank. Maybe it is just their professional poker faces.

"He left me there." It sounds so ordinary when I say it. Like I lost my mom in the mall. The kind of thing that happens to an average kid on an average day in an average town. "My father."

I stop speaking for long enough that Officer One picks up the cue and throws me a bone. "Well." He shifts his weight as he says it. "That must have been hard for you, too. So." He can't resist reeling this road show back onto its rutted course. "You heard that your father had passed away?"

"Yes," I answer. "I heard that. Actually, I read that. I read it in a letter. It came to me in a letter."

"A letter?"

"Yes. A letter to the set of *The Finger of Fate*. That's a soap opera. I was on it. I get letters there all the time. I mean, got. Fan mail."

"A fan sent you this information?"

"In a manner of speaking."

"Go on," he says.

I look to Howard. He nods. He thinks this is some sort of cure.

"Um. He died. He'd been living in California. Here. All that time. But he…it wasn't until he died that someone found me." I don't know if I am meant to go on. It would seem to be enough of the story to satisfy his question about the bad news I received last winter.

"Who found you?"

Man, this is a lot of questions! This reminds me of Dr. Blanchard. Why? Who? How? When? What? Where?

"There was a woman. A friend of his. He had told her about me."

"And this woman contacted you?"

"Yes."

"Why did she contact you?"

"Um. To let me know."

"Is that all?"

Is that all? Isn't that enough? I don't have to tell them anymore. But it is so easy now that I've started. I can just say it out loud. They all want me to. They all think it would be the perfect form of therapy for me. Would cure me of my ills.

"Miss Russell?"

"To also let me know I had a sister. Have a sister. My father had another child." I look at all of them watching me. Howard, who calls me Kitten. These cops, who call me Miss Russell. And, yes, there is someone out there who, if she knew me, might call me sister.

"Does your sister know about you?"

"No."

"How do you know that?"

"That is what the woman told me. The one who sent the letter. My father had confided in her about me. The woman. Not my sister. He had seen me on the soap opera and recognized me. Because I look like my mother. And…my name. He knew my name. And confided to this friend. She was that kind of friend. You couldn't really keep secrets from her."

"Did you know this woman?"

"I…" How can I explain to them that I know Dottie? That I came to know her when I arrived here. That I came to love her. That she knows things about me in precisely the same way she must have known things about my father. He was her friend and then I became her friend. They will not understand. They will focus on the seemingly—falsely—apparent fact that Dottie died, too, before I arrived in California. They will think I made it up or dreamt it all when I was sleeping.

But for someone like Dottie, death is the most diaphanous of doorways.

"What brought you to California, Miss Russell? Were you looking for your sister?"

And, here we are. I did not want to be here, but here we are, nonetheless. Proof positive, yet again, that I have no control over the course of human events. Or of superhuman events, either.

"Miss Russell? Have you contacted your sister?"

Now, that is a tricky question.

"Miss Russell?"

I look at Howard. "I don't know how you would define 'contact.'"

"Lemme ask you another question, then. Who was the man you hit with the desk?"

That's it. I'm done with them and all these questions. I start to rise but Howard holds on to my arm.

"No," I say to Howard. "Please."

"Kitten…" he begins.

"Howard, I just…" This is all coming at me too fast. Don't people understand that you just can't do things so fast and not expect there to be consequences?

"Ellie, it's okay," he squeezes my arm again. "It is going to be okay. I promise."

So I sit back down. For Howard. I am not sure I believe in his ability to promise anything, but I sit back down for Howard. I look at the cops. And I answer.

"He was my sister's husband."

"Did you claim to your mother that that man was *your* husband? Did you tell Mr. Silver the same thing?"

I can only nod.

Howard has laid both of his hands on my shoulders. They all think I'm crazy, but it isn't that. I am not crazy. I am just tired of never having my own. I did not have my own father. Mindy had him. I did not have a husband. Mindy had him. I did not set out to pretend her husband was mine. I just wanted to find Dottie. And, yes, I wanted to see Mindy. To watch her for a little bit. To determine if she was worthy of my friendship. Of my filial bond. Of sisterhood. To see why my father—our father— chose her and not me.

"And the woman who died across the street? The deceased whose house you were trespassing in? Who was she?"

"She was Dottie Robinson," I say. "The woman who wrote me the letter. My father's friend."

"Did you, in fact, know Mrs. Robinson?"

He will never understand the truth of my deep soul connection with Dottie, so I will give him only the type of facts that he can understand. "No. I did not know her."

"And can we go back to last night? What were you doing in the dead woman's house?"

239

"I…um…I went there sometimes to get away from…to get away. The back door was never locked. I liked to sit there."

"And what is Mrs. Menendez's husband's name? Do you know it?"

"Yes. It is Otto Menendez."

"What was your relationship with Mr. Menendez?"

This is so harsh and unsparing. How can I characterize my relationship with him? If I answer this cop with what he wants to hear, it will sound as if we barely knew each other, Orlando and I.

Otto?

What an inferior name for such a man as Orlando. The moment I saw him, I knew that Orlando was a better name for him. And Menendez? Please. Montague has just the right Shakespearean ring. Anyway, that is what this cop is trying to establish. That I did not have a meaningful relationship with him. Everybody in the room knows this is what he wants me to say.

"Mr. and Mrs. Menendez sold me this house." I finally answer. "Mr. Menendez was a handyman. Sometimes I called him to fix things. Hang pictures. Move furniture. Things like that."

"But you told people he was your husband." He doesn't even ask it as a question anymore, just states it flat-out. No soft edges.

"Sometimes."

"Who did you tell that he was your husband?"

"My mother. Howard. A Screen Actors Guild telephone operator."

"Your mother and Mr. Silver say that you told them you met in Europe over the summer? Married in Italy?"

"Yes."

"But you called him by another name?"

"Yes."

"What is that name, Miss Russell?"

"Orlando Montague."

I realize why he is asking all this when he produces a small box of writing paper.

"Did you have stationery made using that name? Montague?"

I can't say it.

"Did you have this made? Where did this come from?" Officer One hands me the box of cards and envelopes. He must have been snooping out here.

"There's a stationery shop on Hollywood Boulevard," I finally answer. "It's called Eddie's. I went there."

"And did you actually travel to Europe last summer?" Officer One pulls us back.

"Yes."

"What countries did you visit?"

"Switzerland."

"Not Italy?"

"No."

"Was there a purpose to your travels? Your mother seems to think you were looking for something."

"No." I will admit no more. I have given all that I am going to give.

Mindy has my father now and forever. He never even tried to contact me. Not once in all those years. He never told Mindy about me. I didn't warrant that. When I met her the day we went to look at houses—the day she showed up with O, let's just call him O—it was plain that she didn't recognize me. She had never heard my name or seen a photo or had an inkling. Nothing.

She laughed a little and told me her maiden name was the same as mine. Russell. "Small world," she had said. "Maybe we're related?"

"Maybe," I had responded.

Mindy has my husband now and forever. All I ever had was a pulp fiction version of a life I wrote for myself. And she did not deserve him. The life I was writing was infinitely more interesting than the bare-bones existence she offered him in the cottage next door.

And they are asking me to give her more? I don't think so. Mindy will not—I repeat, not—have what I found in Zurich.

"Are you sure about that?"

I have lost my place in this interrogation. "About what?"

"You have nothing more to tell us?"

"Yes. I am sure."

241

"So what happened with that actress on that soap opera? I'm going to talk to New York after the holiday, so you can save us all some trouble and tell me now."

The holiday. I realize it must be early Christmas morning.

My mother brazenly appears at the door. What has taken her so long? "Officers, haven't we gone far enough with this tonight? I need to get my daughter to bed."

The two cops look at my mother with what I recognize as pity. They feel sorry for her for having me as a daughter.

"Sure," Officer One concedes, "put her to bed."

They turn to walk away and then Officer Two turns back. "I don't need to tell you. Don't leave town."

"I understand," says my mother, in a weary, worn-out voice. Sadly, for her, I know that she does understand from painful past experience.

Howard, my mother, and I slump into the house. The cops are walking Mindy out the front door, just as we enter the living room, to drive her to the hospital to check on her husband. She turns her head to me and opens her mouth to speak.

"Mrs. Menendez?" Officer Two warns. "Let's go."

She clamps her mouth shut.

And out they traipse. Out the glass double doors of my house in the Hollywood Hills. The house I live in alone. With my little cat, Bel. The rose-covered English cottage I created for myself and my neighbor's—my sister's—husband.

This reality business is overrated.

47

DONA NOBIS PACEM

I wait until my mother is asleep. Howard is long gone. He left the presents next to the tree in a pitiful stab at normalcy. "Bye, Kitten," he said as he kissed my forehead. He does not think that he will see me anytime soon. I know it. Why would he? The jig—as they say—is up. If anything were to happen to me now, the movie could still be released. Smartly, they left these last days of shooting to scenes where I could be cut out. Maybe they knew.

I rise from my bed. I am wearing old college sweatpants and a T-shirt. I grab a cardigan from the chair and slide my feet into my slippers. Bel stretches out but declines to get up with me. I pad through the quiet house. A night-light burns in the bathroom, plugged into the socket next to the sink. My mother has turned off the Christmas tree lights. She would have been afraid of fire. I am not sure why she would see that as an unattractive alternative right now. After all that was revealed tonight, why not go out in a blaze of glory? That is what Mrs. Danvers chose to do in *Rebecca* and I can understand it. Who knew that I would have more in common with Mrs. Danvers, in the end, than I have with the heroine herself? The world has always seen me as the heroine of the story.

But they were wrong. I am not the heroine. The heroine would always have been Mindy.

I trudge out to the office and back to the secretary desk. It is a shame that I had to destroy it. It really did hold a special place in my heart. Up until I heard that my father had a second family. Another daughter. One he chose to have a relationship with when he chose *not* to have one with me. That knowledge really put a damper on my fantasy life. All my cherished dreams that he would return to me someday, that we would go to Zurich together and open Aladdin's cave to see what he had left in my care for the decades that he was away from me. And then I heard he was dead.

If this had been a movie—or even a daytime soap opera—that would have been an anticlimactic end to the story, especially after there had been so many rich possibilities. And I have researched them all—the KGB and the CIA and that deliciously trashy hillbilly mob that is known as the Dixie Mafia. Any one of those outcomes would have proven to be a ratings-generating plotline.

But no.

Emerson Russell simply walked out on one family for another. And then he simply died—felled by nothing more dramatic than age and emphysema—after a twenty-year absence from my life. It was utterly paltry and pathetic. Small and unimportant like me. The one soap opera–worthy twist to the storyline was the presence of an unknown sibling. The fact that it happened to me—a soap opera actress—lends a wry and mocking irony.

I did fall apart when I got Dottie's letter. And I did make life difficult for Sylvia Long. It is not very hard to understand why. I had some long-lost half-sister who had appeared out of the tar pits of Los Angeles. I was playing Sylvia Long's long-lost half-sister on television. What kind of odds would you wager that I would be able to keep it together under such colossally coincidental circumstances?

Yes, I took her wig. Yes, I wet it. Yes, I froze it. Yes, I remember it all. It was really not such a big deal. And then she got so weird about it, as though she was actually frightened of me. As though she thought I might do her bodily harm.

And so I got fired.

Then the court mandated I enter into psychiatric care.

My mother took me to Dr. Blanchard, and I began sessions three times a week.

Finally, Sylvia dropped the charges.

And then, a few months later, I took off for Zurich.

I did go into the Rothschild Bank. I gave my name. I showed my passport.

A banker lady led me to a box and waited with me to open it. I stared at it for a long while. The banker looked around the vault and made a pretense of giving me my space. I did not know the combination. She could tell that I did not know it, but she was too polite—well trained—to come right out and say it.

Finally, it came to me. It was right where my father had left me. Ruby Falls.

RUBYFALLS.

932761331.

My father had led me all this way in order to bring me back to the cave.

Abracadabra! It worked.

The banker led me to a little cubicle and left me there with my box.

I sat for the longest while, resting my hands on top of it, touching the cold gray metal and trying to divine the secrets it held inside.

In the end, I opened it.

And there it was. What I had been waiting for all my life.

A yellowed piece of paper was rubber-banded around a stack of cash. Good old American money in hundred-dollar bills. It looked like a lot of them, at least by the standards of 1968, the year my father would have placed it there.

I reached down to take off the rubber band and it snapped in two at my touch, all dried up and powdery. Of course it would, after all these years.

I set the money aside and turned my attention to the paper. Always, always, always—in the entire course of my life—the world has changed directions for me based on pieces of paper. Odd little fact of my existence.

Gently, I unfolded it. I lay it flat on the table. I looked up for a moment to the ceiling of this little room and—I don't know—hoped to find some sort of answer there as to why this was happening to me. Why it had been happening for all these years and never seemed to stop happening at all.

The ceiling did not answer me.

So I looked back down at the paper.

Dearest Ruby,

Sugar, if you're reading this, I imagine you are a grown-up by now. And, if you are a grown-up, you know I did not do right by you. I hope your life has gone well. I know your mama—and your grandma, that feisty old bird—will have raised you well. Better than I could have.

The truth is, I had problems and I just couldn't face them. I got myself into some trouble. Took some money from some folks I never should have gotten involved with. You don't need to know who they are. But, here, as you can see, is some of it.

I am leaving you so that you can be free of me. I am not a very good man. I don't think I am a very bad man. Maybe, just an average man. But you'll be the judge of that.

Your mama is too good for me. I left someone—a woman—long ago when I met your mama and I left another little girl. Mindy is her name. I did not do right by them, either. They say they'll take me back and I am going to take that chance.

I have decided to leave you in the cave because I know the world will assume I drowned in the bottomless lake. That should put a quick and easy end to anyone's search for me and wrap this whole mess up in a neat little bow.

But you will know that I didn't. I'm giving you the code to find this box and I know you'll figure it out. You're whip-smart, Ruby. Smarter than I am.

I hope someday you'll understand. I hope someday you can forgive me.

I love you, Sugar. Never forget that. Never.

Always, Your daddy.

It is funny how much people don't understand about unintended consequences. If his letter was to be believed, my father thought that his disappearance would play out seamlessly. One disappeared dad. One bottomless lake. Utterly neat and tidy. Must be a suicide. Wrap that one up and put it to bed. He had no clue about the bedlam that followed. The press coverage, the police inquisitions, my troubles. The never-ending troubles that one dad on one day in one cave would visit on one little girl forever.

If his letter was also to be believed on another front, he never intended to find me again. He said nothing about it here. No words like those he said to me in the cave, "I'll be back, Sugar. Promise." That's what he said. But it is not what he wrote. So, which was to be believed? The words he spoke or the words he wrote?

That was obviously a trick question. I mean, he never came back, did he? The proof, as they say, was in the pudding.

So now I knew he was dead because I'd heard from Dottie. I knew what he wanted to say because I'd read the letter. I had some mad money—the bundle of cash from the box. Here was where we could still hold out the fantasy of Secret Service or underworld ties. He got that money somewhere. He said he was in trouble. But maybe he was just full of shit. Maybe he took it from my mother. Maybe it was his guilt offering, a way to buy me off and keep me away from him forever.

I counted the money. I wanted to know just what kind of value he put on a child. On me. And then I put that money and the letter back into the box. None of it was worth the paper it was printed on.

I gave the box to the teller who sealed it up in the wall. I was just about to leave when I remember to ask her a question.

"How long do I have this? I mean, is it paid for? The box?"

"Let me check, Miss Russell," she said as she turned to go into an office. Consulting a higher-up, I presume.

"Why yes," she said on returning. "The box is paid for fifty years."

Fifty years.

He was never, never, never coming back.

I sat with that. I spent some time in Zurich, mostly lying in bed. A few weeks, maybe a month. I never went to Rome.

But I came to California.

I looked up Mindy. In a crazy stroke of luck—will you grant me that since I haven't had much luck in my sorry life?—the cottage next door to hers was for sale and she happened to be the real estate agent. So I bought it. Mindy had no idea who I was. But Dottie knew. Dottie was dead, you say? Please don't be so literal.

I had not factored in Orlando. His green, green eyes. His black, black hair. He was like a character out of a fairy tale, a prince from a magical kingdom. The Anglo-Chinese offspring of a couple who met by destiny at the foot of the Himalayas. A dealer of Asian antiques. Pretty good, huh? In fact, he was a Filipino handyman who'd grown up outside of Atlanta. Now, what can you do with that? You have to admit that an aristocrat from a faraway land is much more alluring.

And, yes, I called him to the house. I asked him to help me with projects that needed to be done. Plumbing and carpentry and the like. It was he who added the glass doors to the office for me. He was tweaking a few final things out there the day I came home from the set to retrieve the costume I'd left behind. Mindy even brought him some coffee, which upset me for the rest of the day.

And, yes, we really did have something of a relationship. Maybe we flirted a bit. Maybe he kissed me once or twice. I mean, considered that way, you can't really say he was a very good husband to Mindy. To my sister in the house next door. He can't have cared that much about her if he was in my house as often as he was, now can you? And you can't really say I didn't know him. You can't.

Did he know that I called him Orlando?

Technically?

I would have to say no.

Once I started filming—you don't know what is real or fake right now, but the movie was real, I assure you—my head got cloudier and cloudier. Dottie was a bright spot.

But Dottie, you will remind me, wasn't real.

And then Orlando became a little upsetting. He said we had to cool it. He said he couldn't help me anymore. He made it all seem so common and tawdry. Like what we'd had was a simple affair. Like he was just plain old Otto and I was just some tart of an actress next door.

But Orlando, you will insist, was not real either.

Real or false, I lived those months in California, on Primrose Avenue in the Hollywood Hills, in a rose-covered cottage with a husband and a cat and a friend. I lived it. You choose whatever reality you wish to choose, and I'll choose mine. What kind of life would this be if things happened to little girls that they had no power to control?

Well?

I leave the office and travel around the exterior of my little cottage. I don't want to disturb my mother or Bel. I circle the other side of the house, on the far side from Mindy's. I don't wish to see her, either. I walk into the road and turn to the east. For a few minutes while I am walking, there is a band of indigo in the sky and another of purple that form a crescent that hugs the hills. The jagged line of trees and houses rises up—a palm tree here, a eucalyptus there, the turret of a Spanish castle, the steep slope of a Norman roof. The fantasy landscape of Hollywood. Then, the sun is rising and streaking the horizon pink. Just like it did that first morning on the terrace of the Chateau Marmont Hotel. Not real, you say? Who are you to say that, I counter.

I move toward the sunrise.

Just as I crest the hill, the full orb of the sun bursts into the sky— fierce and orange—frightening like a Hindu deity. Kali, I think. The one with the tongue and the blood-dripping heads.

It is so dazzling it blinds me to anything else.

I hear the brakes of the car first, and then the tires as they squeal behind me. Do I smell the burning rubber?

In a nanosecond, I realize that the driver of the vehicle must be sun-blinded too.

I do not feel the impact.

"Ruby?" my father says, as he rises out of the sun. Out of Kali. Out of the future I've been seeking for so long. He reaches his hand out and smiles. "C'mon, Sugar."

I take it. I take his hand back in mine. And it feels just the same as it did all those years ago.

Surprisingly soft for a man.

ACKNOWLEDGMENTS

Writing is both a solitary and a social life. That paradox—like all para-doxes—is what makes it so rich and interesting. My profound thanks go, in random order because there is no way to rank the contributions of these friends, family members, and colleagues, to:

My parents, Kathy and Earl, for taking me to Ruby Falls as a child and (without knowing it) scaring the bejesus out of me and planting the tiny seed that lay dormant for decades until it grew into this book.

My incredible publishing team: Anthony Ziccardi, publisher *par excellence* (happily for two books now at Post Hill Press!); Beth Davey, my terrific new agent; Emi Battaglia and Devon Brown, my amazing public relations team; Susie Stangland, my social media and marketing guru; Ellis Levine, lawyer/miracle worker in getting things done; Robert Epstein for securing rights; Maddie Sturgeon, wonderful managing editor; Allison Griffith and Holly Pisarchuk, business Sherpas; Heather Steadham, copy editor extraordinaire; and Linda Marrow, my visionary editor who "got" every part of Ruby and gave me a clearer path to bring-ing her to life.

A rooftop shout-out goes to the cover design team of photogra-pher Melanie Willhide, graphic designer Cassandra Tai-Marcellini, and artist Becky Ford, for yoking it all together. You gave Ruby the cover she deserves, as beautiful and evocative as the one you gave to Mrs. Ford.

Deep thanks go to early readers, advisers, and editors: Scott Swift, Hilary Hatfield, Molly Pisani, Barbara Ellis, Jan Kardys, Mitch Giannun-zio, Ken Tigar, Cyndy Anderson, Susie Baker, Linda Munger, Mary Ann

Henry, Patricia Lovejoy, Iliana Moore, Cee Greene, Cody Kittle, and Adrianne Singer. Your insightful reads and candid comments led Ruby along her Hollywood walk.

Untold thanks go to the following folks who help me every day in every way, as readers/editors/assistants/accountants/lawyers/you-name-it: Leigh Rappaport Michaelessi, Nimfa Timber, Tim Lewis, Adrianne Boynton, Joanne Gaug, Chris Laterza, Nancy Riscica, Djuana Dolan, and Nicholas Moore.

Much gratitude goes to my writing group for your brains, your humor, and all that popcorn!: Melissa Devaney, Becky Ford, Icy Frantz, Claire Tisne Haft, and Katherine Pushkar.

To Kit Kittle for photographing me to look better than my best, to Laurette Kittle for color vision, to Sam Huss for website agility, and to the team at QuickFrame for your gorgeous videos.

And to my family—my husband, Chuck Royce (with extra winks for letting me keep my writing room!), my daughters, Alexandra Kittle and Tess Porter, and my mother, Kathy Goodrich—all of whose insights are always smart and always welcome. The rest of my family—stepkids, kids-in-law, grandkids, cousins—are all equally loved and appreciated, but I refrained from bothering you with endless drafts of Ruby!

To Daphne du Maurier and Alfred Hitchcock, whose book and later film of *Rebecca* were the water and food to that seed planted in Ruby Falls cave.

To a growing group of fellow authors whose camaraderie and support have been thrilling and sustaining: Sandra Brown, Beatriz Williams, Jeanne McWilliams Blasberg, Patricia Chadwick, Maureen Joyce Connolly, Daniela Petrova, Kris Frieswick, Vanessa Lillie, Lee Woodruff, Kimberly Belle, Emily Liebert, Wendy Walker, Elka Ray, Sara Faring, and Elin Hilderbrand (your words of encouragement meant the WORLD to me!).

To all the sainted souls who run the independent bookstores (Classic Bookshop in Palm Beach, the Savoy in Westerly, Bank Square Books in Mystic, Diane's and Dogwood in Greenwich, Elm Street in New Canaan, Mitchell's on Nantucket, Skylight in Los Angeles, Pages in Detroit, RJ

Julia in Madison, to name a few, but ALL of you!). You have had a rough year, yet you have done everything possible to help all of us writers. Thank you!

To Meryl Poster and Kara Feifer, for helping me keep a toe in that water, and to Fred Walton and Jeff Lieberman, for making me want to dive in again.

To my dogs, Georgina and Paige, who write with me every day, to Tess's cat, Sergeant Pepper, who was the inspiration for Bel, and to Alexandra's dog, Puck, who impishly visits us to cast his spell.

Finally, I arrived in Hollywood many years ago after a whirlwind stint on *All My Children* in New York. Many thanks to Susan Lucci for graciously allowing me to be your "soap sister" for a while, and for laughing when you read the fictious Sylvia Long, who bears no resemblance to you.

And just to say thank you to those of you who were with me then in the magical world of movies and who are with us no more (at least in body):

Ana Martinez, college pal and one-time roommate in a tiny apartment on the edge of Beverly Hills overlooking Olympic Boulevard, where the roar of traffic made people think we were calling from a pay phone along the freeway.

Lisa Rigg Knight, fellow Hollywood Hills mama of our little ones. I met you when you ran down Primrose Avenue—looking like the Hawaiian goddess you were—to meet me because we both had babies. And then we had more. And, for a time, we raised them together.

Howard Goldberg, agent, welcomer to Hollywood, advisor, guide, friend.

Grant Forsberg, old boyfriend and friend, fellow actor, fellow wanderer.

You are not forgotten.

ABOUT THE AUTHOR

Deborah Goodrich Royce's first novel, *Finding Mrs. Ford*, debuted in 2019 to rave reviews. She divides her time between the Northeast and Florida, where she writes, reads, watches lots of movies, and spends time with her family.

Deborah serves on the governing and/or advisory boards of the Avon Theatre, the American Film Institute, New York Botanical Garden, the Greenwich International Film Festival, the Greenwich Historical Society, the Preservation Foundation of Palm Beach, the Preservation Society of Newport, and the PRASAD Project. She and her husband have restored more buildings than she can count, including the Ocean House Hotel and the Deer Mountain Inn.

Deborah holds a BA in French and Italian from Lake Erie College and an honorary doctorate from the same institution. In an earlier life, she was an actress in film and television and a story editor at Miramax Films. *Ruby Falls* is her second psychological thriller, and she owes a debt of gratitude for its inspiration to Daphne du Maurier and Alfred Hitchcock.

The author as a child with her father at Ruby Falls

A FINAL WORD ABOUT THE COVER ART

The cover of a book is a window to the story within. And the story of this artwork is one of accident, fate, and a little magic thrown in. Photographer Melanie Willhide was preparing for an exhibition in Los Angeles when her computer was stolen. Though the computer was recovered, the images contained on it had been damaged by an attempt to swipe it clean. When the artist was able to finally retrieve her photographs, the images re-emerged striated and disconnected. This fateful accident became the basis of her show, *to Adrian Rodriguez, with love*, in honor of the man who had taken her computer. This work, *Grace and Thorns*, though not part of those stolen images, was inspired by them. I cannot think of a more fitting image—both literally and metaphorically—to grace the cover of *Ruby Falls*.